Gone Fishing

Alice Calliva

Calliva Books

To Jade,

Thank you for believing, when I didn't.

.

Authors Note

This book is intended for audiences of 18 years old and over.

Gone fishing explores the issues of grief, alcohol abuse and chronic illness. The death of a parent is depicted at the beginning of this book. If you wish to skip this particular scene, go straight on to Chapter 1.

Contents

Prologue

The salt stung my skin, leaving a chalky layer over my face. I gripped the rails, relishing the feel of the waves as they crashed into Saoirse, the sea spray arching over the deck. The wind was picking up, but the sun still pushed through the swelling grey clouds above.

'Oi, Riss. Any plans to do some work today, or are you just gonna stand there sunnin' yourself?'

Some would say working with family was the worst thing you could do, but they were wrong. I'd known as soon as I could hold a straight thought in my head that I was going to be out on the boat with Dad catching lobster. I was made for it. People talk about something being in their blood. Fishing was in mine.

I inhaled deeply, allowing the smell of bait and ocean to fill my senses. *Ahhh*, there it was. Contentment.

Looking back, I should have realised. I should have seen the signs, the subtle cues. The building clouds, the need to steady myself one too many times. But that's the problem with contentment—you don't see shit. It's a relaxed trap, designed to lull you into a false sense of security, and then *BAM!* Everything is taken away from you.

'Yeah, alright, I'm here.' I smiled at Dad as he headed out onto deck

1

from the wheelhouse and busied himself with the gear. His ripped oilskins barely held onto their original purpose of keeping him dry. His once red hair, faded and greyed before its time, stood at random angles off his head, making his unkempt beard look tidy by comparison.

'How'd you feel about bringing her up alongside, and I'll hook on?'

'You sure?' I didn't normally bring Saoirse up alongside the buoy. I was normally the one hanging over the railing hooking on to the buoy, so we could haul the pots back on board and see if our catch would just cover the bills or give us a little extra.

'Yeah.' He said as he cupped his spade-like hands around the cigarette in his mouth, his oversized fingers fumbling with the lighter. 'You got this, Riss.'

My chest swelled with his words, as it always did. I'd been out on Saoirse as soon as I could walk, but becoming a fisherman had been harder. Not quite as simple as hopping on a boat and off you go. And it wasn't just because I had a vagina. There were nautical navigation skills, budget management, a crash course in engineering... The list went on. But whatever the obstacle, Dad had been there. Always guiding, always encouraging.

I made my way back towards the wheelhouse. The key to hooking the gear on the first attempt was practice. Lots of it. I wasn't bad at it, but the waves were bigger than normal. The wind had kicked up a notch, and the sun had finally given up her plight of staying visible. I widened my stance as Saoirse rolled deep into the waves. Dad took a deep drag of his rollie and looked up at the sky, as if his thoughts were mirroring mine. We'd known the weather was going to come in, but the wind was definitely more than we'd expected. Saoirse was a ten-footer, and there was only so much swell she was able to handle.

'If you keep her steady, we'll be fine.' He winked at me as he ran a hand over his cheek. Something in his movement gave me an uneasy feeling. As quick as it arrived, though, it was gone. 'Right, Riss. Let's get this girl earning her keep.'

I stepped inside the relative protection of the wheelhouse and flicked off autopilot before double checking the plotter. All good. I was on the right course. Now we just needed to hope the pots we'd put down a week ago were full of lobster. I let my shoulders relax. It wasn't like I hadn't done this before, but my desire to impress my dad overrode everything. It didn't matter that he was proud of me regardless of what I did. I could have said I was going to join Aunt Val at the pub, and he still would have beamed back at me, his eyes watery with pride. But maybe because I'd chosen to follow him, I felt an imaginary pressure to prove I was good enough. Worthy.

I turned Saoirse around and lined us up nicely, hoping Dad's confidence wasn't misplaced and he would be able to hook on to the buoy on the first attempt. The less time we spent bringing the pots in, the quicker we could get out of this growing storm.

'Looking good, love,' Dad shouted from the deck, his chest bent over the railing, hook in hand. 'That's it. Hold her steady.'

I looked over my shoulder and watched Dad as Saoirse leaned into the next wave with more force than I cared to see. 'You good?'

'Let's go again,' I heard him say over the wind, as he swiped water off his face.

But none of the subsequent attempts were successful. I turned back into the wheelhouse to try and edge Saoirse alongside the buoy. That's when it hit. The wave crashed over Saoirse, throwing me against the wall of the wheelhouse.

'You alright?' I shouted, pulling myself up against the wheel. 'Fucking hell. That one came out of nowhere!'

No reply. A cold shiver trickled down my spine. Why was there no reply? I turned to scan the deck. Nothing. Where was he? Why wasn't he there?

'Dad!' The panic bubbled out of my mouth, and I struggled to steady myself as Saoirse was thrown from side to side.

A flash of yellow oilskins caught my eye as I scanned the water. I made towards it, mouth open, ready to scream out, but it was gone—sucked out as the second wave hit and water smashed into my face, knocking me onto my back. I gasped like a fresh fish on deck, my chest heaving as though trapped beneath an immovable weight.

Chapter 1

I slowly lowered her back onto the bed, careful not to let her body land awkwardly. Her fragile frame crumpled back onto the soft cushions, the tension in her shoulders lifting as the pain of moving subsided.

'Well done, Mrs Lesley,' I said, louder than I would to most people.

'Can we get back to it now?'

'Yes, absolutely. And, as promised,' I said, reaching over to the side table for the plate of brownies.

'Look at this one—I wouldn't mind an evening with him,' she said, crumbs tumbling down her chest as she spoke. She brushed them away absently as she gazed at the photo in front of her.

'Let's see,' I said, leaning in closer. 'Not bad, not bad at all,' I said, nodding in agreement.

'What about you, Rissa?' she asked, her aqua blue eyes piercing into me. Her skin was wrinkled, and ill health had faded her beauty, but you could still see the flashes of it. Her long silver hair, kept in rollers each night, tumbled down to just below her shoulders, and her eyes, unaffected by time, still shone with determination. Mrs Lesley wasn't even *that* old by the Home's standards. At seventy, she was a relative spring chicken, but health had been unkind to her, and her needs had outgrown her own abilities.

'What about me?' I asked, knowing all too well what she was getting at. After all, we had this conversation every time we came across a wedding or baby photoshoot in her beloved magazine.

'When are you going to find someone to settle down with? You're not in your twenties forever.' she said, chuckling with an air of self-disappointment as she flicked to the next page.

'I don't know. Maybe one day,' I said, swallowing hard to loosen the familiar tightening in my throat.

Don't let people in. People get hurt. People you love get hurt.

'You should speak to my son. Now there's a word of warning if ever there was.'

'Your son?'

'Spent too much time building his fancy homes. I blame his father.'

I smiled. Her poor son's ears must be continually burning. There weren't many days when she didn't berate him for something.

'You need to get out more. Stop spending so much time with us old farts,' she continued, after finishing the last of her brownie. Her arthritic fingers pressed on the last of the crumbs.

'I'll have you know, I love my time with you old farts,' I said, moving her empty plate from its precarious position on her chest and placing it on the side table by the bed. It wasn't a lie. I did enjoy my time with the residents. But it was also a great place to ignore my life.

'I'm sure your son is happy with his choices. He must get a lot of satisfaction from his work.'

'Nonsense,' she said, waving a hand dismissively, and flicked to the next page of her magazine with a little too much force.

'Where does your son build his houses?' I asked, trying to steer the conversation towards pride rather than disappointment.

Before she had a chance to answer me, there was a gentle knock at the door.

'I'll get that,' I said, getting up from my chair to collect the plates and half-drunk coffee. I turned towards the door as six foot of suited beauty walked in the room. Dark blonde hair framed a face so perfectly symmetrical it was difficult to look away.

'Saying lovely things about me, Mum?' He smiled with affection at Mrs Lesley, then dark green eyes landed on me. 'You must be Narissa.'

I nodded, words vanishing as they came to mind, my concentration too distracted by the specimen in front of me. He gave me a broad smile that did nothing to help my ability to function as a fully grown adult.

'Then I owe you a huge thank you for the care you have given my mother. She speaks fondly of you.'

'It's— It's fine. Thank you,' I managed, words slowly filtering back into my head. 'I will leave you to it. Mrs Lesley'—I looked back at her—'buzz if you need anything.'

As I walked towards the door, I allowed myself one last look at the man in front of me. His attention had shifted back to his mother, and as I got closer, I went to one side to let him pass, before he mirrored my move.

'Oh.' I laughed, in that polite way you do as you dance an awkward dance with the other person, not knowing who should go first.

'I'll just—' I don't know if I moved prematurely, or whether I should have second guessed the move. But whatever it was, it was wrong.

One step. Side step. His step. My step. *Crash!*

The brown stain of coffee seeped across his white shirt as the soft thud of the plate hitting the carpet had me dropping to my knees to tidy up the mess.

'God, I'm so sorry.' I kept my eyes on the ground as I brushed brownie onto the plate.

'Don't be. It's my fault entirely. Here, let me.' He picked up the napkins and added them to the plate, along with the coffee cup.

'I'm so sorry,' I said again, mortification spreading red across my cheeks.

'No harm done.'

Before I had a chance to reply, my colleague Venessa was at the door.

'Sorry to interrupt. Rissa, there's an *Aunt Val* on the line. Says it's urgent.'

Chapter 2

The train was packed with people escaping the city. I found myself squashed tight into the window seat. Someone had opened up one of those instant noodle pots as we'd left London two hours ago, but the smell still hung in the air like a musty fart cloud. I shifted in my seat, trying to make space for myself in a chair that wasn't getting any bigger, however much I tried. I leaned into the window, hoisting my bag further into my lap. All the overhead space had been taken before I had even got on the train. Thank god for seat reservations, otherwise I'd have been standing the whole five-hour ride to Telbury! My cheek was pressed against the window, but given the temperature in the carriage was definitely creeping steadily towards thirty degrees Celsius, I was grateful for the cool glass...even if I was far too close to some unidentifiable smears, which I really didn't want to think about in too much detail.

'Ticket, please.'

'Hmmm?' I said, peeling my cheek from the cold window to see the overweight frame of the train conductor waiting impatiently. By the look on his face and the sag in his shoulders, the heat of the carriage and the sheer number of bodies he had to navigate past was taking its toll.

'Ticket, please.'

'Right, sorry,' I said, rummaging in my bag, trying desperately not to elbow the woman to my right.

'Thank you. Telbury is in three stops. Make sure to be in the front three carriages, or you'll not be getting off,' he said on autopilot, without looking up at me as he examined my ticket.

I managed a weak smile before I slumped back into the window and hugged my bag tighter to my chest. The butterflies of anxiety started to swell in my stomach again as I stared out the window, watching the sky grow bigger and the houses become fewer as we chugged closer towards Telbury and everything I was running from.

***

Telbury remained pretty much unchanged from its original state some three hundred years ago. Narrow streets, never adjusted to aid modern day cars. A one-platform train station (despite the thousands that descended on it each summer) was positioned on a hill, leading down to the heart of the town at the harbour.

The warmth of the May sun was comforting as I stepped off the train and dropped in line with the mass of tourists moving as one. I allowed myself to be pulled along on the wave weaving down the hill of narrow streets to the cobbled square overlooking the harbour.

Some things might not change, but the revolving door of new shops wasn't one of them. I did a scan of the square and spotted the latest. A fancy soap shop. Two large, perfectly pruned bay trees sat outside its entrance, where a young girl handed out samples to anyone willing to take them. But despite it all, Telbury still managed to hold on to its original charm. You could almost hear the smugglers of Jamaica Inn making their way along the narrow streets by the cover of darkness, their only light that of a full moon.

The group of tourists in front of me let out a range of *ooh*s and *ahh*s when they spotted the brightly coloured exteriors of the old fisherman houses lining the cobbled side streets, pausing to get the obligatory photo. I couldn't help but grimace, knowing that their ludicrous per week price tags rendered them no more than museum pieces for the locals.

My eyes were drawn to the other side of the square, where Mermaid's Fish Bar stood, proud and tacky. Her oversized plastic mermaid was perched above the door, calling all passers-by to come in. I took a deep breath, allowing the smell of deep fat fryers and sea air to fill my nose as gulls prowled the sky above, waiting for their next victim. There was always a tourist to be robbed. I watched a gull perched on the back of a bench throw its head back and screech. Despite everything, it sounded like home.

As the crowd filtered off in different directions, my heart swelled as my eyes landed on the scene that never failed to simultaneously break me and complete me. The sailboats stood tall and elegant out towards the harbour walls, their superiority unmistakable, whilst pleasure boats bobbed up and down in the calm sea. The tide was on the way back in, but the fishing boats left behind still had their underbellies crudely exposed.

'Narissa Williams.'

There were three people who ever called me by my full name, and one of them was Clem.

I turned around, throwing my arms in the air. 'Ah, I haven't heard that name in a while.' I smiled into his broad shoulder, breathing in his familiar scent of vanilla rum and tobacco.

'Let's get a good look at you.' He placed his large, rough hands on my shoulders whilst he gave me a suspicious once over. Clem was of the belief that London was filled with cheats and liars, the home of Hades himself.

After everything happened, he had come to visit me. He'd managed one night, declaring that anywhere that had more people in a train station than Telbury had permanent residents was a dangerous and untrustworthy place to be. Who was I to disagree?

'Need a bit of sea air on you, I'd say.'

'Shut up.' I laughed, batting him away. 'You could do with a haircut.' Despite my five foot ten build, I still needed to reach up to ruffle his shaggy hair.

'That's rich. Doesn't look like you know what a hairbrush looks like, or a colourist.'

I let out a disbelieving laugh. 'Since when do you know what a colourist is?'

'Despite what you think, I don't live under a rock all the time.'

He was right of course. My dark brown roots were past being acceptable, and no matter what I did, my hair always ended up in a tangle of knots thrown into a ponytail.

'Have you been home yet?' All humour disappeared between us, and his eyes looked back at me in anticipation.

'Not yet.' Of course I hadn't. After Aunt Val had dropped her *I'm sick* line, she had reassured me she wasn't about to drop dead on me. I had organised a few days off work and agreed to help with the weekend rush at the pub. I glanced at my watch. I knew I should have been heading straight to the pub, but my innate need to bury my head in the sand was in full swing.

Please god, throw me a bone!

'I'm...stalling? Plus I wanted to see you.' I smiled, pushing the anxiety back down with a swallow and trying to regain some of the lightness of a moment ago.

'Course you did, Rissa. Course you did.' He lay one arm over my shoulder, as the other re-lit the half smoked rollie in his mouth. 'I've missed you. It's not the same without you here. Nav is so much more manageable when you're around. Will you stay this time?'

'Ah, I've missed *that*,' I said, letting out a laugh. Half from relief that the conversation had moved into safer water, but also because the love-hate relationship my two best friends had was nothing short of bestselling rom com material.

'What?' he said, as we fell into a comfortable stride together in the direction of the Shed.

'You know what. Yours and Nav's eternal game of pretending you don't like each other, when in fact, you're more alike than you both realise.'

He grumbled something inaudible under his breath before changing the subject. 'I've got some salting to do. Fancy it?'

'Fish heads and guts. How can I resist?' I smiled to myself as I was thrown my figurative bone. Anything to avoid heading to the pub for a little while longer. I felt my chest loosen knowing the topic of me moving home was finished.

Clem flicked the end of his cigarette before tucking it back into his lips. 'And don't think I've forgotten about you staying this time. I won't give up until you're back out on the water!'

I groaned inwardly. Maybe it was half a bone.

Chapter 3

'You're here,' a voice called, as soon as I entered the bar.

'Bloody guests, bloody guests,' Johnny squawked, bobbing up and down on his perch, wings stretched out. It was common knowledge that parrot was the only one to receive unprompted affection from Aunt Val.

'Hi to you too,' I said, as I looked around. The wooden floors still held their tackiness, and the thick mauve curtains were still drawn, leaving a soft purple glow across the room. The familiar smell of beer and bleach hit my nose as the deep tones of Johnny Cash blasted out from the speakers.

Home.

Aunt Val's back was to me, one hand pressed against the wall as she reached her duster to the top of the curtains. Her skirt was hitched around her thighs, and her blouse had ridden up, revealing the tip of her dragon tattoo. The remnants of a youth I found hard to imagine. Aunt Val was an eternal spinster and proud of it. She'd had one relationship. Said it was enough to put her off for life. The pub was her one true love... And me. Although she'd never admit it.

I watched as she put both feet on the banquette and climbed back down. I swallowed a gasp as she turned. Her skin was pale, and her chest heaved from the effort of her movements. A wave of guilt crashed into me that I had dismissed her calls for help. My mind ran away with unhelpful ideas on what the mysterious illness that had brought me back was.

But it was Aunt Val. Sickness wasn't a word given to someone like her. *Or was it?* I shoved the lingering question from my mind. There was no space for anymore loss.

Aunt Val straightened her skirt and smoothed her hair back into place.

'Alexa, button it,' she said. The music stopped, and Johnny stopped bobbing. I couldn't help smiling.

'Is that even a command?'

'Course. Just customise it in the app. Can't be doing with all the niceties in the basic settings.'

Ah, same old Aunt Val. Her indomitable tone reassured me. I stepped forwards, wrapping my arms around her small frame, ignoring the familiar grumbles of resistance. But then she hugged me back, and I breathed her in. Whatever was going on with her, the truth was that I needed this. More than I had realised.

The moment didn't last long before Aunt Val's innate inability to withstand human affection kicked in, and she grumbled her way out of my grip, diving her hand into her 1980's fanny pack.

'You know you can't smoke inside anymore.'

'Nonsense,' she said, flicking the lighter on. 'Anyway, no one comin' in now. Boats not in till later, and twenty per cent off down at Mermaid's Fish Van.' She inhaled deeply before releasing a plume of smoke into the space between us. 'Tryin' something new again. Tourists not biting as much as usual. So, need us locals in.' An undeniable hint of scepticism shook her voice.

I shook my head and turned to look around the dimly lit pub. The walls were littered with sun-bleached photos of the local fishing fleet, and the snooker table with its four ball pockets missing still stood in the window looking out onto the bay. The pub was as old as the town itself, and Aunt Val had no intention of bringing it into the twenty-first century to appeal more to the tourists. In fact, she prided herself on being a local pub, *for* locals. How close she was skirting to discrimination was anyone's guess, but she'd been at it so long, the tourists who came back year on year liked the story and the quirkiness of it all.

***

'So, you going to tell me what's going on?' I asked, once I was perched on a bar stool, and Aunt Val stood behind the bar. Johnny was on her shoulder, his eyes watching as she dipped a peanut in a dish of beer before handing it to him.

'You got any bags with you?'

'I just have my overnight bag. Don't ignore my question.'

'Let's get you upstairs and settled in. No time to stand here all day.' She dipped another peanut in the beer and handed it to Johnny.

'Aunt Val!'

'What?' She looked back at me with innocent eyes.

'You know what.' I nodded to Johnny as crumbs of peanut gathered on the bar top. Parrots really were the most ineffective eaters.

Aunt Val sighed and slumped onto her stool. 'Now I don't want you getting them frilly knickers of yours in a twist. 'Cause I know what you're like.'

'Spit it out.' My nerves were beginning to fray. Despite her bravado, it wasn't like her to stall.

'There's some property company sniffing around the Shed.' She looked away, taking another cigarette from her fanny pack.

'Are you joking?' I scoffed. This couldn't possibly be the reason for bringing me home.

This was after all Aunt Val's MO. Come up with some excuse to get me home, then bring it all back to the same issue. The joke, though, was on me, because I never seemed to learn.

'This isn't news. People are always looking to buy. It doesn't matter, because it's not for sale,' I said, doing my best to remain calm. The Shed had been owned by the same family for more generations than it was worth counting. There was a long-standing agreement it was for the use of the fishing community in whatever way they needed. It wasn't for sale.

'The old man died a while back.'

She took a deep drag.

'Turns out the sons want to be rid of it.'

Exhale.

'Got a town meeting with the potential buyer. I want you to be there.'

I sat silent, watching the tendrils of smoke twist their way up above our heads.

'There have been offers before, and it's never worked out. This won't be any different,' I finally said, only half convinced myself. We'd all seen what had happened to the fishermen terraces down by the harbour. Eventually money did talk.

'Maybe.' Another drag.

We went back to our silence as I allowed my mind to wander through what this all meant. Despite my dismissal of it all, I wasn't able to shake the feeling there was something in what Aunt Val was saying. And if it was true, and some clueless, rich impostor was trying to buy the Shed... A shudder went down my spine. Was it possible there was a reality in which there was no longer any fishing in Telbury?

No, Rissa. Don't be ridiculous.

'Is this why you called me home?' I wanted to be annoyed by the deceit, but I couldn't quite bring myself to feel it. Instead, I was left with the unsettling feeling that all was not well.

'I'm glad you're home,' she said, before standing up and walking towards the stairs.

***

Dad had been

equal part hoarder, equal part re-user. Whenever things needed repairing at the pub, he was quick to bring out something he had been holding onto for that exact occasion. I reached my hand out to the makeshift banister Dad and I had made when I was a kid. He'd found a plank of wood down on the dock and banged it on to the wall with overly large nails that still jutted out. My hand trailed along the wood, catching on the thin splinters that still covered its surface. My eyes were drawn to the photos that lined the walls either side. My childhood mapped out in the length of a staircase.

Mum had died when I was two. The cancer had been too aggressive. Dad wasn't ever going to be able to cope with a kid on his own, and so Aunt Val had made room. Despite the shadow of a mother never known, my childhood was one of love and laughter. Dad always said I had her brown eyes, but Aunt Val said it was my smile. She said when I smiled it was as though my mum was standing right in front of her again. I turned away, my eyes beginning to swim, as the memory struggled to stay in the light it should be seen. Happy, joyful. Instead, the inevitable tightening in my chest began to rise, and my throat started to narrow.

'I'll leave you to get settled in,' Aunt Val said, as she backed out into the corridor.

'Wait.' I placed my hand on her shoulder. 'Are you going to tell me what's up with you? Do I need to be worried?'

'I'm glad you're home, Narissa,' she said again, her smile not reaching her eyes. 'Plenty of time for all that other stuff.' She stepped out of reach and closed the door with a gentle click.

I flopped down onto my narrow childhood bed and allowed the familiar feelings of comfort and heart-tearing grief to flood over me. Eventually I gave in to the uneasy sleep my body was pushing on me. Disjointed dreams of sun glistening on the sea, my father's laughter filling the air, a feeling of contentment. But then the clouds. Big, grey boulder clouds. Waves, wind whipping hair into my eyes, blurring my vision. Water, why was there so much water? Too much water. Dad. Where's Dad? No, stop. This is not right. Stop. Dad!

Wake up Rissa, it's just a dream.

I felt my brain clicking back into gear as the fear subsided. Each time I had the nightmare, I woke with a sad relief that the worst had already happened. And yet, this time the relief wasn't there. Aunt Val's words played over in my mind, and I started to think the worst wasn't yet over.

Chapter 4

People are amazing creatures in time of need. After the accident, I had been surrounded by them. I'd heard the comments of sympathy and felt the gentle hand on my shoulder. But it didn't matter. It changed nothing. Dad was gone, and it was my fault. Hiding in London, caring for people I could actually help, was my way of pretending Telbury didn't exist. No harbour, no Shed, no boats...no fishing. But the key to numbing yourself is to disappear from everything that reminds you of the pain. I couldn't allow even one good memory to slip through. The problem with my plan, however, was that it didn't matter how hard I tried to remove my past, it was always there.

***

'Rissa! Riss!'

The unmistakable boom of Nav's voice travelled across the square, and I turned to see my best friend's small frame rushing towards me. Both arms were held high in the air, as though on crowd control at a festival.

'Excuse me, excuse me. Best friend coming through.' I watched as she dodged a woman walking backwards, camera to her face, as she attempted to get all six members of her party into the photo.

'Whoa, watch out. Emergency fluids being transported.'

My chest swelled with love at the sight of Nav pushing her way through the crowd. Despite her crazy busy life, she always managed to be a damn good friend. Something I couldn't always say was reciprocated.

'Ah, come here, you,' she said, wrapping her arms around me. 'I've missed a good hug.' Her voice was muffled against me. 'Clem is no substitute! I swear that man is allergic to human contact.' She released me from her grip and stood back, taking me in. 'Don't think I'm not completely pissed at you for not coming to see me the minute you got home, 'cause I am. But here is one *deluxe* fine dining hot chocolate, topped with whipped cream, chocolate shavings, nougat pieces, and something a little extra. Top secret,' she said, handing over the paper cup with all the pomp and ceremony of a royal coronation.

'Thank you.' I put the cup to my face, revelling in the deep chocolate aromas. I had been back a few days and had barely left the pub. Aunt Val wasn't saying anything, but she wasn't herself. Tasks that used to take her minutes were taking her much longer. She wasn't spilling yet, but I knew something was up with her, and I'd be damned if I was leaving before I knew she was alright.

We pushed our way past a group of overexcited teenagers who had just had an ice cream nabbed by a gull to find a space up against the railings.

'Sooo, tell me all. How are you? How long are you here this time? Oh, tell me you're staying forever.'

I dipped my finger into the chocolate-topped cream and shook my head as I scooped it into my mouth.

'Thank god you're back. That man is insufferable. I need you here to stop me from having to deal with him on my own.'

'You two are ridiculous,' I said, more to myself than her. She was already waving a hand, as if to silence any further talk of Clem.

'What girl talk am I walking in on?'

A voice startled us both as Clem appeared by our side.

'Jesus. Seeing you this early in the morning is too much for anyone, Clem. What on earth brings you back to the shore so soon?'

'Hello, Naveen.' Clem beamed at her with unrestrained sarcasm. 'Riss and I have a date with Saoirse.'

'Right, that's my cue.'

'Really?' I asked, disappointed.

'I've got to get back to the restaurant.' She pushed off from the barrier. 'Lord knows I can't leave Dopey Darren in charge for more than five minutes.'

'How is the restaurant?' I asked, all too aware we had talked of nothing but me.

'You know what it's like. It's a restaurant. Strained.' Her shoulders dropped, and I caught what sounded like the beginning of a sigh, before she corrected herself and plastered on her indestructible mask of stoicism. 'It'll be fine. We just need to get through the summer season.' She stopped and looked out at the water. Nav might not say it, but her tone told me she was worried. I wrapped an arm around her shoulder and squeezed.

'It'll be alright. Let me know if I can do anything to help. I'm not a great chef, but I'm sure I can take instruction.'

'Stay,' she said, leaning into my shoulder.

For the first time in a long time, that didn't feel like the worst idea.

'I'm not ready,' I said, turning to look at Clem once Nav had gone.

'You're never going to be ready. You've just got to do it.'

'I know. But can it wait one more day? How about some salting? Salting sounds fun.'

Clem let out a resigned sigh. 'Come on, then. But this is the last time. It's been long enough.'

'I know, I know. I promise, tomorrow.' He was right, of course. I hadn't been down to the boat since the accident. But the longer I was in Telbury, the stronger the pull to her became.

***

The Shed was a large wooden building at the farthest end of the West side of the harbour. When the fish market moved out of Telbury along with the bigger fishing boats—all tempted by the lure of the larger ports—the fishermen left behind took it on. It was fronted with a sliding door the height and width of the building, which looked out to the harbour. Crab pots waited patiently for repair, and rolled netting sat neatly stacked outside the front.

I stepped in through the side door, the smell of fish hanging thick in the air. The plastic corrugated roof poured light into the space; the crackled sound of music playing from a radio struggling to stay in tune drifted across to us.

Each fisherman had their own area. Clem's was to the left of the sliding door. No better place to be in the summer as the fresh breeze blew in, but come winter, the salt in the air would crystallise on your fingers as you baited mackerel lines. Memories of threading lines with small pieces of tinsel as my fingers succumbed to frostbite filled my mind. I smiled as I looked around at the barrels, crates, and fishing gear.

How had I ever turned my back on all this? But as soon as the question came, the answer was too quick to follow. I'd had no choice.

'Val must be happy you're back.' Clem's words jolted me back to the Shed. I watched as he opened the lid on one of the barrels. Clem inhaled the smell as though it contained the delights of some home-cooked meal, not that of mackerel heads and frames.

'What? Don't look at me like that. You know the key to making the perfect bait—'

'Is the extra salt you add. I know.' I laughed, finishing his sentence before passing him the bag of salt sitting on the small table beside me.

'Exactly. Crabs will eat anything. But lobster,' he said, wagging a finger in the air, 'lobster like something a bit special.' He narrowed his eyes in concentration as he poured the salt into the barrel like a chef adding to a sauce.

'How is she?' I asked, the mood between us becoming more serious. I'd always been able to talk to Clem. For the longest time, it had been me and him, out on the boat with Dad. He'd been there through it all—the investigation and the inquest. So had Nav, and she'd done her best, but Clem understood in a way few ever could unless they had been at sea.

'I think that's a question for Val.' There was something in his voice I hadn't heard before, and it sent a shiver down my neck.

'Do you not think I've tried that?' I picked up a new barrel and carried it back to where Clem was now busy stirring his carefully flavoured lobster bait. My body had fallen back into the rhythm of the jobs, instinct taking over.

'She is getting on, and the pub *is* hard work.'

'Clem.' I paused as I used all my strength to tip the crate full of every part of a fish you never wanted to see into the bait barrel. 'I know something's up, and I know it's not just the worry over this potential bid for the Shed.'

'All I'm saying is, go easy on her.'

'Argh! Come on!' I shouted, as a splatter of fish juice hit my cheek.

'Bit rusty, it seems.' He laughed whilst I used my cuff to wipe my cheek.

'How about you go and get the last of the crates? They're down the bottom by the boat.' He nodded to the door heading back outside.

'What's wrong with your arms?' I flashed him a look.

'Nothing. It's yours. You need to get some practice in. Ain't gonna be hauling anything more than a hook line with arms like that.' He grabbed my arm and pressed my decidedly squishy skin.

'You know, if you were anyone else, I would smack you one for that.'

'Yes, but I'm not, so I will continue until you get moving.'

***

Sun in the city was never like sun by the sea. It was a sticky heat. A heat that left me wanting to stand in a shower for half an hour rinsing the grime away. But not here. Here, the heat was calmed by the sea air. I stepped outside into the rapidly warming day and smiled.

Nothing could beat the sight of a fishing boat coming back in from a day out at sea. It felt ancient, sacred. People had fished the waters around Telbury on Cornwall for hundreds of years. No matter how hard I fought against it, a part of me—a big part—craved being out there with them.

When the crates came into sight, I cursed Clem for sending me out to get them. Of course there were three of them. I bent down, tensing my core, then cursed myself for realising he was right. I was out of shape... Fishing shape, at least. I steadied myself, shifting the crates so they balanced just so across my chest, the sharp-edged plastic digging into my exposed arms.

One, two, three. I took in a deep breath, braced my legs, and as I started to stand up, I let my breath out. My arms trembled under the weight, and the crates wobbled against my weak frame.

'Excuse me. Do you think you could help me?'

I shifted my weight and started to turn.

The voice continued, 'Sorry, allow me. Let me help you with—'

With hindsight, I might say I turned too quickly. But how was I to know the mystery voice would be right behind me?

My feet twisted, my ankle rolled, and I felt my legs wobble beneath me. The crates, teetering in a fragile balancing act, started to slip, my arms frantically trying to regain equilibrium like a desperate juggler trying to keep all the balls in the air. But it was too late. My knees gave in, and I landed hard against the man now right in front of me, the crates lying between us on the ground.

I pulled my legs back underneath me and peeled myself off the firm, immovable object I had faceplanted into. I looked down at my now fish-stained jeans and gave them a quick brush, before remembering I still hadn't seen the face of the person I had crashed into.

My eyes caught on a pair of suede loafers, which lead into a very well-fitting pair of chinos. My brain did a flash assessment, and I realised I was dealing with a wandering tourist. Looking up, I saw the horror spreading across his face. I looked back down at his shoes and watched as he shook the skeletal remains of a mackerel from one of them.

'What the...'

'Sorry,' I said, before he could finish. I flashed my best smile. For the first time, I made eye contact with the man who wore totally impractical footwear, and my stomach dropped.

'I'm not sure I even want to know what that is,' he said, his voice deep and cut with the Queen's own English. And a hint of...humour?

'I'm really sorry,' I said again, looking around for something to help brush the unidentifiable fish parts off his trousers and shoes.

'These things happen. I think.' He laughed as he reached into his jacket pocket and pulled out a handkerchief.

Was that still a thing?

He looked back at me, and recognition flashed across his face. 'I'm sorry, I don't want you to think this is some pick-up line, but do I know you from somewhere?'

I nodded. 'We met the other day. I'm—'

'Narissa,' he said, pointing at me as it all fell into place.

'You were with Mum.' He shook his head. 'We have to stop meeting like this.'

'I'm sorry?'

'I think last time it was coffee you threw all over me.' His smile was wicked, and I laughed at how well he was taking it.

'You can call me Rissa.'

'Rissa.' He nodded.

'I really am sorry.' I looked up at him again, taking in his features more this time. Soft creases either side of his bright green eyes suggested a level of life experience, without adding unnecessary years. His lightweight black jacket looked like it had just come off this year's Outdoor Range at some fancy clothing store, pretending they know what's needed for adverse weather.

'What brings you down here?' he asked, apparently unfazed by the lingering smell of fish.

'I'm visiting family. This is where I grew up.'

He looked around the dock and smiled. 'Quite the place to grow up.'

'Yeah,' I said. 'What about you?'

'Right now, I'm looking for a restaurant called Nav's. I was following my phone directions from the hotel, but it died as I came down the hill.'

'I think you might need to head back to the hotel first.' I ran my eyes up and down his clothes.'

He looked down at the mess and laughed. 'You might be right.'

Our eyes met again, and neither one of us made to move away.

'Rissa, what you doing?' Clem's bark broke the spell, and I looked away.

'Coming,' I called, all too aware of the heat rising in my cheeks. I bent down and gathered up the now empty crates.

'I better get going, but Nav's is up in the main square. Take a right up there, and you can't miss it.'

'How long are you here for?' he asked, taking me by surprise.

'I'm not sure at the moment.' For the first time since leaving Telbury, I really meant it. This time felt different. Maybe it was my worry over Aunt Val or the looming meeting about the Shed, but either way, Telbury felt like where I needed to be.

'I'd love to catch a drink if you've got some time. It's nice to see a friendly face. Any local recommendations?'

I smiled at that. 'Yeah, I might know somewhere. The Old Ship. I'll be there this evening, if you fancy it.'

'Alright.' He nodded.

I picked up the crates and looked at him one last time. He really was beautiful.

'Water and vinegar,' I said.

'Hmmm?'

'For your shoes. Should get the stains out.'

'Noted.' He nodded with a smile.

'But maybe you should think about a more practical pair,' I added, as he looked back down at his shoes, shaking his foot once more when he noticed another piece of something stuck to it. He opened his mouth as though to reply, but I turned and walked back towards the shed, forest green eyes stuck in my mind.

Chapter 5

The sound of music and voices merged together as I took the stairs two at a time. The pub was already full with the nightly drinkers, mostly from the boats. I watched as Aunt Val moved from one tap to the next, pouring perfect pint after perfect pint.

'Need a hand?' I shouted over the noise.

'Two if you can,' she said, taking another tankard off a hook.

We worked quickly, weaving past one another. Aunt Val started taking the order, and I started pouring. The mob of men were jovial and patient. They knew whose house it was. They wouldn't dare be anything else.

'You haven't forgotten then?' She smiled as I pulled the hand pump towards me, allowing the beer to fill the tilted glass.

'Never!' I stood the glass straight and flicked the tap off. My teenage years had been spent behind this bar, and before that, clearing tables of the empties. If I wasn't at sea with Dad, I was serving drinks in the pub.

The door swung open, and Clem strolled in along with Geoff. Geoff was the fisherman of books long out of print. He looked as though the ocean had spat him out half a century ago to live his life on the unfamiliar place of dry land. A life at sea had not been kind to him. His face was etched with the wind and sun it had been exposed to, making him look almost as old as the fleet itself.

'You're a natural,' Clem said, slumping into the bar stool in front of me. His sea salt-stained hair was textured in a way that people would pay a lot of money for in an upscale salon. Clem was, in objective terms, a catch. He had a permanent bronzed glow from being outside, and he always managed to make his old, weather-worn clothes look more fashionable than they were ever intended to be.

'Why, thank you. But it's not my first rodeo,' I said, giving a small curtsy.

'Well in that case, I'll take my usual.' He raised an eyebrow in challenge to my cockiness.

Dammit!

I walked back over to the till to buy some time, and Aunt Val appeared by my side, a glass in hand.

'Bottle to the left of the fridge. One ice cube.'

'I thought Clem was staying off the hard stuff?'

'Mmmm, he was. But been slipping recently.'

'Not bad. Not bad.' Clem nodded as I placed the amber liquor in front of him with a smug grin.

'On the hard stuff already?' I asked, as he knocked it back, signalling for another.

'It's been a fucking year of a week.'

'Gotcha.' I poured him another and decided I would check in with him another time. Drinking came with the industry, but Clem's history was never too far out of our memories.

Aunt Val's voice carried across the bar to me. 'You can take that one.' She nodded towards the tall frame of a man with his back to us. I rolled my eyes at Clem, who took his chance to join Geoff on a corner table.

I knew who it was without even seeing his face. It was impossible not to appreciate the rise and fall of his shoulders against his jumper. Don't get me wrong. I might not have been very active in the whole love scene in recent times, but I still had a pulse...as did my trusty vibrator, which was as close to intimacy as I got these days. His unstained, not threadbare jumper and lack of battered rain coat made sure everyone knew he was not a local.

That explained why Aunt Val sent me over. Although she didn't encourage tourists in the pub, she couldn't exactly kick them out. But she sure as hell didn't need to serve them if someone else could do the task for her.

'What can I get you?'

He turned around, and my stomach lurched. His rusty-blonde hair was short but hinted at curls if allowed to grow long. And those green eyes...

'Hi,' I said, for want of anything more interesting.

'Hi,' he said, looking around the room as though in a museum. 'This is quite the place.'

'I'm going to guess this isn't your usual sort of drinking hole.'

He laughed. 'Thanks for the tip, by the way. Vinegar and water. Who knew?'

'What can I get you?' I said again. The suspicious glances from the locals were turning into murmurs, and I had no intention of encouraging them.

'Do you have a wine list?'

'Probably as likely as you now wearing appropriate footwear.' I lifted myself up on the bar and peered over. 'That'll be a no then.'

He let out an amused sigh and pointed to the nearest tap.

'I'll take one of those, and something for yourself...by way of an apology.'

'That seems fair—you did walk into me.' I forced my eyes to focus on the beer filling the glass and not the way his jumper clung to his chest.

He laughed again, and boy, did it feel good to make him laugh. 'Maybe,' he conceded. 'The shoes might not have been a great choice.'

I raised an eyebrow and flashed him a look, 'And they are now?'

'OK.' He nodded. 'Not a suede shoe fan.'

'Is anyone?' I tipped the glass upright and flicked off the handle, placing the beer in front of him.

Another smile and more soft creases by those green eyes.

Stop looking at them, Rissa! You know the rules. No real feelings. Emotionally unavailable with a hint of deadbeat was more my style. *Make a list; lists always help.*

1. Too old for me. (I'm not normally age discriminatory, but I'm prepared to give it a go for this argument.)

2. Not deadbeat enough. Has a successful career and loves his mum.

3. He is a walking poster for an Italian men's fashion label...however perfectly his jumper fits him...or smells. He really does smell good. Cotton and...

I took an involuntary sniff, as I tried to capture the something extra. Nope, no idea. But given everyone else in the pub smelt of fish and a day's sweat, I could convince myself that was why he stood out.

'And you?' He gestured towards the drink now in front of him.

'Thank you, but I'm fine. I've still got work to do.'

'OK. Maybe later.'

'Maybe,' I said, already regretting it. 'I better get back.' I waved a hand in a feeble gesture of goodbye as I moved off to the next customer, all too aware of the queue that had built up.

'If you change your mind, I'm over there in the corner.' He smiled, pointing to the window seat.

'Looking to catch yourself an out of towner there, Riss? Us local lads not to your liking anymore?' Clem hollered at me from his seat with Geoff. He knocked the rest of his drink back before flashing me a mischievous smirk. I grumbled my disapproval and turned away before anyone saw the pink flush that had developed on my neck under his gaze.

'Another two when you're ready,' he said, raising his glass to me, encouraged by Geoff, whose shoulders rose in heavy shudders as he laughed at Clem's teasing.

***

It was fair to say I didn't think all my decisions through with the greatest care. Kissing Tommy Newell in Mermaid's whilst we were both metaled up with braces at sixteen was definitely one. Committing to celery juice every morning for a month because some health expert told me it would *change my life* was another. Total. Bullshit. Placing two fresh beers down on the table in the corner was beginning to feel like one of those bad decisions too. My only excuse was curiosity. It's like when the new kid would turn up at school. There was always a level of mystery surrounding them.

'Seat taken?' I said, sliding uninvited onto the banquette opposite him.

'Hey,' he said, sounding genuinely pleased I had come over.

We both glanced out at the evil looks being laser beamed from the regulars and laughed.

'Charlie,' he said, and stretched out his hand. My hand tucked into his, and I did my best to ignore the unwelcome flutter of butterflies that took hold at the feel of his skin on mine.

'I realise I never actually introduced myself when I met you the other day with Mum, or earlier today down on the dock.'

'Of course it is,' I said, after my stomach had come to heal again. This lack of control over my feelings was not helping my nerves. I took a long sip from the glass in front of me and waited for the alcohol to hit my brain.

'It is?' He cocked his head to one side.

I took another sip of beer and regretted having no filter.

'Sorry. I just meant, well, someone like you would be called Charlie.' Another sip. 'Or Hector maybe.'

'Ha, I see. Shoes and names. Quite the list.'

'List?'

'The list of things you have an issue with.'

'I don't—' I stopped myself from going any further. 'Fair enough. But there's nothing else on the list.' I paused. 'Actually, can I add gherkins? I really don't like gherkins.'

'Gherkins.' He nodded. 'Done.'

'What about you?'

'What's on my list?' He smiled.

'No.' I laughed. 'What are you doing here? You're not the typical tourist. You're a bit far from home, no?'

'A typical tourist? Now, what does that look like?'

'You know.' Another gulp of beer. Either Aunt Val had turned the heating up again (she said it made people thirsty, so they drank more) or his gaze had a direct link to my internal thermostat.

'Baggy shorts, a little too long to be acceptable on a grown man. Open sandals, with feet on display that only come out once a year, and quite frankly shouldn't. Ice cream-stained children in tow...and of course, the canvas bag carrying a month's supply of food and drink for an afternoon on the beach.'

He paused, as though thinking about his answer. 'No, I'm not that tourist.'

'A woman? Sexy weekend away.'

He coughed on his beer, and his eyes widened. 'Definitely no woman.'

'Man then. Sorry.'

'No man either. Work. Just work. What about you?'

'Me?'

'I know you hang out down on the dock and enjoy assaulting unsuspecting, non-traditional tourists. You have a knack for pouring a pint...even if it isn't a full-bodied red. And you also have the skill of putting up with my mother's trashy magazine habit.' His mouth did that thing again, and my stomach took another turn.

I will not swoon.

'This is my aunt's place. I grew up here,' I said, looking around the pub.

'Quite the place to grow up.'

'Yeah, it was.' Memories of summers past flooded my mind. The inevitable sadness that now coated each memory of Telbury made it hard to keep the melancholy from my voice.

The pub had entered its "comfortable buzz zone." Drinks were in hands, and even Aunt Val had perched herself on the stool behind the bar, deep in conversation with Clem and Geoff. Her beloved Johnny Cash was singing in the background. Every now and again, a group picked up the chorus and ran with it.

'Do you play?' I said, looking over at the pool table, wanting to change the direction of the conversation.

'I haven't...'

His words were cut off by the muffled sound of a phone ringing nearby.

'Sorry, I better get this.'

I waved a hand in casual acceptance and turned my attention back to the beer in front of me. Charlie stood up and walked towards the door. It wasn't long before he was back at the table and reaching for his coat.

'I can't believe I am going to do this, but I have to go. I have some work that can't wait. I'm sorry. I feel like tonight was about to get a whole lot more fun.'

'No problem. You would have been crying into your beer by the end of the evening after I'd whipped your ass at pool.'

He let out a genuine laugh, and I couldn't help but smile at being the one to make it happen.

Pathetic, Riss. Just pathetic.

'Thank you,' he said, looking straight at me.

'For what?'

'Keeping me company. There was a moment back there when I thought I was about to be kicked out.'

'Aunt Val never does that to money. She might discourage those that aren't local, but your pound is as good in her till as the rest of them at the end of the day.'

He nodded and stretched his hand out. I reached mine out in return and barely kept my intake of breath inaudible as sparks fizzled across my skin when his fingers wrapped around my hand. His touch was firm, but not harsh, and the gentle traces of veins mapped his hand. Turned out I was a hand fetish kind of gal. I snatched my hand back a bit too quickly to be normal and smoothed it down my jeans, as though trying to dampen the sparks still flickering off my skin.

I'd never considered myself a sap, but as I stood watching Charlie's back as he walked out, I would have to disagree with myself. A man who bore no resemblance to anything I would ever find attractive had me hooked after some mild flirting and a handshake that had my lungs cutting out too fast on a breath in.

Chapter 6

'You're still in bed!'

I threw my head up to see Aunt Val enter the room, Johnny the parrot perched comfortably on her shoulder. I clasped my hand to my head, as my brain took a few seconds to catch up with the speed of my movement.

After Charlie had left, I'd played too many rounds of pool and drank too many drinks to be considered acceptable. I'd known in part that I needed the distraction from the lingering threat hanging over the harbour, and I thought Geoff and Clem were pleased for the distraction too.

The miniature Thor and his hammer started up a relentless attack on my skull, telling me I needed water fast. I chugged the water I'd had the foresight to put by my bed the night before. 'Seriously?' I gasped, dribbles of water running down my chin.

'I thought you might have died.' She shrugged in answer to my obvious annoyance. 'It's seven-thirty. You should be up.' She ignored my groaned reply and walked over to the window, throwing the curtains open. My eyes winced as they tried to adjust, and I rubbed them in an attempt to adjust to the light pouring in through the open window.

'Fuck off,' I groaned, pulling the duvet back over my head.

'It's common knowledge. Anything past seven-thirty is considered sleeping in. And you're not here to sleep in. You're here to help me.' Aunt Val whipped the duvet back off me before settling on the ledge by the window.

'And how do you want me to do that?'

'You can start with the floor downstairs.'

'Aunt Val.'

'Uh, I don't want to hear it.' She took a cigarette out of her fanny pack and lit it. Her head turned to the open window, as if that did anything to prevent the smoke from wafting back into the room.

'Do you mind?' I growled.

'What?'

I glared at her as she took another drag.

'You know, you're a right nag,' she said, stubbing the cigarette out. 'Have you had a chance to think about what I said?' She moved towards the door, her hand resting on the handle.

'About?' I pressed my head into the pillow. The effort of keeping my head upright proved too much.

'Staying for the town meeting.'

Not that I would ever admit it to Aunt Val, but I couldn't imagine being anywhere else but home.

The truth of it was that the same things which stirred all the pain were the same things that held him close to me. Allowed me to feel him near me. Without the fleet, without the boats, where was my connection to Dad?

'Of course,' I said.

'Good.' She nodded.

'But how about you tell me what's going on with you?' I shuffled myself up a little higher, the flush of water into my system easing my head.

'What do you mean?' Her knuckles whitened ever so slightly as her grip on the door handle tightened. I sat a bit straighter and looked at her. She had evaded my questioning so far, but she wasn't going to today. Despite her tough act, something was different with her.

'Aunt Val.'

'I told you. I'm not getting any younger, and this place is hard work.'

'I'm not buying it. You've been at it for years. Let's be honest, you're not *that* old.'

'Maybe it's time for a change.'

'A change?' I looked at her as her eyes skittered around the room, determined to focus on anything but me. 'Aunt Val?'

'I've got some toast for you downstairs if you fancy it. Or are you still recovering after your night of debauchery?'

And just like that she shut down, the door closing behind her. I dragged the duvet up over my head and scrunched my eyes shut, pressing a palm into my forehead. An alarm went off by my ear, and I slammed a hand down on my Kermit the Frog clock.

***

Saoirse came into view. All ten feet of flaky paint work, dodgy electrics, and a hundred other unfinished jobs. I had no memory of Mum, but

Dad naming the boat after her was his way of keeping her with us.

'I've done my best to keep her out there. But it's hard. I know you don't want to hear it, but she needs someone on her all the time.' Clem paused, as though deciding whether to say what he was about to. 'Preferably two people.' He watched my face for a reaction, and when I didn't give one, he pushed on. 'Plus, now I have Tinman...' Clem's voice trailed off and I allowed my mind to focus in on the steady slap of water hitting the keel.

His words stung, causing my chest to tighten. Of course she was meant for two. I knew he wasn't trying to be cruel—he was right; Saoirse was a two-person boat. There was a sad irony that we had called her Saoirse in memory of Mum, so Dad and I could feel close to her. Now it was the one place I could feel close to both my parents.

'If I'm honest, Riss, she's gonna need to come out the water. The cutlass bearing has gone, and she needs a new paint job, and a whole bunch of other jobs that I haven't had a chance to get to.'

'What are you saying, Clem?'

'You might need to think about selling her.'

I sucked in air, as though I'd just been hit with something hard and heavy. I knew Saoirse couldn't sit unused in the water, but I wasn't ready to hear those words.

The breeze picked up, and the whistle of the sailboats filled the air as their strings rattled against their masts.

'You alright?' One of Clem's hands came to rest on my shoulder as I stood halfway between Saoirse and dry land. There's no rush, I said to myself, allowing the screech of gulls above my head, and hint of engine oil in the air to slow my breathing.

'Like I said, she needs a bit of love.' He ran his hand along her hull.

'I mean.' I let out an involuntary laugh. 'That might be an under-statement.'

I looked at the cracked and peeling paint of the wheelhouse, my eyes moving from one repair job to the next. Boats were a continual list of repairs and improvements.

However, the longer she sat in the water doing nothing, the harder it would be to get her going again.

'Looks worse than it is.' Clem backtracked as he watched my eyes dart from one thing to the next. 'A week on shore and we'll have it all done.'

Maybe he was right, but what was the point? My mind sat some-where between an inability to let go and move forwards, and a desperate urge to hold on to everything I once had.

'I'm gonna leave you to it. Got some stuff to sort out back at the Shed. You going to be OK?'

I nodded, distracted. We both knew I had to do the next part on my own. I held onto the metal railing and took the long overdue step on board. The pots were stacked, and the deck was clean and clear. Clem had done a good job keeping her afloat. The hum of the pump whirring in the background told me I really did need to get her ashore and replace the cutlass bearing. I turned and looked towards the wheelhouse. It was small, but still capable of holding two people.

I moved with the water beneath me, and a flicker ignited in my stomach. Excitement? Yes. Yes, there was happiness here too.

I let my fingers stretch out over the wheel, feeling the gentle rock as the water moved. She had everything you needed for a day's fishing—GPS, plotter, radio. The bubble of excitement grew at the thought of heading out to sea.

My eye caught on the thin scribble of handwriting covering the papers stacked up on the side, and my breath caught in my throat.

Breathe. They're just old notes, Rissa. No biggie.

I forced my fingers to grip them and make my eyes read through a life I couldn't bear to admit I still yearned for.

- **What to do when coming aboard**
- **Where to find the best crab**
- **How to drop the gear**
-**How to bring her in on the tide.**

My stomach lurched, and I stuffed the papers away. Each time I thought there was a chance to move through the pain, something else crept up on me, a whack-a-mole hammer sending me back into the sadness, the guilt, the grief. Dad's voice jolted me back from the edge of self-pity: *Focus on the mundane. It clears the mind of all other thoughts. That's what helped when we lost your mum.*

Whenever he had something on his mind, a problem to be worked through, a worry to put aside, he would be on the boat. I made my way back outside, running on muscle memory as my brain ran through the checks Dad had drilled into me. Check gear, check pots...

Some things are just too ingrained, eh, Riss?

I bent down and opened the trap to the engine. Nothing like a bit of grease and metal to clear your mind. And if the state of the exterior was anything to go by, god only knew what needed fixing inside.

***

'Get out you piece of— Urgh. Gotcha!'

I couldn't tell you how long I'd been there. Bent over on my knees, feeling had disappeared from my waist down.

I couldn't imagine what state I was in, but what did it matter? I was alone. Besides, Dad had been right. It was total therapy. I had my tool bag by my side, engine oil in my hair and on my face, and I was pretty certain I had given a front row seat of my ass to every passing gull. But boy, did it feel good.

'Rissa?'

What the—

The smooth, deep tone jerked me from my work, and in my haste to unexpose my bum, I knocked my head on the hatch door, sending small stars dancing across my eyes.

'Oh, god, I'm so sorry.' He rushed onto the deck and knelt at my side. 'Are you alright? I didn't mean to startle you.' I could feel the warmth of his hand on my shoulder. 'How many fingers am I holding up?'

I know it's three, but I'm still seeing stars, and you can't blame a girl for enjoying the moment.

'Rissa?'

His voice stopped my thoughts getting more out of control, and I looked him up and down.

'Are *you* going to be alright?' I asked, feeling the pain subside along with the dancing stars, as the warmth and weight of his hand on me increased.

'What do you mean?'

'You're kneeling in oil. Water and vinegar won't help this time.' I laughed as he flinched at the sight of his blue chinos, which were now

47

sporting two black knees.

'All in the name of chivalry,' he said, recovering and holding a hand out to me.

I straightened myself and made a poor attempt to wipe the grease from my face with my T-shirt, only succeeding in spreading it to places it hadn't been before.

'You missed a bit.' He stepped forwards. His handkerchief appeared and, before I had a chance to react, he'd wiped a gentle path across my cheek. 'Perfect,' he said, his eyes fixed on my face.

Charlie took a step back as though catching himself. Breaking the spell of the moment.

'You're quite the anomaly, Rissa,' he eventually said, as he looked around the boat.

'I'm not sure how to take that.'

'Well.' He stopped and looked at me again, his word holding more than it should.

I felt my cheeks blush beneath the smears of oil.

'What are you doing down this side of town? Fancy a career change?' I said, humour my only deflection from the unfamiliar feelings this man stirred inside me.

He let out a short laugh that brought me far too much pleasure.

'I was snooping, if I'm honest. Not stalking, I can assure you. Although'—his eyes caught mine and held them—'running into you again is definitely no bad thing.'

I took in a breath and reminded myself of the basics of breathing. *Keep it together, Riss!*

'This is quite a boat.' He turned away again. 'Is it yours?'

'Family boat,' I said, fiddling with the neatly stacked crab pots. This was one conversation I wasn't prepared to have. I let the silence fall between us.

The hum of the pump and steady slap of water against the boat was the only noise left. I watched as he moved his large frame around my small deck. His fingers ran along the rail as though inspecting. His confidence was infuriating and intoxicating in equal measure.

'I should get back to—'

'I'm glad I've run into you.' He turned to face me, his deep green eyes looking straight at me, sending a buzz through my body that shouldn't have been there. 'I'm on my way to find some of Telbury's famous fish and chips. I can't tempt you, can I?'

'Oh.' My voice went up like some love-struck schoolgirl.

'The guy at the hotel reception said a trip here wasn't worth it without sampling the fish and chips.'

'He's not wrong.'

'So, what do you say? Fancy a temporary tour guide position?'

'I could give you a map, if you like?'

Really?

'I'm more of a personal tour kind of guy.'

His voice lowered and was dripping in unsaid words.

'Right.' My voice came out strangled and altogether lacking the smoothness of the man in front of me. Did people like him go to some special after school classes to learn how to be so goddamn put together?

'Thanks, but I better keep at it,' I said, twirling the spanner in my hand in explanation.

'Fair enough.' He nodded. 'How about dinner then?'

I stared back at him, as his lips lifted into that stomach-turning smile.

Say yes. Say yes!

'I've got a lot going on at the moment.' It wasn't a lie.

'Do you not eat?'

'Funny.'

'It's a date, Rissa. Not a marriage proposal.'

'A date?'

'I think they're still called that. I admit, I haven't been on one in a while, but things haven't changed that much.'

'I think I remember you telling me you were too busy for such things the other night.'

'True.' He nodded, sliding a hand into his pocket. 'But like I said, you're quite the anomaly.'

I let out a laugh. I should have known he'd be the persistent sort. Clothes like that and confidence like his didn't point to a man who took no for an answer. No, Charlie was one of life's achievers. Before I had a chance to reply, he put his hand out to stop me.

'It's just food. If it makes you feel better, we can split the bill.'

'Promise?'

'Scout's honour.'

The wink he gave me told me everything I needed to know about how far from a scout he really was.

'OK then.'

'Good.' He nodded before turning and stepping back on to the jetty.

'Mermaid's.' I called after him as he walked away.

'Pardon?'

'If you're looking for a fish and chip shop. You're looking for Mermaid's chippy, up on the square. Best deep-fried sausage this side of Scotland.'

I watched as he walked back up towards the town, my eyes paying far too much attention to him walking away. To hell with it, maybe a bit of handsome distraction was exactly what I needed.

What was the worst that could happen?

Chapter 7

'Nav, aren't we meant to be heading over to the town hall?' I asked, looking around at the busy tables and the kitchen full of chefs. Nav's restaurant not only held the title for best restaurant in Telbury, but it had the best view. Floor-to-ceiling windows allowed customers uninterrupted views across the water. Dark leather banquettes lined both walls, and the kitchen sat at the rear of the space. Despite it being late afternoon, the tables were still full with people enjoying long, boozy lunches, and the restaurant had that buzz that only somewhere with happy customers can.

'I know, I know. Five more minutes... No. No! Does that look right to you?' she shouted. Her attention turned to the young chef who had just placed a—from what I could see—perfect panna cotta in front of her.

I took a step out of the way. Nav might weigh no more than your average spaniel, but there was a great green Hulk hidden under those immaculate chef whites.

'Five minutes, Riss. I've got all the nibbles ready. All we have to do is plate them when we get there.'

Another mouth-watering plate landed in front of her. This time a beautifully presented lobster. She bent over with a pair of tweezers, placing delicate blue petals onto the dish.

'How's Val? Have you spoken with her?' she asked, not looking up.

'That feels loaded.'

She mumbled something inaudible before sliding the now complete dish to the waiting hands of the server.

'What does that mean?' My concern piqued.

'Nothing.' She dismissed the words with one of her tiny hands, before looking back down as a new dish was placed in front of her.

'Nothing?' I raised a suspicious eyebrow.

'Just speak with your aunt.' Her hand touched mine, before she turned and barked out some more orders.

Nav was one of life's anomalies, thriving off stress and pressure. However it sure as hell didn't mean she worked calmly in it. I was convinced part of her success was because people enjoyed watching her rage around the kitchen like some irate gorilla in a cage. That, and the fact her food was sublime.

'Next time your best friend tells you she's opening a restaurant, just shout *no*!' Her short black hair momentarily fell from its position tucked behind her ear, before she quickly corrected it.

'That bad?' I asked, unable to suppress a laugh.

'I swear I'd be better doing it all myself sometimes. Darren! How long for table five?' She spun round to face the mere boy coming towards us. Her fingers tapped out an impatient tune on the stainless-steel counter as he hurried over, the plate shaking in his sweaty hands.

I watched in awe as she squeezed puree onto the plate in front of her in ever growing circles.

'Now that you're staying this time...' Her eyes didn't look up from the plate, and her voice trailed off. Not that she needed to finish the sentence. I knew where she was going with it. It was the same old, same old. I kept my eyes on the mesmerizing blobs of pink puree being squeezed onto the plate in the hope she'd get distracted and move on. 'I'd love a new supplier.'

Or not.

'Clem is your supplier.'

'Exactly!' She snorted.

She was trying to help... Everyone was, but the truth was, all it did was make the knot in my chest twist tighter. My mind wandered as thoughts of the boat came back to me. Dad's face when he realised I really did want to be a fisherman. The sun bearing down on us; the gulls' impatient screeches as they waited for the pots to be hauled in. Then clouds. Wind. The cold hit of water in my face. Water, everywhere. Too much water.

Nav caught the look on my face and grabbed my hand. 'But you know what, it doesn't matter. You're here now, and that's all I care about.'

I shook down my shoulders like a boxer before a match and let out a breath, shrugging the thought of Dad out of my mind.

'You're right.' I smiled. 'Now let's go and find out how much of a threat this property-developing devil is, before they ruin us all.'

Chapter 8

The town hall was off the main square and possessed all the appropriate characteristics a town hall should. Running along the front of the building, shallow stone steps led up to large wooden double doors. An overhanging balcony jutted out at the front, supported by four small pillars.

The evening was still warm, and the late sun flooded the hall in a honey glow, making the crowd on the top steps look heaven sent.

Once inside, I looked across the hall. Chairs had been set out in rows, covering most of the room. Despite its grand exterior, the inside was far more basic. The rectangular space had wood panelling with a few overhead lights serving as a spotlight for the stage. Other than that, the stage was either lights on or lights off. Normally the stage was reserved for the Christmas Nativity or school concerts, but it was now set up more like a fancy Silicone Valley AGM. A row of three armchairs, each with its own side table, filled the stage. A glass bottle of water was on each table, accompanied by a glass tumbler.

A large projector was in the process of starting up, but the frustrating message of *ERROR* flashed repeatedly on the screen.

'Ladies and gentlemen, if you could all now take your seats. The presentation is about to begin.'

The lights dimmed, and the last few stragglers took their seats as a hush came over the hall. The projector screen that had been flashing *ERROR* not long ago was now beaming out an aerial view of Telbury from the sea.

'God, it's beautiful, huh?' Nav whispered to me. 'Still gets me.'

'Me too,' I said, staring back at the images. 'Although, it's giving me definite early evening soap opera feels, with the drone camera swooping through the town in opening credits.'

She let out a snort of laughter, and I covered her mouth with my hand as a few grumpy faces turned to look at us.

Three men entered stage right. The first I recognised as our local councillor, Mr Rooney. He had been in the position since I was a teenager. He was a small man with a slight frame. His greying hair, thin and wiry, and his half-moon spectacles did nothing to quash the idea he was actually an elf moonlighting as a human. The next two I hadn't seen before.

Both wore suits that surely cost more than an average yearly salary here in Telbury, and both were carrying leather folders. The kind that zip up all the way round and almost always have their initials embossed on the side.

'Who are the two with Mr Rooney?' Nav asked, squinting at the stage.

'Good evening, everyone, and welcome. Thank you all so much for taking the time to join us here tonight and hear about our exciting proposals,' one of the leather-folder men said. I couldn't be sure, but I would swear Mr Rooney was sweating. He seemed more uncomfortable tonight than usual.

'This is all a bit serious, isn't it?' Nav leaned in as we watched the mystery man move with confidence across the front of the stage and look out into the darkened hall.

'We hope that with our plans, Telbury will secure its future for generations to come, whilst opening it up to even more people to enjoy,' the man continued, seemingly unfazed by low grumbles that travelled across the room like a Mexican wave. Nav and I turned to look at each other, and for the first time, I saw the flicker of concern that was building in me mirrored in her eyes.

I looked back at the stage, and the aerial view of Telbury had vanished. It was being replaced by an architect drawing with large words in bold at the top. I could feel my heart rate quicken as I read the words in front of me. There was an audible gasp from the audience, and Nav grabbed my hand as she read the screen.

LUXURY APARTMENT COMPLEX
HARBOUR SETTING, SEA VIEW

'What on earth—'

'I don't understand,' Nav said, shaking her head. 'What is happening? Who are these people?'

'It can't be true,' I said, more to myself than anyone else.

'Next slide, please,' the man on stage said, looking out to someone right of stage. A new image filled the screen.

'Is that—?' Nav cut herself off as the next image came into focus.

'No way. Is that meant to be Telbury?'

'Where's the fishing fleet?'

My eyes scanned the image in front of us, and my heart rate picked up. This wasn't real. It couldn't be. Where were the crab pots, even?

Nav let out a high-pitched squeal and grabbed my hand tighter. 'What have they done?'

A luxury building complex, where a two-bed sea view apartment will start from £400,000.

My head filled with too many questions, and I was struggling to keep them all in. The man on stage started talking again, ignoring the gasps and ever louder mutterings from the audience.

'And without further ado, let me introduce to you the mastermind behind this amazing development, Mr Charlie Caulson.'

Fuuuuck!

My body stiffened, and all the noise around me slipped away. The room was moving in slow motion, and I watched as those unmistakable suede shoes moved out onto the stage. It couldn't be. It wasn't possible. I would know. I would... Perfectly fitting chinos, gave way to a grey jumper with a turned up zip collar.

No! How did I not know? How, how...

'Riss, what's happening? You look pale.'

'Charlie,' I said, my voice coming out as a gasp. My eyes fixed on the man now standing in the middle of the stage, that smile beaming out at the audience, as effortless as breathing.

'Who's Charlie?'

'Charlie,' I repeated. 'That's Mrs Lesley's son.'

'Who's Mrs Lesley?' Nav gripped my hand tighter.

My face was on fire, and I leaned back into the table hoping it would prevent me from sinking to the floor.

'Thank you, David.' His voice was loud and unmistakable as he took the microphone and walked to the front of the stage. 'And thank you all for coming here tonight. I'm sure you have lots of questions about our plans, and we want to be as open as possible with you all. After all, this is your town. As many of you will know, this project is still at the bidding stage. However, we feel it's important to engage with you all from the beginning.'

'How about engaging with the door then!' came a shout from somewhere in the dark. A cheer rose up, followed by more shouts. Charlie didn't flinch. From his expression, it looked like he didn't even hear it. But once the hall had been hushed back to quiet, he placed a hand in his pocket and nodded his head as though agreeing with the crowd.

God, he was like some self-help coach from L.A.

'I understand your frustrations, trust me. But that is why I'm here. I want to reassure you all and give you all the information I can.'

***

The sound of chairs scraping on the floor as people began to move from their seats brought the room back into focus.

'Chef, do you want the mousse now?' Darren appeared in the door, his white-knuckled hands clasped in front of him.

Nav had been stunned into silence and just about managed a cursory nod.

'I'll come and help bring them out,' I said, desperate for something to do, other than visualise the many ways I was going to inflict unbearable pain on Charlie.

Darren and I silently placed the pots of mousse onto the trays and carried them back to the table. Small groups had started to form, all having the same hushed conversations.

'Riss, incoming.' Nav nodded in the direction of the men walking towards us.

I ducked down under the trestle table as the group approached. I had forgotten about the bin bags I'd stuffed under there right before the presentation started. They were now blocking my hiding place.

'Thank you for the spread, Nav. Excellent as usual.' I heard Mr Rooney's voice moving closer and took my chance. I gave the bags one big push and wiggled myself out of view before anyone caught me.

'Thank you.'

'And Narissa? Is that you?' Mr Rooney's voice was bordering on concern.

Dammit. *Can't a girl just hide and pretend the world doesn't exist anymore?*

'Are you OK there? Here, let me help you,' the now all too familiar voice of Charlie said.

'I'm *fine*,' I said, unable to sound indifferent. I reversed myself back out from under the table and pulled myself up. Of course he caught me crawling under the table. How else was my shit luck going to play out?

I took a second, allowing myself to compose my face before turning around. When I did, Charlie's smiling face was looking back at me, a distinct look of amusement in his eyes. The soft wrinkles by his eyes crinkled as he smiled his gorgeous smile. Although, I could see how if you squinted your eyes and tilted your head, it was more Disney villain than Adonis beauty.

'Hey,' he said, taking a step towards me that I matched with one backwards into the hard edge of the table. 'I can't tell you how nice it was to see a friendly face out there. Not exactly the easiest crowd.' He raised his eyebrows and gave a quick look around the room.

'It's you.'

'It is.' His look turned from amused to quizzical. 'Are you OK?'

'You're the monster wanting to destroy our town.'

'Rissa?'

'How could you?'

'Rissa, I—' He went to say something and closed his mouth before opening it again.

'It's not my intention.' He reached out towards me, and my stomach lurched as his hand touched mine, but my mind was in control now. No more swooning.

'It seems like we have a lot to discuss. How about we get that dinner? We can talk everything through.'

Arrogant son of a—

'You think I'm going to go and have some cosy dinner with you?

'I just meant—'

'You are trying to destroy our fishing fleet. Do you know what that will do? Do you have any idea?' People were starting to look, but I didn't care. I was only saying what they all wanted to. 'You never said anything. You lied to me.' I shook my head, hoping it might shake me from the nightmare I had found myself in.

'I never lied. I just never told you what I did for a living. But neither did you. This isn't the deceit you think it is.' His tone had lost its playfulness.

'I have to go. I'm sure you have lots of people who want to talk to you.'

'Rissa.'

I didn't know if he said anything else after that. I was halfway across the hall already. To hell with hanging around to hear him spew more lies.

Chapter 9

Clem had a 1990 Lee Fisherman. The hull was bright turquoise with a black stripe on the top and bottom. The single man (two if you were hugging) wheelhouse was at the front of the boat, and the deck was kitted out for fishing. We chugged out of the harbour, the sound of the engine soothing me. I closed my eyes and inhaled deeply, a mix of diesel and sea salt filling my nose. The sea was calm, and the only movement was the boat, pushing the water away like rippling honey. The sun glistened on the surface, and a few candy floss clouds dotted the otherwise blue sky.

As we pulled around the head of the bay, the craggy rocks of Harry's Jump came into view. The early jumpers were already there. There were a number of ledges jutting out from the cliff face, many that could only be reached by climbing up to them from the water. But if you were daring enough to jump from the top, you could reach them. I smiled as I watched more brave souls hurl themselves off the ledge. The distant sound of bodies hitting the water reached us. No fear. No worry about the consequences. I was envious of that.

'You caused quite the stir last night,' Clem said, once we were past the worst of the sand banks and into deeper water. It was a short trip out to fetch the pots Clem wanted to bring in, and I could see the buoys in the water up ahead. 'I got the tail end of it. From what I heard, you gave him what for.'

'He deserved it. I mean, who the hell does he think he is?'

'Rich.'

I let out a knowing laugh and turned back to the water. My anger over the town meeting had done a good job of distracting me, but as the buoys came into clear view and Clem moved around the boat in preparation, I could feel my muscles tense.

'You good?'

'Yeah,' I said, without breaking eye contact with the water.

The engine slowed and we came up alongside the first buoy.

'How 'bout I'll get us going and you help on deck.'

I nodded, grateful Clem wasn't one to probe.

Clem flicked a switch, and the winch came to life. I had learned at a young age that when the machines started up, you needed to have your wits about you. There were too many horror stories of limbs getting caught in the gear to not pay attention.

'You ready?' Clem shouted to me over the noise, as he pulled on his gloves. He had hooked the buoy, and he was about to start hauling up the pots.

'Bring it on.' I smiled. Fake it till you make it, right?

The first pot flung up out of the water, and I waited, hands ready, for Clem to push it my way.

'I think we have a couple of good ones,' I said, as I opened the hatch and pulled the first lobster of the day out. I moved quickly, taping its claws and placing it in the already prepared box.

'Chuck that one,' Clem said, as I pulled out the next.

'Too small?' I asked, holding it up.

'Ah, like riding a bike, isn't it?'

'Lobster are biting today.'

The excited anticipation I'd had as a child started to creep back in.

'Let's hope it continues. Another ten to go!' Clem shouted over the noise of the winch. I had forgotten how noisy the boat was once the all gear was on and pots were flying up onto the deck.

It was a relatively simple system. The pots were on a line and spaced certain distances apart, between two buoys. Each fisherman had their own, and the number one rule was not to interfere with someone else's pots. But once the pots started coming on board, you had to be ready. Not keeping a tidy deck could mean some pretty nasty accidents.

***

After another hour, Clem lit his rollie, and I leaned back on the railing, letting my arms drop to my side. A dull ache built in my biceps from hauling pots around.

'We've got to stop him, Clem. He can't get away with this.'

Clem looked back at me and chuckled.

'What?'

'Just good to see that fight in you, is all. Gonna need it.'

I might have had my issues with Saoirse and what that meant for me fishing again, but over my dead body was I going to sit back and let some jumped up rich idiot steal what wasn't theirs.

'We need to stop them.'

'You know what the answer is then, don't you?' Clem leaned back on the railings next to me, his head tilting back, eyes closed.

'What?'

'Better call an emergency FFL meeting.'

***

Johnny sat on his perch by the window. He knew something was up and so had spent the best part of an hour hurling abuse at whomever walked through the door. For a creature that lived by the ritual of routine, the unusual gathering of people in a circle of seats in the middle of the pub was causing all sorts of problems. The Fisherman for Life meeting had been called.

'Here you are, my love,' Aunt Val said, opening her fanny pack and taking a handful of nuts, before dipping one in a small bowl of amber liquid.

'You've got to stop doing that,' I said, walking over.

'Hush your moaning. It's a stressful time. Johnny feels it all, you know.' She shook off the drips of beer, before handing it to an excited Johnny, who bounced up and down expectantly on his perch.

'Oh, we know. He's introduced me to swear words in the last hour that I didn't even know existed.'

'Ignore her,' she said, thrusting her face towards the parrot, one finger stroking the soft grey feathers on his chest as he crunched the peanut. 'She's just grumpy that lover boy turned out to be the evil mastermind behind the destruction of our town.'

'Or maybe I'm annoyed with my aunt who brought me home under false pretences. After swearing it was nothing to do with getting me out on the boat. You lied and told me you were sick! But you're right. You are sick, in the head.' It wasn't my finest moment, but I was running out of ideas. She was giving me nothing on her health, so she left me no choice. Baiting was my best bet.

'I didn't lie,' she said, her gaze not leaving Johnny as she continued to stroke his chest. 'And we didn't know for certain. You saw everyone's faces at the meeting—they were as shocked as you. It was all hearsay before that... Besides'—she looked up at me— 'would you have even come if I'd told you there was a rumour about the Shed being sold?'

I opened my mouth to answer, but she cut me off. 'No, exactly. You might not want to accept it, Rissa, but you are meant to be on the water. You can't run from it forever. What happened was not your fault. You need to stop using it as an excuse and face up to it all. You're not going back to London, and you're not running away anymore.'

She left a space for me to reply, but instead I said nothing.

'No. That's what I thought. You're sticking here, where you *belong*. You know it's the right thing.'

OK, so baiting was a fail.

'Rissa!'

I turned, thankful for an easy getaway from Aunt Val as Nav appeared in the doorway. Ever the feeder, she was carrying two large hampers full of provisions for the long evening ahead.

'Let me get that,' I said, rushing to help her. 'You didn't need to do this.' I took one of the loaded hampers from her and guided her to the nearest table.

'Don't be stupid. It calms me. Besides, a room full of angry fishermen...who then turn hungry?' She grimaced face and shook her shoulders in a shudder. 'I don't want to be here for that! Anyway, how are you doing?'

'I'm fine,' I said, already knowing my tone was too defensive to be believed.

'Rissa.' She put the final tray of sausage rolls out and looked up at me. 'You're allowed to be hurt. It will take a moment.'

'I'm fine,' I said, with as much confidence as I could. 'There's nothing to move on from, I promise.' I avoided her glare and continued emptying the contents of the hamper in front of me.

'It was sneaky and downright dishonest. You are allowed to be pissed.'

My head spun round to face her. 'It was, wasn't it?'

We both laughed as we tore Charlie apart, allowing some of the tension I had been carrying around since seeing him at the town hall to dissipate.

There was a growing circle of hardy, weather-worn men filling the space. Most had come straight from the dock, their thick soled wellies still on, the smell of sea and fish competing with the warm, spiced aromas coming from Nav's picnic. I watched Geoff march in and make his way to the bar. A skinny young man shuffled in behind him. I didn't recognise him, but there was no mistaking the family resemblance to Geoff.

'Who's that?' I asked, loud enough just for Nav.

She looked from me to Geoff and laughed. 'You sure you're feeling alright?'

'No, the kid.'

'Oh.' She sucked on a finger and released it with a pop of pleasure as she tasted the dip she had prepared. 'Geoff's son. Luke. Not surprised you don't recognise him. He's never about. Not a fishing fan.' She whispered the last bit as though uttering words of treason. 'Imagine this is the last place he wants to spend his evening.'

***

'How did this happen?' one of the younger lads asked.

'That idiot son of the Marshalls' saw a winning payday, that's what,' Clem answered.

'That wasn't ever the agreement. We were told that was for us to use. They know without the Shed we might as well stop now,' someone else added.

The questions descended into noise, with no clear direction. I found a seat next to Clem and let the conversation take shape around me.

I snuck a quick glance at Clem, who'd finished off his first beer and was cracking the lid on another.

'What?' he said, when he caught my eye, his annoyance obvious.

I shook my head and decided it wasn't the moment. Since when was I the alcohol police? It was two beers, not two bottles of neat whisky.

'This is bullshit.'

'Is it even legal?'

The loud voices of the skippers broke through my thoughts, and I looked out at the group around me. Their voices were getting louder, as though to cover up the real fear that lay beneath it all.

'Enough!' Geoff's voice brought everyone to a stop. 'We need solutions, not this.' He waved a giant hand around at everyone. 'We need to work together.'

'What's she doing here then?'

'Who?' Geoff's brow furrowed at the question.

'Her.' The young fisherman from earlier nodded at me. My mouth went dry at the attention. 'She ain't one of us. She's been away years.'

An unhelpful gasp was let out by the room.

Welcome to the Jerry Springer of Telbury.

I opened my mouth to reply, but nothing came out. Clem nudged me in the side, trying to jolt me into a response.

'Rissa is one of us, you twat.' Clem laughed, as though the comment was absurd. 'She's got more fishing blood in her than most of us in this room.'

'Yeah, but she's not been here. What, she just happens to turn up now? Can't deny it's a bit weird. He's from London. She's been in London. Then they're all cosy in here the other night.'

'There's nine million people in London,' Nav said, her disdain obvious.

'And yet she knew him.'

I slid deeper in my chair in a desperate attempt to melt out of the situation now unfolding. My desire to stop any more eyes burning into me was building at a dramatic rate.

'Well, Narissa, do you have anything to add?' Geoff looked at me, as though challenging me to stand up for myself.

'I didn't know who he was. Trust me; if I had, I wouldn't have had drinks with him.'

'Yeah, she might be a spy sent to trick us.'

What?

The conspiracy theory picked up pace, and comments were being thrown out from every angle. I scanned the room for a friendly face, briefly making eye contact with Luke, who looked as desperate to be out of the pub as I did.

'Right, how about we think about this rationally. Rissa is one of us. She wants what's best for Telbury too. She is not a bloody spy!' Nav pushed in to the circle of skippers.

'You a spy, Rissa?' Geoff said, his suspicions meeting in the deep gully between his eyebrows as he frowned over at me.

'Geoff, come on.'

'See! She is a spy!' someone shouted.

Geoff said nothing and kept his eyes on me.

'No, Geoff. No, I am not a spy. I am from here. This is my home. I am as upset as the rest of you.'

Being there was starting to feel like a big mistake. Who was I kidding? I hadn't been back for any real length of time in years. They had no reason to trust me. I twisted the oversized watch on my wrist, resisting the urge to run.

'I'm not...' I started to defend myself again, but the voices drowned me out. I found my legs pushing my body out of the circle before I knew what I was doing.

'Riss, sit down. You need to stick this out. They'll burn themselves out of oxygen in a bit.' Clem looked up at me. But I was already making towards the door. I needed air; I needed space to think. Maybe they were right. Maybe this was a big mistake. Why on earth would they want *me* involved, for Christ's sake? I could feel the rising knot in my chest and grabbed for the door handle. I pushed it open and sucked in large gulps of evening air.

Chapter 10

There are some facts in life that are irrefutable. One of them is that a deep-fried sausage will ease even the most troubled mind. Lucky for me, Mermaid's Fish Bar sold the best deep-fried sausage south of Inverness. My stomach growled as my nose got the first whiff of grease and chips. I checked my watch. Nine P.M. It was a risk arriving this late, but it was a weeknight, and I banked on most of the tourists going traditional. Mermaid's had an annoying habit of only having a certain number of sausages available. Once they were gone, that was it.

'You alright, love. I'll be with you in a minute,' the man behind the counter said, before turning back to what he was doing.

'No worries.' I slid onto one of the headache-inducing red banquettes and sent a little thank you prayer to the man upstairs as my eyes locked onto the deep-fried sausage behind the glass counter.

The door behind me swung open, the computer-generated doorbell sound ringing in my ear.

'I'm just putting your fish down now, mate. Won't be a minute.'

'Thank you, no rush.' There was no mistaking that voice. No erasing it from my memory and casting it out into the coldness of space.

I turned slowly around. There he was.

I'd act like nothing had happened. Say nothing. Maybe if I turned to face the wall, he wouldn't notice me. That was the answer.

'I was hoping to bump into you.'

Say nothing.

'Rissa?' He stepped forwards, and I focused my attention on my watch, twisting it one way, then the next.

'You had the same idea, I see.' He nodded towards the counter. 'Late night fried food. Sometimes it's all that will do.'

Say nothing...

'Why are you talking to me?'

Too late!

'Can't you see this is not alright?'

'Getting fried food, or talking with you?' He smiled.

Ugh, the smile.

'Seriously?'

'Sorry.' He put a hand up in acceptance. 'I know this is a little hard for some of the town. But I promise this is a good thing.'

'A good, a good...' I stuttered. 'Are you insane? Do you have any idea what you're doing?'

'I'm hoping to build some wonderful homes, whilst also bringing more money to the area, securing Telbury's future.' There was a decisiveness in his tone. A hint of the businessmen who had made him who he was today.

'There are other options you know. Other places to build. How about the cliff side? Have you explored that?'

'There are always other options, but this is the best. Rissa, I have been doing this a long time. Trust me when I say, this is the best place.'

'The best place for you, maybe, but what about us? What about everyone that lives here? The community you're impacting?'

For a moment, he paused. For a moment, I thought he might be about to agree. But my optimism was short-lived. Whatever I thought he was going to say never came.

'You know what?' I jumped up from my seat. 'I just want to order my deep-fried sausage and go home.' I turned and faced the counter before I did some permanent damage to the man's all too perfect face.

'Are you heading back to London?'

Come on!

'No.' I turned back to face him. He was closer this time, and the scent of sandalwood and fresh linen invaded my nose.

'So you're going to be around for a while?'

'Yes, yes I am.' Resolve set in. I took a step back, desperate to get my shaking voice under control.

He nodded.

'I would rather bath in fish guts each day than let you get away with this.'

'Vivid.'

'And you know why?'

'At this point I'm pretty sure I can hazard a decent guess,' he said, his mouth still teetering on the edge of a smile.

'Because people like you are always getting away with this stuff. Thinking you're doing us small country people a favour, helping us out. But guess what? You're not! I am going to make sure you never get your entitled, *arrogant* hands on our Shed.'

'Erm, excuse me.

We both turned and looked at the man behind the counter, his eyes darting back and forth between us.

'What can I get you?'

I let my shoulders drop, relieved at the reprieve to my verbal diarrhoea.

'Deep-fried sausage and chips please.'

The man's face paled, and his gaze settled on the paper bag that had been placed on the counter.

'Unfortunately, we're all out of sausage, but maybe you'd like...'

'You!' I spun round.

'Me.' Charlie held my gaze.

'You've taken the last sausage.'

'I had it on good authority that this was the place to eat, and I'm a sucker for a deep-fried sausage.' Barely contained amusement filled his face.

'Is there nothing you won't take?'

He stepped closer, and the words I was about to speak melted in the air. My body stiffened as he leaned his head towards me, his breath on my ear.

'I would offer you mine, but I'm pretty sure you believe chivalry to be dead.' His voice was no more than a whisper.

Charlie straightened and walked over to the counter whilst I had a word with my overactive heartbeat. Why couldn't my body get on side with accepting the fact that hating Charlie Caulson was the only option?

'And Rissa?' He stopped at the door and looked back at me. 'You won't win. I will build these houses. But I do love a good fight.'

***

I burst back into the pub, the door swinging in my wake.

'I know you don't believe I'm the right person to help. But give me a chance, and I'll show you I am.' Heads spun around to see who the crazy person was. 'I want these dickheads out of here as much as the rest of you.' My dramatic, Hollywood-esque speech was not received with the loud cheers of applause I would have liked, but rather a lot of stunned faces, eyes blinking back at me. I waited a beat longer, hoping one of the startled faces would break the now very awkward silence.

'You're fine, Riss. You're on the team,' Clem said, looking up from the pieces of paper strewn across the table they were all crowded around.

'Fine?'

'Yeah, fine.' He walked up to me and flung an arm over my shoulder. 'I told you, everyone just needed to say their bit. You and the melodramatics.' He shook his head and guided me over to everyone.

'Shut up.' I mumbled, as I allowed my shoulders to relax, the tension draining away. I was on the team!

The next few hours passed in a blur of ideas and planning. Aunt Val had volunteered (a little too enthusiastically) to do a parachute jump. The next pub quiz would donate all proceeds to the cause, and Geoff had begrudgingly agreed to do a day out on the boat for a silent auction winner. But we still needed more.

'More will come up. We can always do some good old-fashioned fundraising in town with a bucket. Tourists love shit like that. Like to feel they're helping the poor little country folk,' Nav said, while packing up her picnic baskets.

'Maybe we can add more to the parachute jump? Stalls, donkey rides, make it a whole day thing,' I added.

A grumble of agreement went round the room at my suggestion. If we were going to beat this, we needed to throw as many things as we could at them. The worst thing we could do would be to stay silent. We needed to make them aware that this was the wrong town to invade.

'Right, Narissa.' Geoff's voice commanded the silence of the excited chatter, and everyone turned to look at him. 'You know what you've got to do?' He posed it as a question, but his tone told me I should be in no doubt about what I was doing. 'You need to be the main point of contact, Rissa. All these things we've talked about require organisation and time. Something we don't have much of. We need to understand what they're after. Find the flaws in their plan.'

'Flaws in their plan. Got it.'

'Riss.' Nav leaned into me, lowering her voice. 'Is this a good idea?'

I flashed her a look that told her all she needed to know about that statement.

'OK, OK. I'm just checking.' She put her hands up in surrender. 'We all need to have our wits about us. These developers don't pull any punches you know. They have one interest, and it sits on the bottom line of their pockets.' She shut the lid of the picnic basket with unnecessary force.

'We will not lose this town to some second home monstrosity,' I said a little louder, making sure for everyone to hear.

'Alright then. It's settled.' Geoff nodded with finality. 'But let's keep it democratic. Show of hands—who's in favour?'

Like all decisions in the FFL committee, all things were by majority vote, and all by a show of hands. For the most part, this was a fair approach to take.

I watched as the oil-stained hands rose in the air, and I took in a sharp breath as the knot in my chest tightened by an inch. But not from the usual feeling of despair and grief, no.

This was a feeling of belonging, a feeling like I was with my crew. I hadn't known I was coming here for the fight, but I'd be damned if I was going to lose!

Chapter 11

'You're sure this is legal?'

'I mean, it's a bit late now,' I deadpanned, causing Clem to blink one too many times. 'I'm kidding! Of course, it's legal. We have a right to protest... Besides, I got the all-clear from the council. Told them it was happening. They just wanted to make sure it was all civil. Don't want any trouble.' Despite the vagabond look most of the fishermen tended to take, giving them an unapproachable appearance, they weren't about to start trouble. We were making noise. It had been a week since the FFL meeting, and we had agreed we needed to get as much exposure as possible for what we were fighting. The more noise, the more people we could reach who might be able to support us.

'Right.'

I slipped under the rope we had strung up, blocking passage to the tall wooden structure of the Shed and the boats beyond.

Our picket line.

'Get your signs ready, you lot,' I called out to them. Geoff, Clem, and Aunt Val stood resolute at the front. If anyone looked like they were going to cause trouble, it was those three. But as I looked out on the rest of the assembled protesters, it was warming to see how many non-fishing folk had shown up. 'They are due down here in the next few minutes. Aunt Val, get your camera ready.'

She had suggested setting up some social media accounts to track our fight. For a woman whose pub wouldn't look out of place a hundred years past, she sure did have a way with technology.

'They're coming!' someone called from the crowd.

'Camera on,' Aunt Val said.

I nodded as my stomach jolted, and I took in one more shuddery breath. I wasn't an activist by any stretch. I didn't sign up to save the penguins, or march with my peers on worthy causes. But here I was, front and centre, with a loudspeaker raised to my mouth.

'We don't want it! We don't need it! Take your second homes and beat it.'

Everyone around me joined in, as boards with neon-bright painted messages were thrust into the air. The group of men kept coming. One took out a phone to avoid eye contact as another swivelled his head in any direction but forwards. Charlie kept focused on us. If he was shocked by our blockade, he didn't show it. His head was held high, shoulders relaxed.

We chanted louder this time. I looked over at Aunt Val, then Clem, giving them both a knowing nod. There was a bubble of excitement rising up in me. My usual dislike of putting myself in the spotlight was gone, replaced with an unwavering anger towards the man walking towards us as we continued chanting.

Charlie and his cronies slowed as they reached our picket line.

Ha, now what's your plan? I thought.

'Smile, you're on camera,' Aunt Val said, thrusting the camera forwards.

Charlie responded by leaning in close to the man on the phone and saying something audible only to him. The man nodded and started stabbing away at his phone again.

Charlie walked up to me, and my stomach made an unauthorised response.

'Nice turn out,' he said, looking straight at me. The crowd continued chanting, some of the words becoming a bit fruitier without the loud speaker to keep them in check.

'I told you. We're not going down without a fight.'

'Maybe,' he said, his expression unreadable. 'But you will go down.'

I looked straight at him, his hair ruffled from the breeze and his lightweight jacket open, exposing his fitted white shirt. Why did such an innocuous sentence sound so damn sexy coming from his mouth?

He was the devil sent to taunt me.

'This is just the beginning. Don't make the mistake of underestimating us.'

He leaned forwards slightly and lowered his voice. A secret to be kept between the two of us. 'Oh, I wouldn't dare.' His eyes never left mine, causing the hairs on my neck to stand on end. Charlie took a step back and straightened. He waited a beat, as though thinking through his next sentence.

'It was nice to see you again, Rissa.' A polite smile tugged at his mouth, but it felt wrong, in the same way as the words leaving his mouth. Was he about to say something else? The polite tone of his voice and the stunted words from his mouth didn't match the intensity swimming in those deep green eyes. But before I had a chance to come back at him, a flash of something flying through the air caught my attention. I realised too late what was happening and could only look on.

The sound of egg shell cracking, followed by bright yellow yolk dripping down Charlie's immaculate shirt caused me to gasp.

Splat.

The second one struck him squarely on the chin. For someone who had just been attacked—by egg, I admit—he didn't flinch. Instead, he took his handkerchief (I was starting to see the benefit of them) from his pocket and started dabbing his face.

'Oh no!' I groaned, watching as the mood shifted in the crowd. A cheer went up as some of Charlie's group started to move away. The man who had spent most of his time stabbing at his phone marched quickly over to where Charlie and I stood.

Me staring, mouth agape, unsure as to my next move.

Charlie trying and failing to remove the egg from his shirt and face.

'This is assault! Don't think we won't be looking at all our legal options for this,' he said, pointing his short, stubby finger at me. 'I'll be expecting a copy of that as well.' His attention swivelled to Aunt Val, who stood with her camera hanging by her side. No doubt the whole egg throwing incident was caught in perfect HD.

My brain grated into gear, and I put my hand out in a sign of peace. 'I'm sure we don't need to go that far. Emotions are heightened, and after all, no one got hurt.' I flashed a look at Charlie.

'Rissa will get you cleaned up.' Aunt Val's voice cut through the growing noise.

'I'll what?'

'Go get Mr Caulson a damp cloth and a towel. There'll be something over in the Shed.'

I tugged on Aunt Val's arm and pulled her towards me. 'What the hell are you thinking? I can't be seen to be helping him.'

'And we sure as hell can't be seen to be assaulting him either,' she hissed back.

I stood straight and looked up at Charlie, who had an amused sparkle in his eye.

'I do feel a bit of a bruise coming up actually.'

'Oh for...'

'Rissa will take you over to the Shed now,' Aunt Val butted in.

***

'Here.' I dropped a towel into his lap.

The shouts from outside were muffled inside the Shed. I had left Aunt Val and Clem to calm the rookie protesters. Turned out a bit of anarchy was too much for some.

'I would have thought you'd be trying a bit harder to placate me. After all, I will be looking at my legal options.'

I opened my mouth to respond, but the smile that played at the corners of his mouth stopped me, and I felt the sides of my mouth caving in to match. I took a seat next to him and did my best to ignore the heat of his body so close to me. A silence fell between us, until I could stand it no more.

'Why are you doing this?' I sighed.

'I just don't think egg yolk looks great with this shirt.'

I rolled my eyes and pushed on. 'I'm serious. What can we do to make you stop?'

Charlie folded the towel and placed it on the barrel to his left, before turning his whole body towards me. 'I'm not going to stop, Rissa. This is a great deal, and I think you and the others will come to agree with me on that. The world is changing. Telbury is lucky—it has the chance to move with it. Don't ignore that.'

'This deal will kill the fleet. You will ruin the livelihoods of countless people.'

'And create hundreds more jobs in the process. No one will be out of pocket.'

'You don't get it.' I shook my head, already exasperated by his complete ignorance. 'This has nothing to do with money.'

'Then I suggest you change your approach.'

'What are you talking about?' My patience for our conversation was waning with every word out of his all too perfect mouth.

'Whether you like it or not, money talks. The sooner you realise that, the easier this will all be.'

'Your mum told me you were a workaholic, but she never mentioned you were plain mean.'

I felt Charlie's body still. It was the first time I had mentioned Mrs Lesley since our meeting. The heat of his body was gone as he stood and brushed down his chinos. When he started talking again, whatever nerve I had touched had been quashed, and his steely confidence had returned.

'Like I said, I admire your determination, but you will lose. I am happy to work with the community as much as possible, but don't fight the tide.'

'Well, I guess we're done here,' I said.

'I guess so.' He stretched out a hand which I found myself taking. Damn him and his old school manners. His fingers wrapped around mine, and a jolt of electricity shot through me, hitting a spot somewhere between my legs as he pulled me to my feet. He kept my gaze, and neither one of us pulled away.

'I better be getting back,' I said, a beat too late.

'Of course.'

I snatched my hand back, rubbing my fingers as though they'd been burned on hot coals.

'Let's just keep this about business, okay?' I said, more for the oversized butterflies in my stomach than anything else. The sooner my body got the message, the better.

'Absolutely.' His answer was clear, but the unwavering intensity of his gaze told me something far more dangerous.

I turned back towards the door, determined not to be dragged under by those eyes.

'It's a shame, you know,' I said, and looked back to where Charlie stood, his eyes still focused on me.

'What's a shame?'

'I had a really fun evening with you the other night. But I guess it's on me, thinking you were actually interested in spending time with me.'

Charlie opened his mouth to say something, before changing his mind and nodding.

'May the best man win,' I said, and walked away.

***

'Nav.' I pushed open the restaurant door. 'I need your finest of finest hot chocolates ASAP. And before you start your preaching, I have a plan and it's all going to be OK.' I had left the Shed and headed straight for Nav's. The door hadn't even shut behind me before I stopped in my tracks. The usual hum of the commercial fan and chatter of a busy kitchen were missing.

'Nav?'

'Mmmm,' came the reply. 'I'm here.'

I walked around into the kitchen, trying to make sense of the clear worktops and lack of bodies.

'Nav?'

'Welcome.'

A slurred voice came from below the counter. I look down to see Nav sitting cross-legged in a pair of baggy grey sweatpants and her favourite oversized Duran Duran hoodie.

'Jesus, Nav, are you alright? Are you hurt? What happened?' The questions tumbled out of me as I did a quick scan of her to check for any obvious signs of injuries or open wounds.

'He left,' she said, shrugging her shoulders, before tipping the bottle of wine cradled in her arm into a wine glass.

'Who left?'

'Darren.'

'Ah.'

I crawled under the counter and squished in next to her.

87

'Will he come back?' I wrapped my arm around her tiny frame. For all her confidence, Nav was still capable of crumbling every now and again.

She pushed a crumpled piece of paper at me. 'Don't say anything,' she said, nudging me, 'I know you think I was too harsh on him.'

I read the note which Darren had left and sighed. If I was honest, I was surprised he'd lasted as long as he had. Not that this was the moment to impart this particular *I told you so* comment.

I pulled my fingers over my mouth to show I wasn't even going to go there before she leaned down to her side, bringing a fork up to her mouth.

'Is that caviar?' I asked, as she shovelled a large forkful of scrambled egg and caviar into her mouth.

'I'm comfort eating,' she said, before taking a large gulp of wine. 'And comfort drinking.'

'At least you're doing it in style.' I reached up to the counter and grabbed a glass before pouring myself some of the overpriced white wine. 'Although I would expect nothing else. Toffee popcorn and tequila were never going to cut it.'

She managed a smile. But I was all too aware of how losing her right-hand man would put even more pressure on her. The summer season was upon us, and finding staff at this point in was almost impossible.

'Why are you here anyway? You've not come to tell me we're about to be sued, are you?'

I let out a laugh at the look of horror on her face. 'No. We live to fight another day.' I leaned back against the wall behind and took another large gulp of wine.

'So, tell me, how tempted were you to rip his clothes off?'

'Nav!'

'Oh shut up with your piousness. I'm not saying you're gonna do it, but don't tell me you haven't thought about it.'

I took another sip of wine. Whatever my overactive butterflies thought about Charlie's physical appearance was irrelevant. As much as I wanted to slowly undo the next button of his shirt, exposing the light smatter of hair I knew was waiting for me, I also wanted to chop his balls off and feed them to the crabs. Logic would prevail!

'He's gonna fight us,' I said finally, shaking my mind from the gutter.

'We're ready.'

'It feels like an impossible feat. We're not even sure if we can buy the Shed yet.'

'Maybe. But maybe not,' Nav said, threading her arm through mine. 'We have things planned, and we can organise more. I was thinking about a summer ball. Sell tickets at some ridiculous price. All the holiday home lot will be here by then, and if there's one thing second homers hate more than locals, it's new second homers.'

We both drank to that.

Bring it on!

Chapter 12

Pubs are like all-seeing eyes. They have a front row seat to some of our most intimate moments. First kisses—mine was wet, a minute too long, and involved my sampling far too much metal from braces. Fights—a pub isn't a pub if there haven't been some good fights held there. Wedding receptions, birthday parties...wakes. Like I said, an all-seeing eye into every aspect of people's lives. The good and the bad. But tonight, it was good. It was filled to the rafters with people all coming together for a common cause. The feeling of support rippled through the room, making even the most cold-hearted feel warmed. In addition to the already planned pub quiz and day in the life, new ideas from the past week had included a karaoke night and a beach day that would facilitate Aunt Val's parachute jump.

Tonight was the pub quiz, and the locals had not disappointed.

'Right, button it, you lot,' Aunt Val shouted across the pub. She turned down the sound of Mr Cash to below a whisper, quieting her obeying subjects. She'd thrown herself into the fundraising and, in particular, the preparation for her sky dive. Most mornings she could be found splayed out on the pub floor, practicing positions she wanted to recreate in the air.

'Welcome, all of you,' she called out, taking a small bow in response to the whistles of approval at the canary yellow leotard she was wearing. 'As you know, we got some bastards think they can come and take what's ours. But we're all here to say that ain't the case.'

The crowd responded with a resounding *yeah*.

'Every penny counts. Rissa mentioned it on the flyer, but I'll tell you all again. All profit tonight is going straight into the war chest, so I expect you all to get smashed. Not one of you should be walking straight by the end of the night.'

Once again, the bar crowd voiced their approval.

'Also, if you want to see this goddess-like body in this outfit again, go buy your beach day pass. Nav over there has tickets. I don't want any excuses.'

It was impossible not to be carried along by the crowd. Aunt Val had done quizzes in the past, but this was something else. We were operating on the O2 Arena level now. It was standing room only, and people were crowded around tables, pens at the ready.

'You all have your pen and quiz sheet in front of you. I'll do a final round of drinks now for them that want it, then we'll get going. Ready, steady, let's get pissed!'

A wall of excited fishermen moved forwards as one, and I watched Aunt Val disappear behind the bodies.

'I better get over there before they start climbing over the bar.'

'I'll come. Could do with some distraction.' Nav jumped off the bar stool. After her kitchen floor reset the other day, she'd rallied and decided she didn't need a sous chef after all. She was in the denial stage of grief, but I was going to let her sit there for a bit.

***

'That'll be £7.50 please.' I pushed the machine across the bar, and the man in front of me tapped his card.

'Have you heard from he who shan't be named?' Nav came up beside me, taking the card machine and pushing it in front of her customer.

'No, but I'm not expecting to.' There was nothing to discuss. 'We need to focus on raising the money. Then he can scuttle off to destroy another town,' I said, moving away to the next customer.

I had called the care home to check in, let them know my plans to stay down here for the foreseeable future. Venessa told me that he had been in to see Mrs Lesley. I supposed there was no need for him to stick around now that he'd swooped in and done his big reveal. He would have minions that could do the lowly work of liaising with the locals. It wasn't as though I *wanted* to see him. But the thought of not ever seeing him bugged me. The way a fruit fly does. No matter how hard you try to grab and crush it, it always slips through your fingers, reappearing right in front of your face.

'Are you not just a little bit curious?'

'Nav!' I flashed an apologetic smile at the man in front of me, who was giving me his best disapproving glare.

'What?'

'I am one hundred per cent not interested in him that way... I am completely uninterested.'

Convincing, Riss.

'Whatever you say.'

'Yes, it is what I say. I am focused on saving our town, if you hadn't noticed.' I swung my arm around the room before setting the pint of beer I had just poured onto the bar with more force than necessary. 'Besides, if you didn't notice, the guy used me. He was just checking out the locals and trying to butter me up.' Not that I wanted to admit it—it stung.

'Well, you better keep that focus right now, because you're going to need it.'

I gave her a quizzical look, and she nodded towards the door that had just swung open.

The unmistakable shape of Charlie Caulson filled the door. My lungs took an involuntary gulp of air, and the mutated butterflies I had wrangled into a cage started to thrash around.

His eyes scanned the room as suspicious faces started to turn and look at the man standing in green suede shoes and a pressed white shirt. The rolled up sleeves exposed his muscled forearms.

'What the hell is he doing here?' I managed.

'I think that is what everyone is thinking,' Nav said, as the grumbles of discontent started to become audible.

His eyes moved across the room before landing on me, and a heat flushed my cheeks. I felt everyone's eyes flick from Charlie to me as his large frame moved with the ease and confidence of someone in complete control of their surroundings. Did he not feel the looks? Where was his shame?

'Why is he here?' Aunt Val shouted from the other side of the bar, with no intention of keeping her voice down.

I flashed her a look before she replied, 'You better deal with that. And quick.'

'Seriously?' I said, as he reached me.

He smiled and leaned over the bar, apparently oblivious to the near riot about to start behind him. 'Charming as ever. Good evening, Narissa.'

Why did I get the feeling he enjoyed these interactions?

'Get back here now,' I said, swinging the gate open and ushering him in to the cellar.

'Really, right now? So impatient.' His voice was low and annoyingly seductive.

'Shut up,' I said, trying to keep my distance as we squeezed through the door together and shut it behind us. My hand reached for a light switch that wasn't where I'd thought, and the darkness engulfed us, intensifying how close his body was to mine.

'Come on,' I said, trying to keep the panic at bay, as I scrambled in the dark. My fingers brushed against his stubbled jaw in my desperate search for the light.

'As much as I like this foreplay, it honestly wasn't my intention for tonight.'

'Will you be quiet? Where is that bloody... Aha! There!' I let out a sigh as light filled the room. In my desperate state to make space between us, I stumbled back, knocking into an empty keg.

'You alright?' He let out a laugh, enjoying how uncomfortable I was.

'No, I'm not alright. We are holding a fundraising quiz night, and you'—I prodded a finger into his chest, immediately regretting it as the caged butterflies I had done well to keep under lock broke free at the feel of him—'the reason for this fundraise, have just waltzed in like you're here to put your tenner down and grab a pencil.'

'Can I?' He raised his eyebrows, and the mischief in his voice was undeniable.

'No! This isn't funny. Why are you even here?'

'Can I have your number?'

My patience broke, and with it my self-control, at not giving him a piece of my mind.

'No! Are you really going to hit on me? You think a quickie in the cellar and I'll call off the dogs? Where should we go for? Here?' I tapped the keg I had stumbled into. 'Not very comfortable, but I doubt you're one for stamina anyway.' I gave him a look up and down, before biting my lips shut, stunned at my outburst. But the man was infuriating; he provoked me. Silence fell between us, and only my breathing was audible.

'What? Nothing to say?'

The smile I was growing to love and hate all at once creased his mouth, before he ran his tongue along his bottom lip with a nod.

'Why are you looking at me like that?'

'We have a meeting tomorrow morning,' he finally said.

I looked up at him as he allowed my embarrassment to fill the small space.

'A meeting,' I repeated.

'At ten.'

'You came down here to tell me that?'

'I don't have your number.' He was enjoying this. Watching me squirm under his gaze, under the gaze of everyone in the pub.

I shook my head, annoyed at myself for being dragged into this.

'So,' Charlie said, talking slower now, as though handling an unpredictable animal. 'As'—he paused, considering his choice of words—'tempting as your offer is, I wanted to send you the details before tomorrow. I didn't have another way of contacting you. After our chat in the Shed the other day, I thought it would be considerate to keep you up to date with any developments.'

Was I ever going to learn to stop running my mouth off? I was starting to think it was a chronic illness. I should get someone to have a look at that.

'Right.' Pink heat stained my cheeks. 'I—' I stuttered, my accusation of him wanting a quickie not minutes before replaying in my head. 'Yeah.' I swallowed hard. 'I can give you my number.'

Charlie held out his phone, and I silently tapped in the number, before taking up my interest in the floor again when I'd finished.

'I will send over the details.' His hand reached past me for the door handle, and he stilled as his body came in line with me.

'And Rissa,' he said, as he leaned forwards, closer to my ear, the warmth of his breath igniting an unwanted heat between my legs, 'I don't do *quickies*. When I get what I want, I take my time.'

The door opened, and the sound of the pub rushed in. Charlie was gone, and I was left clutching at the wall for support.

Chapter 13

I wasn't a nervous person. I didn't need to imagine everyone naked or follow a strict breakfast routine of some unthinkable smoothie the day of a big event. However, as I paced the length of the pub, twisting the small bait line in my pocket, I was beginning to think I needed to re-evaluate that.

After Charlie's surprise appearance at the quiz, I had been able to think of little else. Despite what a small voice in my head said, it had nothing to do with how his mere presence seemed to leave me breathless. Or how when his eyes met mine, I had to find a force greater than gravitational pull to tear myself away. No. None of the above. After a few too many espressos and some deep diving into the *upcoming projects* section of the Caulson Properties website, I had discovered all wasn't quite right.

I knew how much investment was being put in, when the project was planned to begin, the name of the architect, the exact site plan, and the projected time frame for phase one of the development. That's right, phase one. Turned out there was a whole second phase that hadn't been mentioned.

'Let's go through this one more time.' Clem's voice jolted me from my pacing.

'No. No more times. I get it.' My midnight research had me riled up, and Clem and I had been running over the options available to us for more than an hour. I knew his intentions were good, but it was doing nothing to help my growing nerves.

'Do you, though? This is important Riss.'

I glared over at Clem who was lying flat on the cushioned bench by the window.

'What? I'm just saying.' His voice was hoarse from not enough sleep. His usual ruffled model look had been replaced by unkempt. The smell of vanilla rum replaced by something stronger.

'Are *you* OK?' I ventured, keen to change the subject, but also worried that something was off.

'Just burning the midnight oil is all. Lots of work. You know how it is.'

'Should I be worried?'

'Not today.' He smiled, a sparkle still reaching his eyes, calming my growing concern. 'Back to you, missy. Are you sure you've got this?'

'I'm here, aren't I? I'd say that's pretty committed.'

'OK,' he said, staring up at the ceiling. The morning sun caught the tiny dust particles above his head. 'We need to find a way to get them to agree to a fair fight. We need to appeal to his human side.'

'I'm pretty sure he doesn't have one,' I said.

'We could always go with plan B,' he said, hoisting himself up onto his elbows.

'Clem.'

'I'm just saying. It's not like you hadn't thought of it before.'

'Before I knew who he was, and before I knew what he had planned. And anyway, it was just that, a thought. I thought he was attractive. Nothing else.' Clem's other plan had been more...base level in its approach. *Flirt, fuck, free the town.* The leap to the last was just that. A leap. How he thought it would happen wasn't clear. Regardless, I didn't even think of Charlie in that way. Whatever my overactive hormones felt had far more to do with my lack of physical intimacy with anyone over the past few years and nothing to do with the suede shoe-wearing man who was set on turning Telbury into some second home monstrosity.

Clem slumped back down onto the seat and closed his eyes. Despite our playfulness, the enormity of the situation was never far from our minds.

The sound of glass hitting the floor had Clem leaping from his window seat and breaking our moment of contemplation.

'Oh no, oh no.' Johnny stretched out his wings and flapped frantically on his perch.

'Aunt Val?'

'I'm fine.' Her voice sounded weak, her usual defiance dented.

'It doesn't sound fine. What happened?' I said, rushing round the bar to where she was slumped against the fridges, her hand wiping her sweaty forehead. 'Shit, are you alright? Should I call someone?' I knelt beside her.

'I'm fine. Just had a dizzy spell is all. Stop fussing,' she said, with a wave of her hand. 'Where's that broom?' She tried to push up from the floor, but her body couldn't take the weight, and she collapsed back down.

'OK, that's it, we need an ambulance.'

'No.' Her body may not have been able to muster any strength, but her tone was certain. 'I told you I'm fine. I need to clear this mess up.'

'Don't be daft; I can do that. What can I get you?'

'If you want to help, you can get me a tea with honey.'

I went to stand as Clem appeared at our side.

'Already on it,' he said, passing me a steaming mug.

'A regular situation?' I flashed a look at Clem.

'Just a couple of...'

'Stop your nattering, you two,' Aunt Val said, hugging the mug between her hands.

'Here, eat this,' Clem said, avoiding eye contact with me and passing a chocolate bar to Aunt Val.

'Does someone want to explain this to me? I'm getting the distinct impression this is not a new thing.'

'I'm fine,' Aunt Val said, the colour returning to her cheeks. On her next attempt to stand, she managed to find the strength in her legs to help her up, and Clem and I lifted her from either side.

'You are not fine. I'm going to cancel this meeting. I need to know what is going on.' My eyes moved between Clem and Val.

'The most important thing right now is you get to that meeting,' Clem said, after he and Aunt Val had exchanged glances.

'I'm fine, love.' She placed her hand on mine. 'I promise. Not enough water probably. You know what I'm like. You just get to the meeting and give them what for.'

'I'll stay here,' Clem said, when I made no move to go.

'Are you sure?' I squeezed her hand. 'I can rearrange.' Everything in me said I wasn't getting the whole truth, but I knew better than to push her. She shook her head and smiled. 'We need you at that meeting love. Go get 'em.'

***

The Townhouse Hotel was tucked away on the outskirts of the old town, looking out to the sea. Some said it had the best view in Telbury, but they were wrong. I walked up one of the narrow streets off the square, smiling at the colourful fisherman's houses. They were squashed in rows, side by side. The only way to know when one house ended and another began was when one colour stopped and another started—a kaleidoscope of colours framing the square below and the harbour beyond. *That* was the best view in town.

I glanced at my phone to see an update from Clem on Aunt Val. He had promised to stay until I got back. Satisfied with my latest medical check in, I pocketed the phone and turned to face the hotel.

'Narissa?'

A tall, skinny lad stood in front of me. I recognised him as Geoff's son.

'Luke, right?'

'Yeah.' He nodded and looked down at the box in his white-knuckled grip.

I waited for him to continue, but he said nothing.

'Well, it was nice to see you again. But I have a meeting.' I pointed towards the Townhouse.

'Wait.' He looked straight at me. 'I wanted—' He stopped, looked down at the box as though questioning his decision to come here. 'Dad said you were comin' to the meeting today. I just. I just wanted to give you this.'

He thrust his hands out in front of him and stepped back. I looked from him to the box, which happened to have a heavenly smell wafting from it.

'They're coconut and honey financiers. I thought you might be able to give some to Nav. You know, if you like them.'

My brain caught up, and I nodded my head in slow motion.

'Right. Yes. Yeah, sure. I can do that.'

'OK, well, thanks. I'll be seeing you,' he said, and walked away. I stuffed the box into my bag and turned back to face what was coming as I headed to the conference room.

Unless there were another twenty people coming to the meeting that I was unaware of, the varnished, banquet-length table in front of me was being used as an intimidation tool. Large windows allowed the morning light to flood in from floor to ceiling.

I walked round the room, my hand trailing along the table. A coffee machine and a tray of biscuits had been set up in the corner in front of the wood-panelled wall, and I decided to top up the now lagging caffeine levels in my system and make my acquaintance with the biscuits. I stuffed one into my mouth.

'You must be Narissa Williams.'

'Mmmm.' I crunched rapidly, trying to dislodge the last of the biscuit from my teeth before speaking.

'Call me Rissa.' I chucked the words out as though the man who had just entered the room might walk away if I didn't speak.

'Rissa.' He nodded, like he was storing my name away onto his naughty list. 'David, I work with Charlie.'

He walked over to me, one hand outstretched, the other scrolling through his phone. Of course it was him. His eyes briefly reached mine as he took my hand in a limp hold. But it was enough to catch a glimpse of something that made me itchy. He had been the one throwing threats of suing us at the protest. He was shorter than Charlie and older. His features were softened from carrying a little too much weight. If I hadn't been certain before, I was now. I did not like him.

A short, firm handshake and look them in the eye. Let them know you're there. You can tell a lot about a person from a handshake.

Dad's words rang in my head as I took my hand back and stored away my new information.

His eyes still focused on the phone in his hand. 'Quite the show you put on the other day.'

'Just exercising our constitutional right.'

'Hmmmm, yeah. Course.' His face was still glued to his phone as his fingers swept over the screen. Unless the guy was organising the final details of world peace, I couldn't think what would be so urgent that he couldn't give me a few minutes.

'I was just about to make a coffee. Do you want one?' I said, leaning my head to one side, determined to catch his eye.

'No. Just sit down, and I'll do it,' he said, moving past me, head still down. 'Charlie is on a call; he won't be long. How d'you take it?' He turned and looked straight at me.

Finally!

'Black is fine,' I said, leaning against the banquet table. Having gotten his attention now, I wished I hadn't. Something in the way he looked at me gave me the feeling of being tested. Challenged.

'My apologies. I got held up on a call,' Charlie said, as he appeared in the doorway. The sun coming in from the windows made him look like some celestial being.

Christ, the man had a knack for finding good lighting.

'Rissa.'

'Charlie,' I said, ignoring the tingle of unwanted excitement that fizzed through me as his fingers wrapped around my hand.

A firm shake. Dammit!

'I see you've met David,' he said, placing the cup of coffee David had just made in front of me.

After a few minutes of coffee making and small talk about what a beautiful part of the world Telbury was, we took our places at the oversized table. Me on one side, Charlie and David on the other.

'So,' Charlie said, pressing the palms of his hands into his mono-grammed folder.

'So,' I said. I placed my dad's watch out in front of me. I drew in a breath and counted it out to the subtle tick of four seconds.

Set a time limit. Anything that scares you. Anything that you need to do but don't want to. Set a time limit and stick to it. Don't go over, and don't go under. It's the discipline that will get you through the tough times. People call it bravery, but that's nonsense. They are disciplined.

My fingers found the bait line in my pocket, and I rubbed it hard between my fingers as I kept Dad's words in my head.

'We're going to buy the Shed.' It came out before I had a chance to think through my strategy.

'So am I,' Charlie responded. His eyes found mine. No emotion visible. Just fact. 'How about we start by going through what we see as the best way forward, and then you can let us know where we might make improvements?'

Charlie's voice was all business. This was the Charlie who had built a multimillion pound property empire. The man who took no prisoners, had never settled down to have a family. But he was also Mrs Lesley's son. He took the time to see her every week. There was a softness to him. I just hadn't seen it yet.

'Your plans don't work for us,' I said, keeping eye contact and a calm voice.

'Which bit? That is the purpose of this meeting. We can go through what you have issues with, and we can hopefully come to a solution that works for us all.'

'All of it.'

'All of it?' He ripped a sugar packet open and tipped it into his coffee.

'By cutting the size of the Shed by half, or even a quarter, you will be condemning fishermen to their death.' I could feel the anger growing inside me with each word, but pressed my fingers harder to the fishing fly and kept my voice steady.

'I think that might be a bit dramatic.'

'No. No, it isn't.' I shook my head. 'You are playing with people's lives. These men don't have jobs on boats. They have their *life* on those boats. It's who they are. It's like...' I paused. 'It's like ripping a daemon from someone.'

'I beg your pardon?' He stopped stirring his coffee.

OK, so my example may have been misplaced, given my audience. But in my defence, who hasn't read *Northern Lights*?

'It doesn't matter. The point is, we are going to buy the Shed, so there is no need for you to be here.'

If David was still in the room, I didn't know it. Charlie and I were locked in a stare-off that had my rational brain fighting the invading thoughts of how he might look without that creaseless white shirt on.

I opened my mouth to break the connection when a phone burst into life on the table, turning in slow circles as it vibrated in pulses.

'Sorry,' David said, in a stage whisper. He held up the phone as though we had no idea what he was referring to. 'If I could,' he said, placing the phone back on the table, having cut off the call, 'maybe it's best to be up front here.' My attention swung from Charlie to David, whose tone held far too much superiority for any one person. 'Let's be real. This deal is going to go through.' He let out a joyless laugh and exposed a withering smile. 'It's cute that you want to save the fishermen, fisher people? Do you fish? I don't even know if you are one of them or not.' He waved a hand in dismissal of this thought. 'Doesn't matter. The point is that this is a good thing.' There was that smile again. 'You can't see it now, but this is going to be great.'

I shifted in my seat and swallowed hard. If Charlie had riled me, I was straight up ready to lodge a fishing hook through this one's tongue and yank it right out of his mouth.

'Besides,' he continued.

'David.' Charlie's voice left no room for negotiation, and his attack dog was silenced.

'I can see this conversation is not going to be of any use to either of us.' I picked up my coffee and chugged it as if it were tequila.

'Rissa, I do believe we can sort something out. Maybe we could relocate the fleet, or—'

I spat out a laugh and shook my head. 'How can you be so'—I struggled to find a word that wasn't outright rude—'ill-informed?'

'What do you mean?' Charlie looked at me with what appeared to be genuine interest. Was it possible there was a chance?

'You can't just *move* the fleet.'

The phone on the table started its slow, vibrating turns, cutting me off. This time Charlie nodded. David shuffled out of the room, leaving Charlie and I looking across at one another.

I broke contact first and looked down the long table, wishing there were in fact another twenty people in the room. My thoughts were jumbling together, and my confidence from earlier was washing away quicker than low tide artwork. I needed to regain control.

'There are other sites,' I finally said.

'Not like this one.'

'You don't know that.'

'I do.'

I looked back down again, my words failing me, and my patience waning. I ran through all the points Clem and I had discussed, and I came up short on all of them. This didn't feel like a meeting for negotiation, but rather a bulldoze to confirm their proposal.

'Look at it this way,' Charlie said, his tone lighter than before, 'fishing is a dying industry. Best to jump now and allow the town to grow.'

His words hit with all the unintentional power they held. He had no idea. The adrenaline running through my body sent the fizzing sound in my ears into overdrive, and as much as I twisted the piece of bait wire in my pocket around my finger, I couldn't contain my anger any longer. I slammed my folder shut and stuffed it in my bag.

'What are you doing?'

'Leaving.'

'Why?'

I said nothing. I hoisted my bag over my shoulder and walked around the side of the table.

'That's it?'

'That's it. I'd say our discussion is over, no?' I reached for the door handle.

'That's not exactly what I would call a discussion,' he said, standing up and moving towards me.

'You weren't ever really here for a discussion. You came here to tell me what you were going to do. Not negotiate.'

'The same could be said for you.'

That wasn't true, was it? Should we be negotiating? Was there even a compromise that would work? Was I authorised to discuss that? That was the thing with this man—he made my mind fog over. How was I expected to keep everything clear?

My internal bickering was stopped short by Charlie's hand landing on top of mine as I pressed down on the door handle.

'How about you come and sit down, and we can go through some things.' He was so close now, too close. Sandalwood and cotton mixed into a heady blend. 'I need a chance to counter.' I grabbed my hand back and pressed my body into the door as I tried to create some distance from this person who seemed to make me want to remove all the space between us.

'We're done here.'

'Are we?'

I looked straight into his eyes, flecks of yellow glinting through the green. Before I had a chance to respond, the door behind me pushed open, and I jumped forwards. Charlie wrapped his arms around my waist and moved me out of the way. A bolt of unwanted heat ran down through my body.

'Sorry about that,' David said, as he walked back in.

I brushed my hands down my jeans and smoothed my hair back, desperate to get out of the room.

'Ah. Off so soon?' He looked between the two of us standing by the door, before looking back at his phone. 'Sorry about the deadline change. But these things happen, I guess. Owners want a quick sale, and we're right there for it.'

'Deadline change?'

'We have initiated talks with the council, who seem—'

'I'm sorry. What are you talking about?'

'Always a solution, eh?' He looked up and winked, before heading over to the coffee machine.

His words came to me in snippets, as the reality of what he'd said smothered me.

'Rissa.' Charlie reached a hand out to me, but I pushed him away. How dare he?

'Is this a joke to you?'

'I'm sorry?'

'Is this some silly little game of cat and mouse? When were you going to tell me? Us! It wasn't in any of the documents you sent over.' There was no way I missed this. 'What deadline change? They can't do that.'

'Oh, they can do what they like.' David's chuckle came from the other side of the room.

'David,' Charlie replied, flashing him a look.

'It was confirmed this morning. I was going to discuss it in this meeting.'

'No.' I cut him off. My voice was struggling to remain steady, but I pushed on. 'This is wrong! This isn't a fair fight. You never had any intention of working with us. We're just a bunch of hillbillies who need to be placated.'

'Rissa, stop.' Charlie ran a hand through his hair. 'This is business. I admire your determination, but this is bigger than you and Telbury. This is a boulder rolling downhill that you can't stop.' His tone was pleading.

David walked back to where Charlie and I stood staring each other down. The feeling of his hand on mine not moments before, now completely erased by the pure and unfiltered rage that ran through my blood stream.

'Can we sit back down? I'm sure we can come to a solution that works for all of us. It doesn't have to be one or the other.'

I raised my hand to shut him up. I couldn't listen to another word.

'Do you know what? Damn you and your arrogant, entitled self. And fuck your sidekick here.'

I slammed the door behind me and allowed my body to slump against the wall. I needed space and air and to be as far away from that man as possible. My thoughts whizzed round my brain as though stuck on an ever-speeding carousel. As my jagged breaths came back under control, the muffled voices of Charlie and David had me stopping mid-step.

'There was another way to handle that.'

'Charlie, come on. She needed to hear it. Besides, we can't have her and her bunch of merry men screwing this up. The investors have been clear. No drama. We don't need anything spooking them.'

If anything else was said, I missed it. The rattle of the door had me taking the stairs two at a time until I was out of the hotel.

Chapter 14

'What's the current total standing at now?' I asked, as I poured one of the six bowls laid in front of me into the mixer.

'Not enough,' Nav said, passing a critical eye over my cake batter. Not that I could have done much to screw it up. All the ingredients were in assigned bowls. Nav had already weighed everything out and had it lined up in the order they should be added.

My phone had buzzed non-stop since leaving the Townhouse, but I rejected every call from that Satan. What was there to say?

Nav looked into the mixer and turned it off.

'What ones have you put in?'

'This one and this... Oh.' I flashed her a limp smile. 'Sorry, they looked the same.'

'You're as bad as Darren,' she chastised me. 'Here.' She handed me the next bowl. Great, now my cooking skills had been downgraded. The task had at least done the job of tempering my raging anger.

'We will just have to push even harder,' she said, as she watched me pour the final bowl of ingredients into the mixer. She was right, of course. The timeline had been moved up, and it was just another reminder of how precarious the whole situation was.

I pushed the mixer handle into place before glancing at Nav for confirmation it was good to turn it on.

'I told him we are planning a summer ball, and tickets are selling fast.' I sighed my confession.

'Christ.'

'I know. But he panicked me. I needed something. It just came out.'

'Although...' Nav said, pointing a finger in the air, the cogs of a plan turning over.

'Yes?' Hope rose in my voice that there was something salvageable from the disaster of a morning I'd had.

'Don't get me wrong. You running your mouth off, *especially* to Charlie, was still stupidity of the highest sort...' She narrowed her eyes in a knowing scowl. 'But it might be a genius idea.'

'It is?'

'Of course. It will be height of tourist season.'

'True.' I nodded, trying to keep up with her thoughts.

'It adds a lot on our already full plates, but hey, you know what they say? Necessity is the mother of all invention, and we will bloody invent!'

'Yes,' I said, feeling encouraged by my best friend's unwavering enthusiasm.

We fell into a comfortable silence, me enjoying the distraction of watching Nav in her element. She ran her spoon through the mix and watched as it pooled in thin spirals before sinking and disappearing back in on itself. I'm sure she could see something I couldn't. She gave a quick shake of her head, and I turned the mixer back up again.

'How you doing though, Riss?'

I let out a sigh and leaned back against the cold stainless steel counter. 'I'm fine. I'm just focused on the job at hand. Raise the money and help out Aunt Val. That's it. It was one stupid moment where I thought something might happen. But that was it.'

Nav said nothing, and I felt an uneasy need to fill the space. 'I mean it. I have no thoughts, other than evil ones about that arrogant, ru—'

'Gorgeous?' Nav interrupted, as she pushed the lid down on the dishwasher before moving back to her chopping board.

I groaned. 'Don't remind me.' The memory of his body pressed against mine in the cellar, the crackle of electricity that ran through me as his hand landed on mine... Nope. Not happening.

'Like I said, raise money and help Aunt Val.' It was my new motto, and I was sticking to it. 'Anyway, aren't there rules around sleeping with the enemy? Like don't!'

Nav came back to me and turned the mixer off before deftly pouring the content into a tin. The level of concentration was no less than that used by a surgeon performing groundbreaking brain surgery.

'If you say so. But don't pretend there's not something there. You never know—it might work.'

'I don't think so. Aside from the obvious, the man already has his one true love.'

'He's married?'

'His job.'

'Oh.'

Nav was a contradiction when it came to love. For her, the closest she would get to a relationship was one night of mind-blowing sex. She chased the buzz of the beginning of things. However, when it came to me? Nav lived in constant hope that I would meet *the one* and that would be it. But here we were, Sunday morning, in her commercial kitchen. There wasn't a hint of a hangover to prove we understood what Saturdays were for, and our chances of true love were getting slimmer by the day.

'How's the chef search going?'

There was still no replacement for Darren, and although the rest of the team had been good at keeping things going, if Nav ever wanted to see daylight outside of the kitchen, she needed help.

'Meh,' she said, fiddling with the cuff of her chef whites.

'Maybe I'll just come and work with you full time. That way we can be single and lonely together,' I said, wrapping an arm around her tiny frame.

'Or you could get out on that bloody boat,' she said, as another timer went off on the other side of the kitchen. 'And we are not going to sit here two lonely old spinsters, thank you very much. I for one am not about to let myself go any time soon. Nor should you.'

She gave me a quick once-over.

'What's that for?'

'I'm just saying. Those roots are not a fashion statement.'

'Charming!' I laughed. 'I've been a little busy, if you hadn't noticed.'

We fell into companionable silence before Nav tried again. 'But seriously, Rissa, what is the plan?'

'I'm working on it,' I said, aware that this was not a satisfactory answer for someone like Nav. The irony of it all was, I knew what I wanted. Always had. But the fear was paralysing; the guilt was choking. I didn't have a plan. But I was here; I hadn't run. That would have to be enough for now. I leaned in to my best friend and sighed. Everything was so far from perfect, but this moment was one I could cherish. A moment in the mayhem.

'What's this?' She nudged the Tupperware box I'd carried back with me.

'Oh yeah.' I opened the lid and watched as Nav closed her eyes to heighten her other senses. 'Luke gave them to me. Wanted me to pass them on.'

'Hmm,' she said, taking one of the delicate financiers from the box. 'Let's have a taste, shall we.'

I watched her face for any clues. She said nothing and took another from the box.

'Thoughts?' I said, when the suspense was too much.

'I think you might have found me my new sous chef, Riss.'

***

There was no breeze. The smell of dried seaweed clogged my nose. The blood had long been cut off from my knees down, due to the awkward half-squat position I had taken up under the bow of Saoirse. The boatyard was filled with fishermen desperate to get paintwork finished and any other jobs that needed the help of a few dry days. I pushed back on the clump of metal in front of me and was met with the disappointing sound of movement.

'There's a lot of play on this bearing. Jeez, it's amazing she went at all, Clem,' I shouted over to him, where he reclined, sunning himself.

'You sure you can take it out? Geoff is nearby if we need him.' He managed to lift his head, reaching a hand down to retrieve the beer nestled into the cool box next to him.

'Clem,' I said, pulling myself up and out from under the shadow of Saoirse. 'For the millionth time, yes.' I swiped a sweaty hand over my sweaty face, smearing grime around like moisturiser. I walked over and grabbed the bottle from his hand and took a swig. 'If at any point you want to get off your ass and have a look, by all means, be my guest.' I swung my arm loosely in the direction of Saoirse. 'Otherwise, I will continue sweating my tits off, whilst you work on your tan.' I rolled the beer bottle over my head, smudging the oil and dust that had stuck to my face over the last hour.

'You know what, I think I can hear Geoff calling me over.'

'Is that right?'

'Yeah, what's that, Geoff?' He cupped an ear towards where Geoff was chatting with some of the older vintage. 'You need some help with the pressure washer?'

'Oh, fuck off.' I slapped him on the shoulder and suppressed a laugh, before ducking back under Saoirse.

My phone buzzed in my pocket, and I slipped it between my shoulder and ear.

'You got it back yet?' Nav asked.

'No,' I grunted, half in response to the rusted bolt I was trying to loosen and half in response to my own cowardice at what Nav was referring to. In my haste at storming out of the meeting, I had left my dad's watch on the table. I had called the hotel, and they had assured me someone would go in and retrieve it for me. It would be at reception to collect. That was yesterday. I was waiting to make sure I wasn't going to have a run in again, but I would swing by later and collect it. See, not hiding. Self-preservation.

'Chicken.'

'I'm not; I just have some things to do first. Ow!' I grabbed at my foot as the aforementioned lump of metal landed on it with laser accuracy.

'What are you doing?'

'I'm underneath Saoirse. Those jobs Clem mentioned?'

'Hmmm.'

'Bit more than he said.'

'Yeah, that's Clem. Says one thing, means another.'

'Should I probe?' I asked, spraying some lubricant onto the now exposed bolts.

'Nope.'

'Got it.'

Clem and Nav had always had an indifferent/hate relationship, although since being back home, it was clear this particular hate phase was longer than most.

The sound of someone approaching had me zoning out of Nav's continued rant about Clem. The steps got closer, before the unmistakable flash of suede caught my eye.

'Nav, I'm gonna have to go.'

'Don't forget we're on leafleting tomorrow, one o'clock sharp, in the square.'

'Got it. I'll see you there,' I said, before ending the call. I shuffled out backwards from underneath the hull and straightened.

'You're still here.'

'And you're as charming as ever.'

'What are you doing here? I thought you would be back in London by now. I can't imagine there's much need for you to hang around anymore,' I said, determined not to let my internal organs make decisions for me on how to react to this man. So what if he was wearing a crisp white shirt rolled to the elbow, exposing his toned forearms? Or that he had a day's stubble covering his jaw—that sent an unexpected shock through me. Or that the fresh smell of cotton, mixed with something made up just by his skin, gently filled my nose. All traces of the seaweed were gone.

'Can we talk?' His usual cockiness was gone, and the muscle in his jaw twitched as he stood looking at me, waiting for my answer.

'You realise you're on a boatyard?'

Charlie gave a quick look from side to side, before pinning me with his gaze again.

'There were some clues.'

'And yet you're still determined to wear those shoes?' I turned away from him and back towards the plastic chair Clem had been lounging in, before the sparkle that danced in his eyes did anything more to my insides.

'Is that a yes?'

I said nothing as I took cloth and dipped it into the ice box before wiping my face in the hope it might do something to improve the state I was in. Which as of two minutes ago I was now acutely aware of. I let the tinny echo of metal hitting metal, accompanied by power jets and electric tools, fill the space.

'I don't have long. I have to get back to the boat.' I turned back to him, my composure in place.

'Right, of course.' Another pause. 'It suits you... What you're doing, I mean.' He nodded at the boat. 'Woman of many talents, it would seem.'

He smiled with a genuine warmth that caught me off guard. I said nothing. His shoulders hitched, and he sunk his hands deeper into his pockets. Good, it was about time he looked uncomfortable. This was my territory. Not his. Time for him to squirm like a jellyfish on the beach.

'I wanted to apologise.'

That was unexpected.

'For which of the many things you have done since you got here would you like to apologise? Trying to destroy our town? Letting your attack dog blindside me in that meeting? Or for the crimes you commit against practical clothing?'

His mouth curled at the edges, and amusement danced in his eyes. It shouldn't have enraged me. I should have had more self-control, more poise. But the man was insufferable. Even in a moment of apology (which I had the distinct feeling came few and far between for someone like him) he was mocking me, taunting me. *How dare he!*

'You shouldn't have found out about the deadline change like that.'

I let out a snort in reply.

Attractive, Riss. Real nice.

'Despite what you might think,' he said, as he pressed on, 'I really do want us to find a way forward together. It would certainly make my time here a lot easier if people didn't want to hurl things at me every time they saw me.' He smiled in a way that fed the overeager butterflies in my stomach.

'Ah, well, I'll send a note out to everyone. Wouldn't want *you* to feel put out, now would we.'

'That's not what I meant.' He sighed.

'Charlie, I'm sure in another world and another time, you're a nice guy. But in this reality, it's just not possible.'

I watched as he reached a hand into his back pocket, before holding it out in front of me.

'I believe this is yours.' My dad's watch hung over his fingers. 'You left it at the meeting. I tried calling.'

'I blocked your number,' I said, an embarrassment inching through me at my childishness.

'I get the impression it's of some importance to you.'

Had it been another day, another scenario, another *person*, I would have been impressed at their intuitiveness, but it wasn't and I wasn't. Instead, I took the watch from his fingers, ignoring the jolt of electricity that passed over my skin as we touched.

'I'm not the devil you think I am, Rissa.' Charlie looked straight at me, his eyes urging me to believe him. I turned away, breaking contact. There was a rising feeling inside that told me the longer I looked into those deep green eyes, the truer his words would become.

Chapter 15

'Then what did you say?'

'Nothing. I walked off and got back to what I was doing.'

'Narissa Williams!'

'What? There was nothing left to say.' A thank you might have been an option, but that was reserved for people who deserved it. Charlie was not such a person. Had he and his sidekick not dropped the bombshell of losing about three months on our timescale to get the funds raised to secure the Shed, maybe I wouldn't have been in such a fluster.

'You know what, as much as it pains me, and it does pain me,' Nav said, turning to look straight at me, 'I think Clem is right. You should just sleep with him. Get rid of all this sexual tension between the pair of you.'

'Tension, Nav, just tension. Nothing sexual about it at all.'

'Liar.'

It was two in the afternoon, and we had been handing out fliers since midday. To our surprise, the number of people who wanted to stop and ask questions or sign up to donate far outstripped the nonchalant tourists who couldn't care less what happened where or to whom, as long as they got their ice cream and day at the beach.

'You're kidding yourself. The air crackles between you two. Don't even try and deny it.'

'He doesn't date. The guy is a cutthroat villain who should be banished to pages of a good YA fantasy.' I took in a deep breath and smiled sweetly at the woman who looked my way before handing her a flier.

'He asked you out, didn't he?' She raised an *I win* eyebrow and looked away.

'Anyway, no more Charlie Caulson-talk. How are we doing on the fundraiser?' I asked, shaking my shoulders off as though I'd just done three rounds in the ring.

'We are a quarter of the way there.'

'Shit.'

'Don't panic yet. We still have time... Maybe not as much as we'd like. But this is Telbury. We pull together in a crisis. And this is a crisis.'

'We still have Val's jump. Tickets are selling fast for that,' I said, more to reassure myself than anything else.

'You know, for a woman who actively discourages people from her pub, she's doing quite the job of bringing them out for this beach day. She's managed to get the regional newspaper to cover it. I'm out,' she said, looking over to me with her hand in the air. I reached down to the bag by my side and handed her another clump of leaflets.

'How's she doing, by the way?'

'She's being Aunt Val.' I sighed. Since her fainting, she had systematically avoided me, even locking herself away to do 'accounts.' Something she had avoided all the time she'd had the pub.

'The weirdest thing was it felt like Clem knew what to do. Like it had happened before.'

Nav nodded and looked away to hand another leaflet out.

'After the jump, we have karaoke and the summer ball. We're doing our number, remember? For the karaoke. You're not going to back out, are you?'

'Are you kidding?' We broke out into our best synchronised dance routine, the one we had put together too many years ago to still be acceptable, causing heads to turn as we committed to the full routine.

'Uh-uh, not yet.' I waved my hand in the air whilst maintaining my best running man posture. 'We've got another set to go.' Nav looked past me, her eyes wide as she stood with her arms hanging by her side. 'Nav?'

'*Strictly* have no idea what they are missing out on.'

I stumbled to a stop, spinning round in the same motion, to find Charlie looking back at me, his panty-dropping smile brightening his whole face.

'I think I'm gonna head back to the restaurant. You've got this, right?'

'Nav,' I said, as I nudged her in the side.

'Mr Caulson.' She nodded in his direction, before darting off towards her sanctuary.

After what felt like an eternity of staring at my feet composing myself, I looked back out onto the square and slapped my best fake smile on, whilst holding out leaflets.

'If you don't want to see Telbury lose its soul, and if you want to have our fishing fleet survive for the next generation, then please sign up here.' I cringed inwardly. I wasn't one for town crier behaviour, but the mere presence of Charlie Caulson had me needing to vent my anger loud and clear for all.

'Lose its soul? You sure do like the dramatics.'

I was about to spin back around and give him my best glare, before my vow I had sworn to myself down at the yard rang out loud and clear in my head.

No eye contact.

I could feel the smile on his face, even though I couldn't see it. Even without touching or looking at him, I could feel him. Feel the air between us thin, leaving me breathless.

'Well, I suppose if you're doing it, I should too. I was going to go more subtle, but your way has its advantages I guess.'

My curiosity was piqued, but my determination to remain focused on my task and not give in to look his way was stronger. I held my ground.

'All those interested in finding out about Telbury's potential new development, head this way. Exciting new housing opportunities.'

'Just listen to the twisted lies you are spewing. You do realise when they walk over to you, you have a ninety-nine percent chance of getting an egg in your face again.'

'At least you'll be here to dab my brow.'

It took everything in my body to remain facing forwards. He was taunting me. I could hear it in his voice. This was all just a game for him.

***

'What's this about new houses?' a woman in her mid-fifties asked, her brown paper shopping bags laden with expensive organic products from the new soap shop down the street.

My blood boiled, and heat radiated up into my face. I called out again, louder this time, gaining a glance from the woman now perusing the leaflet Charlie had handed her.

He had leaflets?

'Ah. You must be one of the one per cent,' he said. I knew his eyes were on me; I could feel it.

'Pardon?'

'You have great taste, madam.' His voice was smooth, lulling her into his trap. 'As you can see, the properties will face south out on to the water. There will be all around windows, giving you uninterrupted views out to sea.'

'Oh yes.' She nodded, her enthusiasm doing nothing to temper my rage.

Out of towner. Did she have any idea at what cost those views were going to come?

'My team is always available to talk through any questions you might have about the project, or if indeed you might be interested—'

'Don't believe him,' I blurted out. I didn't look at Charlie, but I moved closer to the woman. She looked at me, waiting. I'd started now; I had to follow it up.

'Has he explained how the building of these homes will be on the site used by our centuries old fishing fleet?'

'Which we have tried to discuss moving, but I'm afraid the communication levels from the other side have been...limited.'

'Limited? *Limited?*' I sputtered. My control was evaporating as fast

126

as the space between us. 'Has he also told you the cost of these homes?'

The woman's eyes flicked between me and Charlie. We stood side by side now.

'Hmmm, yeah, didn't think so. Let me give you a rundown—'

'Actually,' she interrupted, 'I think I can hear my husband over there. Thank you.' She turned and smiled a weak smile in Charlie's direction.

'Well done.'

'Me?' My voice was two octaves too high, and my resolve was all but a crumpled mess on the floor. I whipped around to face Charlie and came face to face with the opening of his shirt—tanned skin and a tease of chest hair greeted me. I jumped back and glared at him.

'What the hell are you even doing here? Is this not beneath you? Shouldn't you be back in London, plotting your next town destruction?'

'It's important that the project has a face. People need to feel like this is personal.' He sounded like a robotic advert. 'Besides, sparring with you is quickly becoming my new favourite thing.'

I let out a bitter laugh.

'That's right, isn't it? All about the optics. Well congratulations, publicity stunt complete. Now you can run on back to your glass tower in London,' I said, ignoring his parting comment, which had my cheeks flushing from more than just the afternoon sun. I took a step forwards, regretting my decision within seconds, as the smell of soap and something just *him* invaded my nose. Charlie didn't budge, leaving me no choice but to hold my ground. I couldn't back down now; that would prove I was affected by him. That his presence had an effect. That my need to feel his body against mine was almost too much to handle. Our eyes were locked in a silent battle of words. The goosebumps shivering up my arms told me I needed to taste that strip of skin exposed by his unbuttoned shirt. Charlie leaned closer, and my heart crashed against my chest.

'I'm not going anywhere.' His words were like a silk scarf slipping down me, smooth and weightless. But they hung in the space between us, both a threat and a challenge.

'Where do you get off?' I mustered the strength to push the unwanted thoughts from my mind. 'What childhood issue have you not moved past to make you this much of a dick?'

For a split second I could swear I saw the muscle in his jaw tighten, his eyes flicker as though caught off guard, before he regained his composure and laughed.

'This isn't one of your YA fantasy adventures. Not all antagonists need to have a bad childhood or a lover to avenge. This is just business.'

My fingers flexed from my palm as my anger spread through my body. But my mind was battling the desire to wipe that arrogant smile off his face or press my mouth against his. Feel his tongue on mine, a nip of his lip.

'You will regret the day you ever stepped foot in Telbury.' My voice was no more than a whisper.

'You know what the trick to winning is?' He straightened, stretching the air between us, and I sucked in a desperate breath.

'Enlighten me.'

'Pick fights you know you can win. The more fights you pick that you know you can win, the more you do win. Before you know it, you're winning big and small. In case you weren't sure, I always pick fights I know I can win.'

Definitely wipe that smile off his face, definitely no kissing!

My fists tightened, and my nails dug into the palms of my hands. I fixed him with one last look, then turned and walked away. I would not be beaten.

We would not be beaten.

***

'I'm not sure how else you saw that going. I mean, it's not news that the guy is one giant— *Ooof*, that's a stretch,' Aunt Val said, as she lay on a yoga mat. 'Why are you so surprised?' She looked up at me, her eyes blinking from a position I struggled to see a way out of.

'I thought after he came to apologise, maybe we had reached a level of understanding. Is that completely necessary?' I asked, unable to ignore the sight in front of me anymore. Aunt Val's canary yellow leotard did nothing but highlight the difficult position she had forced her body into.

'I have to be limber. I can't go pulling something as I'm flung from that plane.'

'You're strapped to someone else. They're not just going to chuck you out. Besides, I hate to break it to you, but limbering up now ain't gonna do jack for your bendiness.' I let out a laugh as she rolled herself onto her front and tucked her head underneath her before she started rocking back and forth. *Lord, give me strength.*

'While we're on the subject of health, are you ready to talk about the other day?'

Subtlety was neither of our strong points. Aunt Val had remained tight lipped about the whole fainting incident. Aside from drinking more honey tea, she hadn't appeared that different.

'As I've told you, I'm fine. It was just a tired moment. I ain't getting any younger.' There was something comical about that statement, given her current position.

I let her words hang in the air. If growing up with Aunt Val had taught me anything, it was that sometimes you had to plant the question and let it sit for a moment... At least, that had been the case when it came to advances on my tips.

'You know, I was looking at trips to Egypt the other day. Pretty decent prices.'

OK, so maybe I had learned nothing.

'Egypt? What are you talking about?'

'You can do organised trips. They'll show you them pyramids and take you on a boat trip along the Nile.'

'Where is this coming from?'

She opened her mouth to reply as the door to the pub swung open, causing her to catch her breath at the sight of the person who stood there.

'Am I interrupting?' It had been a few days since I had seen or heard from Charlie, and I cursed myself for the split second of excitement I felt that he stood there. His eyes darted round the room, looking for a safe place to land. Aunt Val had taken up another eye-watering position, although this time she had angled her ass high in the air and in Charlie's direct eye line. I was convinced she'd done it on purpose.

'If you mean by walking in here, not particularly. If you mean by being in this town, then yes. Yes, you are interrupting.'

God, I loved this woman!

Charlie had the good sense to stay quiet for a beat. I looked over at Aunt Val, who had now returned to an upright position and was busying herself with giving Johnny a peanut.

'This is close to stalking now,' I said, not looking up from my hands.

'I was hoping we could chat. I brought bribes.'

The smell of fried food gave him away. The involuntary grumble of my stomach told me there was only so long a girl could resist a deep-fried sausage.

'You ain't eating that shit in here,' Aunt Val said, as I turned back to look at her. 'You can take the trash and the fried food out with you.' She nodded in Charlie's direction.

***

Neither one of us spoke as we walked down to the small, sandy beach east of the town. The day's tourists had finished baking under the Cornish sun and had now retreated to their B&Bs and holiday lets. I wrapped my thin camouflage jacket around myself, as the tatty denim shorts that had been so appropriate in the heat of the day did nothing now to keep me warm.

'Are you ready to speak to me yet?'

'Depends. Are you ready to stop your bid to build some god-awful monstrosity and ruin countless livelihoods?'

'Are you always this dramatic?'

'Are you always this arrogant?'

Charlie must have seen me shiver and immediately started to unzip his fancy jacket.

'Don't even.'

'What? Stop you from being cold?' he asked, sounding exasperated.

'Just. Don't,' I huffed, and walked ahead.

Silence fell on us again as we walked a short way down the beach before Charlie stopped and shrugged his canvas bag off his shoulder. He pulled out a Darth Vader beach towel and shook it out on the sand. I raised an eyebrow and glared his way.

'It's all they had left in the beach shop.'

'Fitting.'

If I wasn't mistaken, I could have sworn I heard him let out a small laugh under his breath.

'I'd like to play a game,' Charlie said, once we had settled near the dune grass. 'It's called Fact or Theory.'

'Shame. I thought you were here to apologise.'

Charlie let out a low sigh, not dissimilar to one you might have in a yoga class for calming the mind.

'I might have come across a bit strong,' he said.

'That's it?'

'OK, I should have thought more about what I was saying. But you—' He stopped and did another of those breaths. 'You have a talent.' He took another pause and looked right at me with those eyes.

'I have always prided myself on being good in stressful situations. I have a cool head. But here'—he looked around, then back at me—'and you.' His expression was one of confusion. 'I seem to lose that ability somewhat when I'm around you.'

I waited for the sorry part, but it never arrived. It was something of a relief to know I wasn't the only one battling some internal turmoil.

'I can see this is as close to an apology as you're going to get. Can I have the bribe now, please? I followed you out here.' I knew I sounded like a petulant child, but I couldn't help it. It was a reflex. I couldn't stop it when he was there. 'Unless this is the beginning of a true crime podcast and you're about to dump my body behind the dunes.'

Now Charlie did laugh. An unmistakable, full-body laugh. It took all my inner strength not to join in, because damn, that noise was infectious.

'So will you play?' Charlie said, once he'd stopped laughing.

I said nothing, and he tilted his head to catch my eye again.

'What?'

'If you don't say yes, I will withhold this deep-fried, nutritional-ly-void sausage.'

He held out a napkin for me, and I took it with all the grace of a four year old throwing a raging tantrum.

I played with the idea of grabbing it and running. The element of surprise would leave him in the dust. But part of me was intrigued. Why *was* he here?

'Fine,' I said, sounding like a sulky teenager as I stretched out my hand for my prize.

'Thank you.' He nodded, and his shoulders visibly relaxed. Had he been nervous?

'I think it's fair to say that you and I have some pretty set ideas about one another.'

I rolled my eyes at the understatement of the century.

'This way, we can clear some things up. Maybe we can move forwards with some respect and understanding.' He turned to delve into his canvas bag of tricks.

'Do you have any idea what you sound like?' It was like I'd entered the HR department of the most civil company on earth.

'An adult?'

'Oh please,' I said, as I took an oversized bite of greasy, crunchy batter. I had as much belief in his little game as I did in the TV adaptation of *Artemis Fowl*, but if I was being honest, there were some things I wanted to know. Morbid curiosity, you might call it. I took a chip from the paper and nodded.

'What are the rules to this thing?'

'Simple. You get to name three theories about me and what I'm doing here. Anything you like. If you get them right, I will confirm them as fact, NDAs and company confidentiality be damned. If they're wrong. Well.' He wielded a bottle of amber liquid in front of me.

'That's a Balvenie 21-year-old. Does the occasion call for that?'

'What else would we use?'

'Something cheaper.'

'Not a fan?'

'I'm more interested in the percentage level than anything else.'

'I wouldn't have guessed that.'

I looked up to see a wicked grin on his face.

'I'll go first,' I said, giving him a free pass on his sarcasm. I grabbed another handful of chips and crossed my legs as I shuffled to find a comfortable spot on the sand.

'One: you are so blinded by money you don't think about the human cost of your developments. Two: you came into the pub the other night to make everyone uncomfortable and to show off your dominance. Three: you lied the other day down at the square. Everyone has a story, and you're no different. I hit a nerve when I asked you why you're doing all this. I want to know the truth.'

'Two shots,' he said, pouring the amber liquid into a small shot glass. Of course it couldn't be a paper cup. 'The first one I could take issue with'—he handed me the whisky—'but despite my choice of wording being different, it's not untrue. This is a business deal. Of course, I would much rather everyone was happy about it, but I understand that certain projects will always upset a small minority. I can't please everyone. A good deal is a good deal. So although our wording may differ, you're right. I won't be blinded by emotion.'

'That sounds like a script rather than what you really think,' I said, watching as Charlie's jaw clenched at my words.

'Nope.' He caught himself before giving anything else away. 'One statement, one answer. Drink.'

I rolled my eyes more for effect than annoyance and took the shot, letting out a gasp as the whisky burnt a track down my throat. I didn't care how much that bottle cost; it tasted just the same as any bottom shelf to me.

'I'm a bursary kid.'

'Pardon?'

'Your second point,' he said, by way of clarification. 'I went to the top schools, then on to Cambridge. But it happened because I got to apply at my local school when I was eleven. Some benefactor who had very deep pockets took three kids from the schools in my area every year and gave them a chance. My parents, sister, and I lived in a two bed, fifth floor flat in east London for my childhood. My mum worked as a porter at the local hospital, and my dad worked in the local garage.'

'And you sound like *that*?' I couldn't hide my shock.

'You don't go to a school like mine and keep your accent for long. I learned how to survive. And then once I'd mastered that, I learned how to thrive.'

OK, that was unexpected.

'So the clothes are part of the act?'

His brow furrowed, and he waited for me to explain.

'You know, all the...' My words withered on my tongue as I realised the clothes were all him. 'Doesn't matter.'

I held my glass out, and he topped it up. Our fingers brushed, and the inevitable crackle of electricity that ran through me at his touch ignited.

'Come on then, spit it out. What made Charlie Caulson so...mean?'

Charlie let out a laugh, but his tell was too easy. He scraped his hands through his hair, alerting me to the fact he wasn't as comfortable as he'd want me to believe.

'My dad.'

I said nothing and waited.

'Let's just say, he wanted the best for me.' Charlie stopped and looked out towards the water. The seconds ticked away, and I waited. 'He taught me that whatever happened in life, my work needed to come first.'

'Is that why you have never settled down?'

He turned back to look at me.

'Your mum,' I answered. 'She said work was your one true love. Said she blamed your dad.'

Charlie let out a knowing laugh, the mention of his mother softening his features.

'Of course she did.'

'Is it true?'

He shook his head, and pointed to my still full shot glass. 'My turn.'

I wanted to push further, but the moment had passed, and it was clear Charlie wasn't going to fold.

I knocked back my second shot and embraced the warm rush that travelled down my neck and shoulders.

'My turn.' He rubbed his hands together in anticipation.

The whisky had warmed my skin and loosened my inhibitions. I leaned forwards and narrowed my eyes. 'You're going to be rubbish at this.'

Charlie met me in the middle, a small smile reaching across his face.

'Don't be so sure, sweetheart.'

I swallowed hard and moved away, his words ringing in my ears.

'You talk a big fight, and don't get me wrong, you really are quite terrifying at times, but that oversized watch you wear, that's your give-away. I think it's a special reminder for you of someone or something. Which tells me being this angry isn't a comfortable state for you. You don't enjoy this fighting.'

'Thank you, Lucian Freud,' I quipped.

He ignored me and continued. 'Two: you're fighting to save the town fishing fleet with the passion and drive of a fisherman, and yet you're not out on that water. You're afraid. And three—' He stopped and looked right at me.

'Three?'

'You keep saying you hate my clothes...and my shoes.' He smirked at that last word. 'But the way your eyes travel across my body makes me think you don't hate them one little bit. In fact, I think you like what you see.'

The air in my lungs vanished, and my stomach did a triple loop on the roller coaster it had found itself on.

'That's—' I shut my mouth to save from gawking at him. 'That's not...' I wanted to say he was wrong, tell him he was full of it. Instead, all I managed was an unintelligible grumble.

'You need to pour up two of those shots, Mr Cocky,' I said, once I'd recovered my composure.

'Two, huh? You sure about that?' His tone was sceptical and his gaze intense. I turned away and focused on a blade of grass. I'd always been a crap liar. If he caught my eye now, it would be written all over my face.

'For starters, those clothes do nothing for me,' I said, the twist in my stomach telling me my long-held view on impractical clothes was being tested by this man in front of me.

He made a noise of acceptance, and I stole a glance as he tipped the glass to his mouth. His lips parted, and my mind drifted to what they might feel like on me. His long fingers tracing down my neck.

No. Nope. Not happening.

'It was my dad's,' I said, looking down at my wrist. 'The watch. He died a few years ago. I know I could get it adjusted, but there's something about the weight of it on my wrist. Feels like he's there.'

'I'm sorry,' he said. 'Was he a fisherman?'

I nodded and took another chip to avoid answering any more questions on the subject. I'd said too much already. Dad was off-limits to everyone, even people I cared about. I wasn't about to give this man a direct link to my open wounds.

'He must have been quite the man,' Charlie said, his sincerity catching me off guard. Whenever I thought I had him figured out, he went and surprised me. I dropped the final bite of sausage into my mouth and chewed aggressively. This man wasn't getting any more out of me. Fact *or* theory.

Our now familiar silence fell between us, and I listened to the gentle rattle of dune grass fill the emptiness. I looked at my watch and began to tidy up the now empty papers of our chips and sausage.

'I better get back.'

'Yeah.' He nodded in agreement. 'Thank you.' He took the empty paper from me.

'For what?'

'Taking the time. I know you don't believe me, but I want to find a way to make this work. For everyone.'

'Well, it's good to hear, even if it isn't possible.'

Charlie stilled where he was, a small frown creasing between his eyes. 'I can't believe I'm going to say this, but maybe—' He paused, as though formulating the thought in his mind. 'Maybe we can take a break on moving forwards until we have had a chance to have a meaningful consultation with the FFL?'

My heart skipped a beat, and I was momentarily stunned to the spot. 'For real?'

'For real.' He nodded. 'I'm not going to make promises I can't keep, but I will agree to a conversation. A proper one.'

'Why?' My suspicious brain kicked in.

He let out a laugh that sent a zing of pleasure through me, and ran a hand through his hair. 'The truth? I have no idea.' He laughed at his own admission. 'Maybe this place is rubbing off on me.'

'Huh.'

'So do we have a truce?' He stood and reached his hand out for me.

'What, no more eggs?' I feigned disappointment and took his hand as he pulled me up off the sand.

'It would be preferable.' He smiled.

'OK.' I nodded. 'Truce. No more eggs.' We both stood and looked at one another. For the briefest of seconds, I allowed myself the chance to wonder. Wonder what it might be like if we were standing on this beach without the looming hammer above our heads? But it was just that, a second. The hammer was still looming, and Charlie stood behind it.

'I have to head back to London, but I will be in touch.'

I smiled and turned to walk away before stopping. 'Just so you know, I don't need any help getting off the sand.'

Charlie's face broke into a full smile, and he let out a laugh. My uncooperative pulse quickened at the sight, and I ducked my eyes to the sand to avoid blushing.

'I know. That's not why I did it.'

Do not swoon, Rissa. Do not swoon.

Chapter 16

I t had been over a week since I had seen or heard anything from Charlie, but the universe was determined to remind me she never gave with both hands. Send an evil force to destroy my hometown...but make him unbearably handsome. Rub salt in the wound that he happens to have the sweetest mother on the planet...oh, and of course, is now prepared to give us a fighting chance. I kicked the front tyre of my pick up with no hope of it actually resulting in anything productive, and cursed her latest snatch as the billowing steam continued flowing.

I reached for my phone and cursed.

'Oh, come on!' I held the phone above my head and stared at it, willing a signal bar to appear. 'Damn you, country lanes,' I said, before tossing it on the car seat and reaching for the handbook again. I'd looked through it three times and was no closer to figuring out the source of my problem. Despite my engineering abilities on Saoirse, it apparently did not transfer into automobiles. After a half-hearted poke around, I leaned back against the car and groaned, praying the universe was ready to change my fortune.

The sound of tyres on tarmac coming along the lane told me she was prepared for a truce. I stuck my hand out and waved. The sound of the engine slowing told me my luck was about to change. I straightened my ponytail in the wing mirror and gave a quick attempt to remove the smudged mascara from under my eyes. Having my head stuck under the bonnet had left me looking like a blonde Cookie Monster. I heard the car engine cut out behind me, and I knew. I knew before the door of the car opened, before they had stepped foot on the tarmac. I knew who my mystery helper was. My heart rate kicked up, and I took a deep breath. My body knew on instinct. Knew how the air particles shifted and twisted in his presence.

'You,' I said, as he stepped out of the car.

'Me.' He smiled that butterfly-inducing smile.

'No,' I groaned, more to myself than him.

'Good morning to you too.'

I winced with embarrassment at him hearing me, but it was soon forgotten as I caught the sparkle of pure delight in his eye at finding me in this situation.

'I thought you were in London?'

'I was.'

'Why are you back?'

'Couldn't stay away.' He was looking straight at me now, and I had to stop myself from audibly gasping at his comment. Before I had a chance to gather my thoughts, he was walking towards me.

'Car trouble?'

I didn't make to move forwards, instead crossing my arms and leaning up against the pick-up in defeat. Now there really was no hope of me getting this rust bucket home.

'Nope. Just letting it cool down,' I said, steam still pouring from the bonnet, now coupled with a hissing sound.

'Mmmmm.' He nodded, ignoring my petulance. 'Would you like some help?'

'No. Thank you.'

'Really? Because you had your hand out just a minute ago. I could take a look for you?'

I made some unintelligible grunt that gave all the cynicism required to let him know I had as much faith in his car mending abilities as I did the tooth fairy. Of all the people to wave down, I get long-time city slicker who wouldn't know his way from one end of a wrench to the other.

'I'm fine. Really.' He walked past me as I spoke, his scent catching in my nose and sending my stomach through a loop.

'OK.' He nodded, his eyes not leaving the car as he walked round to the bonnet. He unbuttoned his shirt sleeves and went to rolling each one up with perfect precision. Both of them were rolled on a perfect line, each arm flexing in the most distracting way as long fingers worked the fabric.

'I'm pretty certain there is nothing you can do to help.'

'Is that right?' he asked, quirking an eyebrow before dipping his head below the hood of the truck.

'Charlie.' I pushed off the side door and walked round to where he stood.

'Rissa.' His tone was low and baiting. Daring me to push further.

I threw my hands up in the air and stepped back. 'You know what? Fine. Go ahead, city boy.'

He let out a chuckle and shook his head. I watched as his hands moved across the engine, touching, twisting, lifting. Eventually he stopped and turned to look at me.

'Your air filter could do with a clean, but you can get it sorted once you're at the garage. For now, I'll give you a jump and follow you back into town.'

I looked back at him in disbelief. Who was this man?

'Your alternator is shot, but your battery should be enough to get you back. Have you got any leads?'

No words came out. I said nothing. My lips parted, and I stood gawking.

'Turns out the city boy knew a thing or two, huh?' He left me standing there as he walked back to his car and returned a minute later with a pair of jump leads.

'I'm not sure I know what to say,' I said, shaking my head.

'Thank you, Charlie. You're the best.'

'Thank you, Charlie,' I said, a smile lifting my mouth. It was impossible not to see how ridiculous this situation was. 'I'm sorry, it's just you don't really have the whole...' I paused, thinking about my words, but Charlie beat me to it.

'It's fine. I realise I don't strike you as your usual mechanic.'

'No.' I let out a relieved laugh. 'How? I mean, I just—'

'My dad. I spent time with him on the weekends at the garage. I listened.'

'So you guys were close?' It was an overstep. But something in the way he had shut down the conversation about his dad on the beach had me intrigued.

I watched as his hands stilled on the engine. It was only for a second, before he found his composure again.

'He was busy a lot of the time. Being at the garage was a chance for us to hang out.' Charlie didn't look up to meet my eye.

'I get that. I guess that's why I got into fishing. It was my way of spending time with my dad. Did you ever think about becoming a mechanic?'

Charlie straightened and looked back at me. 'Do you want to give her a go?' He nodded towards the truck. If he was rattled by my question he didn't show it. Only the turn in conversation told me this was not a topic he was going to discuss any further.

I walked back round to the driver's seat and hopped in.

'You ready?' He shouted over to me.

I stuck a thumbs up out the window and turned the ignition. The engine spluttered back to life, and I let out a cheer.

'Yes!' I called, unable to keep the smile from my face. 'I take it back,' I said, as I climbed back down.

He turned to look at me as he wiped the grease from his hand on his handkerchief. Christ, why did he make that look so damn sexy?

'Which bit exactly?'

'The part where I told you to go. Turns out you have a use.'

He smiled then, an ease coming over him at the turn in conversation.

'Mmmm.' He nodded and brushed past me as he headed over to his car. It was hard to keep my cool around this man. Each time I thought I had him figured out, he threw a curveball. It was exhausting keeping him in the box I'd assigned him.

'Thank you.'

'You are most welcome. It's been a pleasure getting to help the most unwilling of damsels in distress. All the sweeter.' He pushed the hood down and looked straight at me. His gaze lingered a beat too long, making my cheeks flush and my pulse quicken.

Damn.

I rolled my eyes to distract from the strange way my body responded to this man. 'Well,' I said, wiping my hands down my jeans for want of something to do with them. 'Thank you.' I smiled. 'Again.' I held out my hand to shake his, immediately regretting it as the touch of his fingers ignited the spark that never seemed too far away. I took my hand back and nodded before making my way back to the truck.

'I'll be right behind you,' he called out.

I smiled a reply and kept my thoughts to myself. Even in a different vehicle, two car lengths behind me, it felt far too close to be acceptable.

Chapter 17

The smell of peroxide and bleach was burning the inside of my nostrils. Nav had promised me it would take no more than thirty minutes, but as the clock ticked ever closer to the hour, I was losing patience. Not least due to the fact that my scalp felt as though it was melting away.

'Hold still.'

'Are you sure this is the best idea?' I asked Nav, looking at her reflection in the large handheld mirror propped up on the desk made of plastic crates. She leaned forwards and took another scoop of cream. The side room off the restaurant's kitchen was not only Nav's office, but her bedroom too. Nav didn't take her work home with her—she never left. Now we could add hair salon to its ever growing list of uses.

'There is literally no excuse for this,' she said, for the hundredth time.

She waved the brush around my head in explanation. She was right, of course. Old leather bag might be a look most of the men in Telbury were going for, but not me. Society (nor myself) were prepared to accept that as a beauty standard just yet.

'Anyway, tell me. Are you going to fuck him?'

'Jeez, Nav!'

'What?'

Nav's ability to jump from one conversation to the next with no warning was something I had gotten used to over our years of friendship, but it still left me racing to catch up.

'Well, are you?'

'No!' I chastised. 'No. I'm not. I said we had a good chat, not that I'm dropping my panties for the man.' Although it was impossible to deny to myself that a small part of me had thought about it.

Small part?

'Just asking.' She shrugged. 'I would.'

'Nav!'

'What? Don't tell me you've never had angry sex?' She looked back at me in the mirror. 'Oh, Rissa. You haven't lived. If I'm honest, of all the different versions, angry-pent-up- overdue-crazy-tension sex is the best.'

At this point I'd be happy to take sex. Plain old sex. Thank god for my trusty substitute. But that was what it was. A substitute. Was there ever a true replacement for the feel of a man's hands on your skin? Their weight pressing against you? Fingers running through hair, teeth nipping at your neck? Heat on heat. My mind drifted, and an image of Charlie replaced the previously faceless desire.

Shit.

'Look,' I said, jolting myself back to the real world, 'just because he seems to have grown a modicum of a conscience, doesn't mean I will be sleeping with the man. I'm just pleased we have a stay of execution for a minute. It seems like he is willing to talk, for real this time.'

'How long does it say to leave it on?' she mumbled, while staring at my head.'

I reached out to have a look at the instructions, but Nav beat me to it. Her small face scrunched up in a frown as she examined the piece of paper in front of her.

'Problem?'

'I don't think we need to panic yet, but I also think we should move very quickly to the sink.'

'Naaaav,' I said, as she hurried me out of the door and back into the kitchen. 'I don't remember the woman in the commercial having this drama. She paints it on, then washes it off.' I hung my head into the large stainless steel sink and squeezed my eyes shut. 'Ah!' I jerked my head up as the water scorched my skin. 'I swear this stuff is burning my scalp.' I winced. It was hard to tell if my light-headedness was from the chemicals or the blood rushing to my head as it hung upside down.

'Yeah, well, you're not gonna have any hair left if you don't let me get this shit off.'

'Nav!'

'Shut up and bend over.'

I looked up at her, and we both burst out laughing.

'Maybe save that for Charlie.'

'Not the time for your inappropriate jokes.'

'Yeah, you're right. But seriously, bend over, I need to get this stuff off.'

By the time we were back in the makeshift salon, my scalp felt like each hair had been individually pulled on by the hands of an overzealous baby.

'Are you ready?' Nav asked. She slowly unwound the towel, and we both stared into the small mirror as though watching the unveiling of baby pandas at the zoo.

'Holy shit! My hair is—is—' I stuttered. 'What is it?'

'A traffic cone?' Nav suggested. Her barely contained smile broke free and she bent over, howling with laughter. Despite my best attempts, I couldn't help but join her. The bottom half of my hair was peroxide blonde, bordering on white, while the overgrown roots were now a very obvious shade of orange. Not fiery red, not strawberry blonde. Orange.

We would have ended up rolling on the floor had it not been for the incessant pings our phones were letting off. Nav grabbed her phone, wiping her eyes of tears while trying to regulate her breathing. The look on her face stopped me from laughing any further.

'What? What is it?'

'You better see this,' she said, not looking up to meet my eye.

I grabbed my phone. Fifteen new messages. I opened the first one, and my brain took a minute to put the image into context. A group of suit and ties sat down at some fancy restaurant. But as the gears in my brain cranked up, the faces in those suits and ties came into view.

'Is that—'

'Yeah.' Nav nodded, as we both stared back at Charlie.

'But what is he— Is that a meeting?'

'That looks like a meeting we should be at. Did he mention anything to you?'

'No. No, he did not.' His words from the beach were ringing in my ears. Was this his idea of meaningful conversations? Just conversations that didn't involve us at all?

'So much for our stay of execution. Looks like the guillotine is on the way down already,' Nav said, looking straight at me.

'Oh no.' I started to get up from my stool. 'Not if I have anything to do with it.

***

This was not the side of Telbury I knew.

My hands instinctively went to check that my head scarf was still in place as I entered the Townhouse Hotel. I didn't care how people perceived me. I was a take-it-or-leave-it-kind of gal. But the traffic cone hair was making me feel self-conscious. Whether the glances in my direction were because I looked entirely out of place in my oil-stained denim shorts, white tank top, and deep blue silk head scarf...or because I stood at the door of the hotel as people tried to manoeuvre past me, was hard to tell. But I pushed my thoughts of not being welcome aside. Who was I kidding? I *wasn't* welcome.

'Excuse me.' I reached out to a lady with a name tag. 'Where's the Caulson party dining?' I watched as her eyes flicked across my body, before I added, 'I have a message for Mr Caulson from his London office. It's important.' I gave her my best smile in the hope that it might take away from my otherwise erratic appearance. She gestured for me to follow.

The restaurant was grand in the way I imagine a royal ballroom is. Chandeliers sparkled above white linen-covered tables. Waiters wafted from place to place, never rushing, but always with purpose. I scanned the room and spotted the group over by one of the large, arched windows.

Show time.

I took my time getting to their table. I stood tall and oozed a confidence that hid my simmering rage. Charlie spotted me first, his eyes finding mine and a flicker of...fear? Regret? Annoyance? Danced in his eyes. He looked back at the table of men and smiled distractedly at something one of them was saying.

'Good evening, gentlemen,' I purred. My hand swept along the back of the seats nearest to me. 'It seems Mr Caulson here has got a little muddled. You see, I understand you're here for an investor chat.' I let the *t* ring sharp in the air, my intent becoming more obvious. 'But there are to be no more negotiations until—'

Charlie's attack dog went to stand up, his fake smile smashed across his face. He made one of those affected laughs to interrupt me. I swivelled my gaze at him, daring him to speak. Charlie's hand found his arm, and David sat back down.

'As I was saying. You have been brought here under false information. I suggest you drink up, and if you're quick...' I gave my watch a dramatic glance. 'You can make the nine o'clock back to London.' No one said anything. The suited men stared back at me with no more than vague annoyance. But I felt it. The change in the air, the shift of particles, as Charlie's body moved. I didn't dare turn around for fear I would be greeted by his chest.

'If you'll excuse us. Ms Williams and I have some things to discuss.'

'Oh, is that right?' My voice rose at being told what to do. David's comments about the investors wanting a quiet, no-drama deal rang in my ears, and I was going to be damned if they got it. Wrong town, wrong girl.

'Are you one of the fishermen?' An older gentleman towards the end of the table spoke up. 'Or fisher?' He let out a laugh before continuing. 'I guess there's a reason women don't fish. What on earth would we call you?' He laughed again, and this time the others joined in. I made to lurch forwards.

'Rissa,' Charlie said, loud enough only for me to hear. 'Please.' His fingers wrapped around my wrist, and my skin burned under his touch. I swiped my hand away as the waiter, oblivious to what was happening, approached the table with a bottle of wine. I picked up the glass in front of me and held it out to him.

'Why not,' I said. The waiter looked from me to Charlie.

'Don't you dare look at him. I'm the one with the glass.'

The waiter had the good sense to nod and pour. I pressed the glass to my lips and downed the ruby red in one.

'Ahhh,' I said, wiping my mouth, relishing the shocked intakes of breath from those looking back at us. 'Not bad.' It wasn't like me to be an exhibitionist, but three shots of tequila before I left Nav's had me wanting to make this table of snobby suits as uncomfortable as possible. The worst thing you could do to posh people? Make a scene. Before Charlie had a chance to respond, I turned on my heels and stalked off in the direction I'd come.

'Not so fast.' His voice was low, and his words sounded more like a threat than a statement. I felt his hand find my lower back as he ushered me out of the restaurant, ruining my escape.

'Where are you taking me?'

'Oh no. You had your turn.'

He grabbed my hand and led me into a small library off the main reception. He gave the room a quick onceover to make sure no one was there before shutting the door behind me. The walls were stuffed with books from floor to ceiling, and a small log burner sat on the opposite wall to the door. A two-seater leather sofa was positioned in front of the fire, a small drinks table to the side of it. There was a soft musky smell coming from lit candles, giving it a secret sanctuary feel.

'Charlie, if you don't tell—'

'We'll get to the shouting part in a minute, but first of all, I'm sorry.'

'Sorry?' The wind of my rage suddenly failed.

'Back there... No one should speak to you like that.'

'Right.' I stood, momentarily stunned.

'But you can't walk in like that. You should have called me.'

'I should have called?' My moment of stunned silence was gone. 'How about you? You saw me yesterday.' I felt Charlie's eyes scanning me, and I regained my anger. 'What? What are you staring at?'

'Can we please talk about this?' He reached a hand towards my head and allowed his fingers to pull gently on the soft fabric.

'Hey!' I swatted at his hand, as unwanted sparks flew off my skin at his touch.

'Interesting.' He smiled as the scarf slipped away, revealing the extent of my hair disaster.

'Go away!' I snatched at the scarf and tried to put it back on the way Nav had shown me. But it was useless. I scrunched it up and threw it down at my side.

'What was the thinking behind this particular look?' His eyes scanned my head with amusement.

'Not that it's any of your damn business, but the dye stayed on too long. *Clearly* it wasn't on purpose.'

'Well, count yourself lucky you can get away with any hairstyle. However...unusual.' He tilted his head to the side, as though examining the look further.

Was he complimenting me? Now? In this moment? I glared back at him, willing the half smile on his face to disappear.

'Can we get back on track, please? To you and your treacherous meeting.'

'Yes. I'll start.' He took in a breath, and I watched his fingers flex by his side. 'What was that, Rissa?' His jaw clenched, betraying his otherwise calm exterior. Despite his outward bravado, he was angry. Good. He should have been. My mission to embarrass was successful. Besides, a good fight is useless if both parties aren't committed.

'Me? How about you? Mr "Let's put everything on hold." What bullshit!'

He combed his fingers roughly through his hair before speaking. 'I *did* want to do that. I w*as* doing that. David had organised for the investors to come down. I didn't know about it until today. I was going to speak with you—'

'No.' I shook my head. 'No, you don't get to do this. I have fallen for your crap before. This was your plan all along. Lull me into a false sense of security, then work quick behind our backs.'

Charlie looked back at me, a look of exasperation in his eyes. 'Dammit, Rissa. Listen to yourself. This isn't some James Bond movie. I'm not some evil villain looking for the destruction of your town.'

'That's exactly what you are.' My voice was rising with each word.

I'd had enough; I needed air. The room was too small, and Charlie was too big. It heightened everything between us to a level not sustainable. I reached behind me for the door handle, but Charlie was quicker. My alcohol-muffled brain had slowed my reaction time down too much. His fingers landed on mine, and I snatched my hand back, desperate to calm the sparks of electricity that danced across my skin. He was too close.

'Rissa, stop.' His voice was commanding and low. I turned around, determined to regain some control and have the final word. But the proximity of his body to mine was stifling. I couldn't think straight, and my normally witty retorts withered with Charlie that close to me. I knew I needed to get out of there. I knew my body's desire was about to overcome the remnants of my rational brain.

'This is going to get us nowhere. Shall we try a different approach?' His voice was calm, in control.

Air caught in my throat, and my body refused to move away, craving his warmth, his touch. It was insane; it was never going to work. But my body didn't care. Wouldn't listen. *Couldn't* listen. My hands moved of their own accord and danced over his crisp white shirt, before finding the hair at the base of his neck. My movements were slow, deliberate. I could feel him watching me the whole time, never once looking away.

If there was a moment for one of us to realise what a terrible idea this was, the chance vanished when my eyes landed on his. Unconstrained want sparked between us. I pulled his face towards me, crashing my lips into his. There was nothing soft, nothing caring in the way our bodies came together. It was all lust and anger. He matched my desire beat for beat. His lips parted on demand as my tongue found his. I took his bottom lip and bit down. I felt his grip tighten around my waist in response. His hard arousal pressing into me only served to heighten my need. My leg slid up along his thigh in a desperate bid to relieve the want. His hand grabbed at my leg, and before I knew what was happening, I was wrapped around his waist, my back to the door. This wasn't me; I didn't do this. And yet I was, and I didn't want it to end.

'Rissa.' His voice was no more than a whisper.

'Mmm,' I said, more from pleasure than communication.

'This wasn't what I had in mind, by the way.' He pressed his lips down my neck, nipping at my skin, releasing a wanting whimper from me.

'I don't hear you complaining.'

'Hell no.' His lips found mine again, and I thrust my hips forwards, desperate for more friction, more connection. More, so much more.

But as fast as it started, it was over. A knock at the door broke the spell, and I pushed off him and onto my own two feet.

'Shit!' Reality crashed in around me at what I had just done. Charlie took a few steps back, realising our monumental error.

'I need to go.' I turned and opened the door, leaving without another word. My fingers drew back to my mouth, the memory of his lips still swelling mine.

I was so screwed!

Chapter 18

I was doomed. Doomed to a day out at sea with some annoying tourist who would repeatedly tell me how much they wanted to be a fisherman. Have a simpler way of life. Gain more work/life balance. God, if they knew! Geoff had showed up at Nav's restaurant while I was filling her in on my most recent encounter with Charlie and had asked me to do him a favour.

Now he nodded towards the jetty, and my true doom came into view.

'Absolutely not. No, no. Not in this life or the next.'

'Come on, Riss. Take one for the team.'

'For the team? You remember it was me at that meeting alone?'

'Good morning.' Charlie's overly confident, crisp English interrupted my ever-heating conversation.

'I'll be getting off then.' Geoff nodded at me and turned and walked away before I had a chance to say anything else in protest. I could run—I could leg it and to hell with the consequences...but that meant letting the town down. Plus, I was a grown up. I could see this for what it was. Charlie had spent a ridiculous amount of money for this experience. I stretched out my neck, readying myself for a fight.

Get it together, Rissa. It's one trip.

'What are you doing here?' I spun around, unable to hide my disdain. I had to take him out, but I didn't need to be nice.

'It's lovely to see you too.'

Why the hell did he want to come out on a fishing boat?

'Look, Rissa.' He took a step on board, and that's when I spotted them. Waxy and green, a neat buckle on the side and reaching just below his knee.

'You have wellies,' I said, stunned by his footwear.

'I do.'

Damn him.

'Didn't come in suede?'

'Salt stains are a nightmare to rub out.'

I rolled my eyes. 'Good for you. But you won't be needing them today, because you're not coming aboard.' My words had force, but I knew my fate had been sealed the minute Geoff had told me how much the (at that time unknown) donor had given for this experience. I took in a breath and allowed myself to be calmed by the gentle rock of the deck beneath me. I bent down and opened the plastic trunk in front of me.

'Catch.'

With effortless ease, he stretched out one arm and caught the yellow oilskins.

Of course he did.

'If you want to stay on this boat, you're going to need to put this on.'

'Roger that.' His smile reached his eyes as he stepped one foot in, then the other. 'Is that what you say on boats?'

'No. It's not.'

'Aye aye, Captain?' His attempt at humour might have been amusing before yesterday, but now I knew him for who he truly was—a liar—it was just plain annoying.

'And I want no mention of last night. As far as I'm concerned, it never happened. I think we can both agree that it was wrong and better left as some horrific nightmare.'

Charlie looked at me, his expression difficult to gauge. For a moment it looked like he was going to argue, then he ran his hand through his hair before nodding. 'Got it.'

***

The sun broke through the swollen clouds in beams, like godly lightsabers. The shadows cast left the water looming black below. I flicked Saoirse onto auto and took in a long breath. We had sailed in silence since we left the harbour.

I had checked the GPRS twice and fixed my eyes to the screen, making sure to stay in the deeper water. The tide was still high, but it was on the retreat. The shifting sand below could cause problems if I wasn't careful. *Never assume.* That's what Dad always taught me: never assume the sea will do what you think it's going to. As I worked methodically through each of the items on the checklist ingrained into my mind, the work kept the tightness in my chest at bay. A flicker of excitement at being out on the water began to build instead.

'You're good at this,' Charlie said, as he walked into the wheelhouse, ducking his head through the door.

'I'm still learning.' My voice wavered with the first words to leave my mouth since we had left shore.

'It's impressive.'

I turned and smiled at him before focusing out on the water again.

'Are you OK?' he asked. The question held all the weight of someone who knew what had happened out here with Dad.

'I'm fine. It's just—' I stopped. I was not about to unload on Charlie Caulson. My eyes darted to his, and I stood stunned. 'How— How do you—' I shut my mouth again, the words giving up on my tongue.

'Your father was quite the hero round here. In between people wanting to throw eggs in my face, they're also pretty keen to tell me the history of the place. Your family features heavily.'

I said nothing, afraid my words were still lost somewhere between my mouth and the air.

'I'm so sorry for what you had to go through, Rissa. I can't begin to imagine how awful that was for you.'

Don't be nice. Don't be that guy. Not now.

I shifted from one foot to the other, looking down to double-check the screens in front of me. I'd avoided situations where I would need to talk about him. But somehow being out on the water with a relative stranger had made it feel different.

'It was calm when we left.'

Stop talking, Riss.

'We knew there was bad weather coming, but nothing we hadn't dealt with before.' I couldn't turn to look at him, but I couldn't stop the words from coming. I heard the stool behind me rub against the floor as Charlie sat down.

'I was the one who usually hooked on. But I guess with the weather, he thought it would be good practice for me to bring Saoirse alongside.' My heart rate kicked up at the memory. 'He shouldn't have been there. He should have been in the wheelhouse. Here.' The thrum of blood in my ears took over, and my hand reached for the wheel as my fingers wrapped tightly around it. 'I...' My voice broke, and I knew there was no going back. Charlie was going to hear it all, whether he wanted it or not. The pressure was rising, and I couldn't stop the words from coming. They were spilling out of me, and there was nothing I could do to stop them.

'The first wave hit and knocked me back. Once I got up, I knew something was wrong.'

Water, so much water.

'I saw him, a flash of yellow against the blue, and I made towards him. Then I was knocked down. The second wave was harder. It hit the deck, and I was crushed beneath it.'

Get up, Rissa. Get up!

'I should have got up quicker. I could have gotten to him. Hauled him out. There was just so much weight, the water and waves. He would be here.' I felt the burn of bile rise in my throat. 'He should be here now. Not me. I don't deserve this fight. I don't deserve to be out here. I don't deserve their trust.' Heavy hands pressed onto my shoulders, turning me and crushing me against him. I let the tears fall silently as the pressure in my chest shifted. The knot didn't twist again; it didn't suffocate me. It was there, but it hadn't taken that last twist as I admitted the truth.

'I miss him so much. This boat is my constant connection to him, and my constant reminder of my failing.'

His arms pulled me even tighter, and he smoothed my hair with his hand. Then Charlie spoke. 'You don't need me to tell you, you are not to blame for what happened. But I can tell you, these people you say shouldn't trust you? They believe in you. You are more than a worthy opponent. You might not be ready to accept that you were born for this, but don't cloud it with the idea you don't deserve it. You deserve everything in this world, Rissa.'

I breathed in his scent on a shuddering breath and allowed myself a moment of calm. There was a strange and twisted irony that the man holding me in this moment was the man who had the power to destroy all I was fighting for. But for just one moment, I would allow myself this feeling. This warm, safe feeling that being wrapped in Charlie's arms gave me.

'Always chase the dream, Rissa. Whatever the cost.'

But it couldn't last. I couldn't let it. I pulled back from his warmth, my body cursing me, and looked at him.

'Maybe,' I said, a little too breathy, before I swallowed down hard. This man was addictive. 'I might not have anywhere to chase my dream, if someone gets their way.'

'You've got a good fight in you. Don't give up.'

I straightened myself and turned back to the screens. Charlie was right—I did have a good fight in me. He may have seen me at my most vulnerable, but I was strong. I had admitted the truth of my guilt, and I was still breathing. If I could face that, I could face anything. Even Charlie Caulson. All I had to do was remind myself of everything that stood between us. This barrier between us was never far away. I didn't want to ruin the moment, but it hung there like the blade of a guillotine, ready to drop any moment and take with it whatever *this* was.

The energy changed as the heaviness of moments before lifted. I looked at Charlie as he took a step back and smiled.

'What?'

'You look ridiculous.' I laughed.

'Thank you,' he said. 'I thought I was wearing it quite well.' He took another step back and turned sideways, as though modelling the yellow oilskins on camera. I wasn't able to reconcile the Charlie in front of me now with the Charlie set on ruining Telbury, but for now, we were at sea, and if nothing else, he had paid some crazy sum to be here. So he better get what he came for.

'Fancy a fish?' I said, after I had recovered from Charlie's impromptu modelling.

'That's why I'm here.'

***

'You know what you're doing?' I said, once I'd baited the lines.

'Do I look very uncool if I say no?' he asked, holding the line as though I had just handed him a grenade with the pin out.

'I'm not sure you could look less cool than you already do.' I looked him up and down with a smirk.

'Noted.'

'The mackerel like deeper water. The waters around this peninsula are close to shore, but deep. Just drop it down and see what comes back,' I said, twisting the final piece of tinsel onto my line.

'Tinsel?' He held the line up, examining it. 'Do we not need worms?'

I let out a snort of laughter and looked back at him. 'No. No worms. Mackerel like sparkly things; tinsel is good.'

Charlie's gaze didn't leave me. And I didn't look away. I had the feeling I was flying too close to the sun, and looking away was getting harder with every minute.

'What?' I asked, feeling self-conscious.

'You're amazing.'

'I know how to fish mackerel on a line. It's no property empire,' I said, flushed by his compliment.

'Don't do that.'

'What?' I said, fixing my eyes on the water as the heat of his gaze bore into me.

'Put yourself down. You are spectacular, Rissa. I've not met anyone quite like you before.'

We stood in silence, the noise of the water slapping the side of Saoirse, and the calls of the gulls coming from the cliffs and swooping low over the water. Not to mention my thudding heart that I was doing my best to protect. But with every sentence that left Charlie's mouth, my resolve was crumbling like the cliffs into the water. All these compliments. Each time they were pointed. Each personal. Just for me.

'What's that?' he said after a minute. 'Up on the cliff.'

I followed his gaze to the top of the cliff. I let out a short laugh.

'What's so funny?'

'That's the cliff hotel I told you about. At Mermaids? Right before you stole my sausage, I told you about it. You told me there was nothing better than the location of the Shed.'

'Firstly, I didn't steal your sausage—it was mine. And secondly, thank you for the reminder.'

He frowned up at the cliff, his voice drifting towards the end, making me think it was a memory he'd sooner forget. Was he regretting his decision? What I believed to be arrogance was now starting to look more like a cover.

'It's been a few things. Hotel, youth hostel. It was a monastery at one point.' The grey stone stood tall and broad high above, the wild ivy reaching and stretching across the roofs that could just be made out from where we were. 'It's been derelict for years. Last owners ran out of money trying to restore it.'

'Hmmmm.' Charlie nodded, lost in his own thoughts. 'I bet it's quite the view from up there.'

'There's a beach at the point.' I nodded to the west. 'The only access is from the hotel. My dad used to take Clem and me to swim there when we were kids.'

'Sounds idyllic.'

'It was,' I said, smiling at the memory. 'You should check it out. If you get the chance.'

'I don't swim.'

I swivelled to look at him now. 'As in...'

'As in I don't. I can. But don't.'

I tilted my head in curiosity and waited for him to continue.

'It was never a thing growing up. My parents couldn't, and holidays weren't really an option. Dad worked all the hours, and Mum was busy keeping me and my sister on track. Swimming lessons were never going to happen.' He paused, as though trying to figure it out for himself. No sense of regret or blame.

'What made you decide to learn? I mean, if you'd gone so long.'

For a while I thought he wasn't going to answer, but eventually he took in a breath.

'My father died a few years back. It was about the time my mum went into care. I decided I needed more balance in my life. Not something I had seen a lot of growing up.' He let out a sharp laugh before continuing.

Whatever was behind that was not for exploring.

'I wrote a list of all the things I wanted to do aside from work.'

'And swimming was on it.'

He nodded. 'I got myself an instructor, and that was that.'

'Wow.'

He looked back at me and smiled. Our eyes kept their hold and neither one of us said anything, the moment stretching between us.

The familiar tug on the line had us both spinning, breaking whatever it was that was happening.

'I think I have something!' he shouted, a look of unbridled excitement on his face. I hurried over, my heart swooning at his childlike glee.

'Reel it in,' I said, moving alongside him. As the line rose from the water, the glint of tinsel was followed by the shimmer of scales as the fish struggled against the hook.

'When it's out of the water, grab hold of the fish tight.'

The fish broke through the water, thrashing against the line.

'Watch your hand on the hooks.'

167

'OK, I've got...' he said, as the fish slipped from his hand and landed on the deck.

'You've got to be quick.' I smiled. The same words said to me the first time I'd reeled in a fish. I reached down and removed the hook. I grabbed hold of the mallet and gave it one solid bash, stunning it instantly, before slicing my knife down through the back of its head.

'Well, I didn't see that coming,' he said, a look of surprise on his face.

'What?' I looked up, holding his fish out to him. 'That we would catch fish to then kill them? This isn't a Disney movie.' I laughed. 'I wish more people saw this. At least they might understand a bit more of where their fish comes from. Not least that this is probably the most humane way to catch and kill mackerel. Not as effective nor as productive as the big trawlers, but always more left for others this way.' I grabbed a bucket and held it overboard, filling it with water before rinsing my hands off. 'But hey, between the new quotas, areas of special interest, and the goddamn price of fuel, it's a miracle we make anything on a fish.' I looked up. 'Sorry.'

'What for?'

'I'm ranting.'

'You're passionate. It's a beautiful thing; don't ever lose it. Without it, there is no point in any of it. What you have here is special.'

I said nothing, afraid if I went any further I would start to believe the small voice in my head telling me this man was more than just an enemy. That he actually cared about what I had to say. That he cared about the town, the people, our lives.

'Can I ask you a question?'

'I think you've earned that,' I said, unhooking the latest mackerel from the line.

'If you could describe yourself as a character, who would it be?'

'Huh?' I let out a laugh.

'Film or book.'

'A character?'

'Go with it,' he said, noting the confusion on my face. 'My first ever investor asked me when I went to raise money for my company. I thought he was mad, but it's turned out to be one of my favourite interview questions. You can find out a lot from a person's answer.'

'OK.' I nodded, my mind now running through potentials. 'God, the pressure!' I laughed.

'Don't think too hard. It's not a trick, I promise.'

'Holly Short.'

'Holly Short?' He raised an eyebrow, and a wicked smile reached his eyes.

'Yeah, she's in Art—'

'*Artemis Fowl*. I know.'

'How?' I spluttered. How on earth did he know about *Artemis Fowl*?

'I have a nephew. Completely hooked on all things magical,' he said, by way of explanation.

'That's unexpected.'

'The nephew or that I read to him?'

'Both.' I dropped the line back into the water and placed a fish on the block. 'And you?'

'Well'—he paused, thinking—'keeping it on theme, I'll say Artemis Fowl.'

I let out a snort of contempt. 'Of course you do. Arrogant and rich.'

Charlie laughed and shook his head. 'I was going for misunderstood, with a true heart.'

Neither of us said anything for a moment, each lost in thought as we bobbed in silence on the gentle sea.

'So what now, teacher?' he said, after a beat.

'Ever gutted a fish?'

***

The sun dipped low, and the harbour glinted like a jewel as the lights of shops and restaurants came on. We had a bucket full of mackerel, and Charlie glowed with the pride of a first-time fisherman. To my surprise, he had been a keen learner, and it wasn't long before he was taking care of his own mackerel.

Damn him.

But as we got closer to the harbour, it was impossible not to let reality nudge her broad ass back in. It had been easy to forget while out at sea. It was a different world, an alternate universe.

'Thank you,' he said behind me, as I turned the key and listened to the chug of the engine rest. He was close, close enough I could feel his breath on my neck.

I turned, the flecks of amber scattered in otherwise green eyes visible. My skin fizzed with excitement at the memory of his touch.

'Charlie,' I breathed, reaching for the wheel to steady myself.

'Rissa.' His tone was low, and my stomach swooped at the sound.

I sidestepped and moved out of his ever-growing gravitational pull.

'You were a good student,' I said, unclipping my oilskins and stepping out of them.

'I had a great teacher.' His flirting was brazen.

I let out a noise that was somewhere between a laugh and a *yes*.

'You should never have stopped.'

'Teaching?'

'Fishing.'

'Ah.' I paused.

'It's clear how much it all means to you.'

His words jolted me. I turned to fiddle with some rope.

'Let's not do this.' I sighed.

'I'm not trying to preach. It's just an observation.'

I rubbed my fingers over the glass watch face on my wrist.

'You can't be both.' I shook my head, finally turning back to face him.

'What do you mean?'

'You don't get to be the evil property developer and the man who holds me while I tell you about my darkest guilt. Who comes out fishing and listens while I relate the history of Telbury. You can't be both. You're not both.' I threw my arms up in the air at the absurdity of it all. 'And you don't get to have an opinion on what I should or shouldn't be doing.'

'Rissa.' He walked towards me again, the line between his eyebrows creasing at the sudden change in mood.

'An afternoon on a boat with me and all of a sudden you know what's best for me too?'

'I didn't—' Charlie moved closer, but I stepped to the other side of the boat. Proximity was the one thing we couldn't have.

'Today was a nice break from reality. But that's all it was. You can't be the good guy and the enemy.'

Charlie let out an exasperated laugh. 'Maybe in some outdated fairy tale. But this is real life, Rissa. You can't tell me you believe you're either one or the other?' His voice was more strained now.

'I do.' I swallowed hard. 'There is not a world in which this,' I said, and waved my hand in the space separating us, 'is a thing.'

'Because I want to build some houses?' He looked confused, the crease between his eyebrows deepening.

'Because you can't begin to fathom how *some houses* feel like a knife to the chest. Because you are entitled and arrogant and appear to never have been told no in your life. Because you refuse to see what we have here is special. It's rare. Just because you can do something, sure as hell doesn't mean you should.'

'You're turning a very complicated situation into something too simplistic.' His voice was firmer now. His frustration was rising to meet mine.

'That's just it.' I threw my arms in the air, letting out a disbelieving laugh. 'This is simple. So simple. There is a right thing to do and a wrong one. You have wholeheartedly chosen the wrong thing.'

'Dammit, Rissa!' He wiped a hand over his mouth, realisation sinking in. 'Life isn't all black and white. There are some fucking scary shades in between, and beautiful ones too. The sooner you realise this, the sooner you'll stop being so damn disappointed in everything...including yourself.'

I went to snap back, but I'd unleashed something in him. My words had cut, and he was on a mission to return the favour. 'I mean, Christ. Your dream is to be fishing, but you are so convinced your father's death is your fault, you won't admit it even to yourself. Do you have any idea how crazy that is? How can you reduce such complicated emotions into something so basic? Life doesn't work like that.'

I stood taller now, determined not to stumble as his words made a direct hit. 'You have no clue what you're talking about. You've been here all of five minutes. Besides, this coming from the man who changes the subject the minute we get close to any conversation bordering on personal for you? You say you love what you do, but I saw more passion, more joy on your face when you were fixing my truck than any time you've spoken about your business.'

'I've seen enough to know you're afraid. You're so terrified of your own misplaced guilt, your grief, that you can't move forwards. I know you have thrown yourself into a cause for the one thing you care about, but still haven't got any blood in the ring. At least have the balls to do the thing you love.'

'What's the point?' I was shouting now. 'You're going to pay your way to destroy it anyway.'

Charlie took a breath and gently shook his head. 'Because to have the thing you love for even the briefest of moments is always going to trump never having it at all.'

He needed to leave. *Now.* I needed him off the boat before I threw all six foot two of him overboard.

'Go,' I said, my voice no more than a whisper, and yet the venom in it could fell a hundred men. He nodded and turned without another word. I gripped onto the railing and bent towards the water, gasping for air. His words had been vicious and thrown in anger, but the tiny flicker of something I couldn't place was igniting in my chest, and I sure as hell didn't want to look too closely at it.

Looked like the guillotine had fallen.

Chapter 19

'He's got balls; I'll give him that.'

I grunted noncommittally at Nav's remark, trying my best to not visualise that particular area of his body.

Since arriving at the beach, Nav had thrown questions at me in a way that would make even the steeliest of interrogators proud. But I didn't have the words to communicate what I was feeling. It was over a week since I had kicked Charlie off Saoirse. He'd left messages, but I hadn't replied. I had been given some reprieve as he had gone back up to London.

What was the point in even considering my very muddled feelings for him? The end had already been written. And yet he had the ability to make me think there was more. More to him. The little surprises. There was just one plausible explanation... Charlie Caulson was an expert manipulator.

Enemy, Rissa, Charlie is the enemy... If I said it enough times, maybe I could believe it.

'This is shit,' I groaned, both in equal measure for the lobster suit and Charlie.

'Button it. You should count yourself lucky. Geoff was all for you wearing the head as well,' Nav said, as we walked (she walked, I waddled) across the sand towards her stall. The lobster suit had sounded great when we were brainstorming ideas for the beach day. Now, as Nav laughed and skipped ahead of me, mocking my inability to move faster than a three-legged donkey walking backwards, I realised my bad decision making was not isolated to manipulative rich men.

We should have people dressed up as different sea animals. We could have crabs and lobsters, and maybe a prawn? They could hand out the programs and help people with any questions. It will be fun!

Yeah. So fun!

'I think you look super cute. And look at this.' She spun around, her arms spread wide. 'Look what we've created.'

I smiled and looked out at the scene in front of us. It was enough to swell my chest with pride and banish (for a moment) my internal turmoil. We had done well. The local farmers market had relocated for the day, bringing with them a feast of food stalls. The girls from Pigs and Pies had already had to head back to the farm to pick up more supplies. There were two Shetland ponies, thick-maned and stubborn, being pulled along the beach by two of the instructors from the local stables. The ponies might not be too impressed about being made to walk up and down the beach, but the shrieks of laughter coming from the children in the saddle made it worth it.

'We still have a chance you know,' she said, noticing my distant look.

'I know.'

'This is massive, and we still have the ball and the karaoke night.'

'Trust me; I will not let him win.' I could hear the anger rising up in my throat again.

'What time is this kid getting here?' Nav said, as she tied her apron round her waist. I looked down at my clipboard and double checked my times. Turned out Geoff's son didn't have the pull to the ocean like his dad, but rather the kitchen. After he'd ambushed me outside the hotel, I'd arranged for Luke to meet us at Nav's stall. She'd been her usual self: stubborn and combative. But the possibility of actual help was a temptation even Nav couldn't ignore.

'Here, Chef.' Luke appeared from the other side of the horse box. I looked back at Nav, who was unable to hide her approval as Luke stepped up in a set of gleaming chef whites.

'Right,' I said, giving Luke an approving wink. 'I guess I'll let you two get acquainted. I have an OAP jumping in a neon yellow leotard in T-minus 5 minutes.'

***

'She's falling. Six minutes to land.' The crackled voice of the pilot came through on the radio. Everyone was gathered around, and Geoff repeated it to the crowd on the speaker. A cheer of excitement went up as people pushed forwards to see the sight of the neon yellow worm falling to earth.

'I still can't believe she's done it,' I said, shaking my head.

'Thank god she has. It's done wonders for the fundraise,' Geoff said, craning his neck skyward.

I looked up and waited for the neon dot to appear. I couldn't help but be in awe of Aunt Val. She was fearless. Her complete disregard for the unknown was something I could only wish for. Part of me wanted to join her in that plane, throw myself out, and see what happened. But like most things in my life, that final step was more like a giant wall I had to climb over.

'What the hell is he doing here?'

'Who?' I asked, looking over at Geoff. His face scrunched into a ball of angry wrinkles.

'Him.' He spat the word out, and I turned to look in the direction he was staring. I felt my pulse quicken and a small flutter pick up in the pit of my stomach. In another reality, maybe I would be honest with myself and evaluate those feelings. But not in this one. Charlie's right-hand man, David, stood beside him, an empty ring of sand starting to form around them as people recognised who they were. Sharks among fish.

'There she is!' someone in the crowd shouted, and I tore my eyes back to the sky. I couldn't think about it now—we were there for the fundraise, for the jump. I was done believing there was an alternate ending to this situation. I let out a shaky breath and straightened myself.

'You alright, love?' Geoff's words caught me off guard, and I opened my mouth to say something, before shutting it again, settling for a nod. I locked my eyes, unblinking, on the tiny Aunt Val falling through the air. Her parachute swayed in the sea breeze. Each second felt like an hour as Aunt Val drifted down to the beach. My eyes may have been on the sky, but my mind was not so easy to control. How dare they show up here? Today of all days! My quickened pulse at seeing Charlie was dissipating as I was left with the quick-setting concrete feeling of disappointment.

Disappointment in Charlie, yes, but mostly me. I knew better. I knew what sort of man he was. I was the one who had chosen to ignore that and allow myself to be lured in by the person he was pretending to be. But I had said my bit; I'd called him out. Now I needed to stay in my lane, and focus on chasing their asses out of town.

A cheer went up as Aunt Val skidded onto the sand, arms waving in the air, her shrieks of delight causing the crowd to cheer even louder. I rushed over to where she was, desperate to create as much distance as possible between myself and Charlie.

'Look this way, big smile.' The photographer was already in position, crouching down to get the best angle of Aunt Val. 'Perfect, perfect. Brilliant, and another from that angle. I love it!' he said, twisting the camera to different angles. If it wasn't for Aunt Val, you'd be forgiven for thinking you had stumbled upon a shoot from *America's Next Top Model*.

'And you must be the famous Narissa,' he said, tossing the oversized camera over his shoulder before stretching out his small hand for me to shake.

'Call me Rissa,' I said, forcing a smile.

'This is quite the event you've organised. Do you mind if I get a couple of words from you on what this is all for and why it's so important?'

I knew he was talking to me, but my attention was on the man in the crisp white shirt with the sleeves rolled up. The man moving in my direction, causing my skin to heat and my sense to scramble.

'Narissa?'

'Yeah. Yeah, sure,' I said, shaking my head, trying to come back to the here and now.

He bent down to a large black box by his feet and pulled out a video camera and a microphone.

'You've got to be Jack of all at these local papers,' he said, in answer to the expression on my face. 'Still get you on the news though. This David and Goliath fight has got quite the traction.'

I nodded, barely able to listen to what he was saying.

'I'm here with Narissa Williams, one of the organisers of this wonderful event. Narissa, I wonder if you might be able to tell us why we are all here today,' he said, finishing with a small laugh.

Charlie was getting closer, his eyes firmly fixed on me. A small cough from the photographer-come-reporter jerked me back. 'Hi. Sorry.' I paused, trying to get my jumbled thoughts into order. 'We are raising money to buy our fisherman Shed, which is in danger of being turned into second homes.'

'Amazing.' The relief in his voice was palpable. 'But as I'm sure you know, this is not a new phenomenon. In recent years, we have seen a huge number of new property developments spring up. All appealing to those sick of the city and looking for a little bit of our magic sea air. Do you think you might be pushing against the tide?' he asked, giving another laugh.

I looked up, and Charlie was right in front of me now. Standing behind the reporter. Nav was right; he did have balls—how long they remained in situ was a different matter. I turned back to the microphone that was now under my nose.

'We are under attack. We are being hounded out of our homes, out of our way of life, all in the name of what? Greed.' The words spilled out of my mouth, and there didn't seem to be any way to stop them.

'Do you think—'

'These people cannot be trusted.' I interrupted the now visibly sweating reporter. 'They are self-serving, self-involved individuals whose sole interest lies at the bottom of their balance sheet.'

'Excuse me.' A hand on my shoulder had me spinning around, my whole body on high alert.

'We have a bit of a problem,' Luke whispered in my ear.

'What kind of a problem?'

'A big one.'

'I'm going to have to go,' I said, handing the microphone back to the reporter, who couldn't have looked more grateful for the interruption.

'Luke, what the hell is going on?' I said, once we were out of earshot of others. Luke was striding in front of me as I struggled to keep up with him in my lobster outfit.

Christ, I did a whole interview as a lobster!

'Clem. Nav. Clem is here and…and Nav and then—' He clapped his hands together and shook his head, before picking up the pace again.

'Luke. Wait.' I moved my feet quicker, but the suit was cut below the knee making it almost impossible to move any quicker than a toddler. But in my effort to match his stride, I pushed too hard and landed face down in the sand.

'Shit, Rissa, are you alright?' Luke took hold of my hands as I rolled onto my back before he pulled me to my feet.

'Yeah, I'm fine.' I said, spitting out the mouthful of sand I had eaten. I looked down to brush the sand from myself, as a pair of suede loafers came in to view.

'Charlie, I'm really not in the mood.'

'I just need a few minutes of your time. I'm not here to fight.'

'I have nothing to say to you.'

'Please! We *really* need to go.' Luke tugged on my claw.

'You know what, I do have one question. What was it? Did you think if you threw me a couple of compliments, a quick touch up, I'd rollover and say "Hey, you guys take the Shed. We don't need the fishing fleet." Or was there more to the plan? Maybe get me into bed, make me come first?'

Luke gasped, and Charlie stood motionless. If there was a sign of emotion, it was the subtle line forming between his eyes. But I didn't care, my humiliation was complete as I stood in my giant felt lobster outfit.

'Look, I don't know what this is. But we really need to go.' Luke's eyes were pleading, and I turned to follow him. 'Maybe you should come too; we might need your help.'

***

I heard Clem before I saw him. By the time I did see him, I could smell the alcohol oozing from his pores. The distinct smell of vanilla rum was now cut through with the harsher scent of vodka.

He was slumped against the back of the horse box, bottle in hand. Slurred shouts and clumsy arm waves completed the look.

'This is not the time or place, Clem. I am not going to discuss...' Nav looked up as all three of us appeared. 'About time!'

I looked from Nav to Clem and got the distinct feeling I had walked in on something more than a drunk Clem. Nav made her way over to us, and I took her to one side.

'I thought this was a thing of the past?'

'So did I,' Nav said, through gritted teeth. 'But until he accepts he's an *addict*.' The last word was said loud and directly at Clem.

His eyes were glazed over, thick, dark bags making them appear swollen. His skin was grey and sweaty, and his hair stuck to his face like cling film. He always looked weathered and a bit rough around the edges, but he had always maintained a sparkle. He was young, and the weathered look had always given him the lovable rogue vibe. Now he was just a drunk.

'Look who it is.' Clem swayed forwards. I couldn't be sure if he was talking about me or Charlie. But from the look in his bloodshot eyes, we were both going to be at the receiving end of his wrath. 'It's the destroyer of lives. Are you happy? Hmmm? Happy making your millions at the expense of others' misery?'

'We need to get him out of here,' Nav said, scanning the beach.

It wouldn't be long before people made their way back towards the stalls for the start of the evening celebrations. A drunk fisherman hurling abuse at people was hardly the image we wanted to advertise.

'Help me get out of this thing,' I said, shaking myself out of my ridiculous costume as Nav pulled the lobster over my head.

'What's he doing here?' she asked, quiet enough for just me to hear. I flashed her a look that said all she needed to know. We would talk about it later. One last pull and I was freed from my sweaty cage.

'What are you whispering about?' Clem went to take another swig and missed his mouth, sending vodka down his face. 'You happy, Riss? Hmmm? Now you're all cosy with the enemy? Destroyer of lives.'

'Clem, let's go hose you down, yeah?' I reached forwards to take his arm. His alcohol-infused spatial awareness had his elbow narrowly missing my face as he went to walk past me.

His eyes narrowed in on Charlie, who up until now had remained noticeable by his silence.

The next few moves happened in slow motion as Clem swung wildly but with intent, the now empty vodka bottle headed straight for Charlie. Charlie launched forwards. Somewhere behind me I heard the gasps of Luke and Nav. Charlie was in front of Clem now, one hand wrapped around Clem's wrist, the other pinning him against the horse box. I steadied myself and moved towards them.

'I can handle this.'

'Rissa, let me help you.'

'I don't need any help. And I definitely don't need yours.' I grabbed Clem's arms and pulled him off the horse box.

'What? Are you shagging him, Riss? You can do better than that pieceoshit.'

'We need to get you sobered up.'

'Get off.'

'Let's take a walk, Clem.'

Despite his drunken state, Clem was still strong, and as I adjusted my grip, he slipped through, taking a final swing at Charlie. I grabbed him by the shoulder, spinning him round, and landed one square on his jaw. He stumbled backwards, and I grabbed hold of his wrist again. Firmer this time.

'Don't give me reason to do it again,' I snarled.

I heard Nav's slow clap from behind, followed by a whistle of approval. Charlie was rooted to the spot. I gave him a warning glare to make sure he got the message I did not want him to follow us.

***

After a battle of wills, I got Clem into his apartment, boots still on, a bucket and a jug of water by his side. Head lifted up on pillows. I had tried to make sense of what had happened between him and Nav, but he was a steel drum. He may have been drunk, but he wasn't spilling on that. I made sure he was settled before I headed back out into the evening.

The muffled music from the beach thumped in the air, and I decided I needed more time. I started walking and ended up in the one place I wouldn't have thought to go, and yet my body knew.

The sound of footsteps on the jetty caught my attention, and I turned to see Charlie.

Not now.

I stepped up onto the deck and said nothing.

'I think we need to talk.'

'I don't have anything to say,' I lied. But the fight had left me and the things I needed to say were too raw. There was only so much humiliation one person could take in a day, and I was well and truly maxed out.

'OK.' He nodded, his voice gentle. 'How about I do the talking.'

I leaned back on the opposite railing in agreement that I wasn't about to walk away. Charlie pressed his hands into the pockets of his jeans, his white shirt still rolled to his elbows in the warm air. I took in a breath and nodded. It was as much as I was going to give by way of reply.

'Fact: kissing you wasn't a mistake. It was never part of some master plan. I didn't know it was going to happen, but it's all I've thought about since.'

He let the words hang between us for a moment. My previously calm heart rate was now tripping over beats in a way I wasn't prepared to think about.

I didn't look up—to look into those green eyes was to fall for whatever he was telling me.

'Theory: your reaction to me being at the beach today was because you feel something. You know there is more between us than some hate-fuelled lust.'

'What are you doing here?' I kept my voice level but short. Anything more and I would give away how what he had just said had floored me.

'Like I said, I think we need to talk.' His hand reached for the side of the boat, before he put one foot up onto the deck.

'I didn't say you could come aboard.'

He took his foot off and took a step back. At least he had the decency to listen to me. But as I watched him move back, I was struck by the unsettling feeling that he might walk away. A part of me was desperate to hear what he had to say, or did I just want him around? I made a brief wave with my hand that said he had permission...just.

I busied myself rummaging in a box for nothing other than some self-preservation.

'Rissa.' His voice was closer this time. 'It might help if you face me.'

I stilled for a moment but didn't turn around.

'OK.' There was amused resignation in his voice. 'I wanted to tell you that the lines of battle have been changed.'

He paused. I wasn't rising.

'Over the last few weeks, it has become clear to me that I have overlooked some pretty important factors in this project, and I need to make steps to fix that. You have reminded me of some things I had long forgotten. I have been in business in a long time, and being here... With you. Around these people—'

I heard him exhale. I twisted the rope I had picked up to stop my body from turning and facing him. This was the most open I had ever heard him, and I wasn't bloody looking at him!

'So I have decided that if the FFL can meet the agreed asking price, Caulson Properties will withdraw their offer. If it were down to me, I would withdraw right now. But I have shareholders I need to appease. This way I can spin it.'

Withdraw their offer. Keep the Shed. It was over?

'Are you being serious?' I dropped the rope and spun round. But I didn't need to wait for him to nod his head. His eyes told me all I needed to know.

'Very.'

'Why?' My initial excitement was being bullied out by my suspicious mind.

'So many reasons, but at the core of it...it's the right thing to do.'

'Wow. Don't go too far, Caulson. You might not recover.'

'OK, I deserve that.' He laughed. 'But I'm serious, I...'

My phone let out a loud ring, and I grabbed it from my pocket and pressed cancel, but not before I saw Geoff's name flash up. 'Sorry, continue, I don't want to miss this.' Charlie opened his mouth to reply, but my phone burst into life again. Geoff, again.

'Sorry.' I held a finger up. 'Hold that very important thought for one second.'

'Geoff, this better be good, because I am in the middle of some life changing shi—'.

'It's Val.' Geoff's voice sounded strained. 'You need to come now.'

Chapter 20

I stared up at the illuminated ceiling of the waiting room. It's funny what you notice in moments of crisis. There wasn't a light in the ceiling, but rather a continual white light that seemed to radiate from the where the strip lights should be. The subtle smell of chemicals and sickness filled my nose, giving my empty stomach a bad reaction.

I walked up and down the small corridor, never moving out of sight of the nurse at her station. I knew she was as anxious to give us news as I was to receive it, if only to get rid of me.

'Rissa, sit down.'

I kept walking and ignored another plea from Charlie. I couldn't be still. I needed to move—stopping meant thinking, and I couldn't think.

'I'm going to go and get us some coffee. I'll be back,' he said, realising his efforts were in vain.

The thought of Aunt Val lying motionless on the beach flooded my brain again. I picked up my pace, doing laps of the small corridor like I was against the clock.

I had hurried past Charlie in a daze when I hung up. My sole intention to get to the pickup, then to the hospital, but he'd insisted on driving me. Charlie had driven in silence, which I'd been grateful for. My brain had had no space for anything other than counting down the minutes to get to the hospital. Which, thanks to Charlie's sports car, had taken a lot less time than it would have in the pickup.

'Rissa.' The whispered panic of Nav had me spinning round and wrapping myself around her. 'I got here as quick as I could. I'm so sorry.' She was rattling through her words, shaking her head from side to side.

'She was fine, and then...then she wasn't.'

'Nav, it's not your fault.'

'I know. I know.' She was shaking her head. 'I just, argh. How is she?' She threw her arms up in the air, and I brought her in for another hug.

'We're waiting on the doctor to come and give us an update. I haven't seen her yet.'

'We're?'

The automatic doors to our right opened, and Charlie appeared, as if on cue, holding two cups of coffee.

'Huh.'

'Let's not do this now,' I whispered to her, both of us still staring at Charlie and the cups.

'You get a free pass on this right now. But it's temporary.'

Charlie held out the cup, and I nodded my thanks.

'Look'—Nav turned back to me, her hands gripped around my arms—'I can't stay. I'm so sorry. The beach party is starting and I need to be there to help. But I needed to see you were OK, and—' She stopped, the anxiety in her voice obvious. 'Well, you know.'

Of course I knew. Aunt Val meant so much to so many different people, and Nav was no different. In the years I had been away, she had leaned on Aunt Val during some tougher times. There was no denying this hit Nav just as hard as me. 'Don't be stupid. Of course you've got to get back.'

She blew kisses my way, then she was gone.

I walked back over to where Charlie was sitting.

'You don't need to be here.'

'I know.' He looked up at me. 'I want to be.'

'I'm sure you have much better things to be doing than hanging round a hospital.'

He took a sip of coffee and winced. 'Well, I could definitely do without this.' He raised his cup.

I allowed myself a half laugh and lowered into the seat next to him.

'I'm here for as long as you want me.' His hand found mine on my lap, and my eyes met his as he gave a gentle squeeze.

'Narissa?' An unfamiliar voice said behind us.

'Yes, yes, that's me,' I said, bursting from my seat, my connection to Charlie broken.

A petite woman with a folder clasped under her arm gave me her best sympathetic smile. She had mousy brown hair scraped back into a tight bun. Despite her pinched lips and curt tone, something told me she wasn't here to deliver bad news.

'Narissa, I'll start with the good news. Your aunt is stable and is going to be fine.'

My chest expanded as I took in a large gasp of air, realising I had stopped breathing when she said my name.

'Like with many newly diagnosed Type 1 diabetics, it can take a moment to adjust and get the medication right. But I will say your aunt's blood sugar levels were surprisingly high. Do you know if she has been taking her medication?'

Diabetes? What medication? The doctor was still talking, but I was racing through my mind trying to figure out how I'd missed this. Why Aunt Val hadn't told me. Was this why she'd collapsed at the pub?

'I think it would be best if we keep her overnight and reassess tomorrow. I want to make sure her levels are stable and she's confident with her injections before she goes home.'

The doctor kept talking, and I kept nodding. My head was spinning so fast I had no way to centre myself, let alone respond to her.

'Thank you.' I heard Charlie's voice and felt him wrap his arm around my waist, rooting me to the ground again.

'For now, though, she is in the right place. Do you have any questions for me?'

I went to speak but nothing happened; instead I felt my body lean into the firm tower that was Charlie.

'Can Rissa see her?' I should have been angry at him, angry that he was swooping in, taking control. But I wasn't. I felt safe. He wasn't being pushy; he wasn't trying to control me; he was helping, supporting me.

'She's sleeping now, and given how late it is, I suggest you go home and get some rest. Nothing is going to change overnight.'

'Thank you.' I nodded, swallowing hard. My throat was on fire, and my voice came out strangled. I held it together as the doctor walked away, but the tears I had tried so hard to suppress escaped my eyes. I felt myself wobble before Charlie's grip grew tighter.

'No.' I wiped the tears from my cheeks and pushed away. 'Don't be nice to me. I don't need you here. I'm fine.'

Charlie said nothing, just wrapped his arms around me, bringing my cheek to his chest. The smell of clean cotton and his deeper, muskier scent played on my nose, and I inhaled deeply. I felt his heartbeat steady on my skin, and an unexpected noise left my mouth. I was sobbing. Not pretty girl tears, but full, heaving sobs. I leaned into it and allowed myself to be held.

***

Once I entered the pub, my body ached and cried out for me to lie down, but my mind was too wired. I had no more tears left. Aunt Val was OK. I turned to face Charlie, who hovered at the door.

'Do you want a drink?' I should have let him go, told him thank you and sent him on his way. But company...his company...was something I didn't want to be without.

'Sure.' He moved into the pub and draped his jacket over a stool before sitting. I slid a large glass of whisky across the bar to him and clinked my glass to his.

'Thank you,' I said again. 'A few hours ago, I would have argued you weren't human.'

'And now?'

'Now...now I think there might just be a beating heart in there after all.'

'I meant what I said, Rissa. I have watched you these past weeks, your passion and determination. There was a time when I was like that. I had that same fire in my belly.'

'And you don't now?' I took a sip of whisky and relished the burn in my throat.

'It's different.' He nodded and held his glass up in the air. 'Cheers.'

'Cheers,' I said, acknowledging his desire to leave that conversation.

'Do you want to talk about it?' he said, after a moment. 'Your aunt, I mean.'

Yes. No. My thoughts around Aunt Val were not fully formed yet. For now, I was content knowing she was alright. She was safe and would recover. Everything else could wait. I walked back around to the other side of the bar, the bottle of whisky in my hand.

'Do you play pool?' I asked, hoping our silent understanding of what we were each not prepared to talk about was mutual.

Charlie turned to look at the pool table. 'I've been known.'

I pushed my pound coin into the rusty slot and grabbed the bucket from under the table to catch the balls as they came shooting out the side.

'You've done this before.'

'A few times,' I said, with a knowing smile.

'Ladies first.' He gestured.

I let out a short laugh and shook my head.

'You're not one for chivalry, are you?' he asked.

'I didn't realise it was still a thing.'

'Maybe just with us old-timers.'

'How old *are* you?'

He didn't rise to my teasing and racked up the balls, whilst I tried to distract myself from the flexing muscles in his tanned forearms.

'Same decade as you…just…' He winked and walked over to pick up two cues from the holder on the wall. My stomach fizzed, and I felt my cheeks flush at his casual confidence. He handed me a cue before leaning forwards over the table. A soft crease appeared between his eyes as he narrowed his gaze and focused in on the balls.

'So this deal. What's the catch?'

'You raise the money, and I'll back off. No underhanded tactics. No change of mind. No catch.'

'Why?'

It didn't make sense. Charlie straightened and looked right at me. A heaviness fell over the air around me under his stare.

'Because what you are doing, what you've achieved, is quite spectacular, Rissa. You have shown me what you are fighting for, and you're right—it's worth saving.'

'I didn't see that coming.'

'Nor did I,' he said, a smile on his lips as he shook his head in disbelief. 'Besides, someone recently told me just because you can, doesn't mean you should.'

'They sound pretty smart.' I smiled, my heart growing with every sentence this man spoke.

'Oh, they are so many things; smart is just the beginning.'

I broke eye contact and stretched a hand out in gesture for him to take his shot. His cue hit the balls, and they splayed out across the table.

'Just so you know, we're going to raise that money, and when we do, we're gonna kick your ass out of town.'

Charlie looked up at me from the table, his green eyes holding me to the spot, not letting me go. The hairs on my arm responded, sending a tingle up my neck.

'I look forward to it. Now if you're done, we have a game to play.'

I turned away, forcing myself to focus on a tear of felt from an overzealous game a few years back.

***

It turned out that even three whisky shots in, my game was still superior to Charlie's. It was game three, and I was playing for the win.

'You could just miss, you know?'

'Now why one earth would I do that?' I said. My eyes flicked up to his with far more sultry intention than I'd meant them to. The whisky had loosened my inhibitions, and the release after the stress of the day had me acting like the seductress I was so far from.

'I don't know, pity? Sympathy? Desire to remain in my company longer?'

I paused, a shiver running over me at his words.

How did he do that?

I watched as he made his way towards me, his hand trailing along the edge of the table as his long fingers tapped casually on the felt.

If he was trying to put me off my game, he had no chance. I was a modern woman, un-swayed by the basic instinct tactics of the opposite sex. But my god, it was hard not to imagine what those fingers could do.

'If you pocket this final shot, I'll tell you my secret.'

My breath caught as I became aware of how close he was to me. It felt like we had moved from light and fun to hot and heavy in one quick beat. The butterflies in my stomach had been genetically modified to have wings the size of elephant ears.

'Is it dirty?' I asked.

It was my turn to hear his breath catch under my words.

Good. At least it wasn't just me feeling this...*thing*.

I leaned forwards and took the shot. The ball tripped up over the snag in the felt but kept speed as it spun easily into the pocket, before landing with a muffled clunk on the carpeted floor below. I took a step back from the table to perform my victory dance, but as I did, my body stilled. I could feel his closeness.

He wasn't touching me. He didn't need to. Every nerve ending on my body was on high alert, receptive to the slightest movement. I was frozen to the spot, afraid if I moved even one inch, the connection would be lost. His mouth moved closer to my ear; the heat of his breath ran over my skin.

I'd been right—it was a dirty secret.

'I have an irrational fear of parrots.'

What?

As soon as the words had left his mouth, his body was gone, and I felt a pang of disappointment that it was no longer there.

'Parrots?'

'In particular, that one.' He nodded over to where Johnny sat on his perch behind the bar.

'Johnny?'

'I swear he has been giving me evils all night.' Charlie had moved to the other side of the table and was returning his cue to the rack.

'Not unlikely. He is a very good judge of character,' I quipped, trying to get my disappointment in check at his revelation. I took a deep breath, doing my best not to let on that that was the most passionate thing to happen to me in about three years. I moved over to the bar and busied myself with the glasses. I turned to see that Charlie had put his jacket on.

'You're leaving.'

'It's late, and you must be exhausted. Besides, I don't think my ego can take another loss.'

I was tired, so tired, but I couldn't shake the thought that if Charlie walked out the door, I would find no rest tonight anyway.

'Stay,' I said, and I meant it.

'Pardon?'

'Stay with me,' I said again, moving closer this time. Charlie took in a breath and let it out slowly. My confidence of moments ago melted away with every second that ticked by.

'I mean— Sorry.' I shook my head and turned back to fiddle with the lid on the whisky bottle. 'Of course you don't want to do that. Forget I said anything.' My voice was too high to be believed as casual.

'Rissa.'

I kept my back to him, but a hand on my wrist had me turning round. He was close, feet almost touching mine. I kept my eyes down, afraid of the rejection I'd see in his eyes.

'Sweetheart, look at me.' A finger found my chin and tilted my face to his. So close, I could smell the subtle scent of whisky on his breath.

'Me not wanting to has nothing to do with it. But you've had a stressful day. You're tired and four whiskies in. I don't want you to do something you might regret.'

I rolled my eyes, unable to hide my annoyance at his excuses. If he didn't want to be there, he could at least be honest.

'Don't patronise me, Caulson. I'm a big girl. If you don't want this, I'll survive...and we both know I could drink you under the table.'

My words were firm, but the conviction was missing in my mind. Would I survive this? Something was telling me this was different, powerful. My pull to Charlie went against everything I held dear, and yet, it was as if I had been circling the edge of a whirlpool that was always going to end up with me falling right into the centre.

'Rissa.' His smile was slow. His eyes trailed down from mine, drinking me in. The finger he'd used to tilt my head was tracing down my neck, my pulse quickening under his touch.

The air was getting thick, and I swallowed hard. I could take rejection. Who was I kidding? I could totally handle it if this whole thing was in my head.

'Do you want this?'

Yes! So much. Too much.

His hand moved up to my hair, wrapping it around his fingers. The hot dampness of his breath on my skin sent shock waves through my body, and I gripped the bar to steady myself.

'I don't need your pity. If this is not what you want, then just go.' My words came out breathless and pathetic.

'Rissa.' His tone was admonishing. His lips hovering over my skin as he breathed me in.

'I'm just saying'—I took another gulp—'you can go. In fact, you should go. This was...I don't know.'

Charlie's mouth flattened into a line. His eyes didn't leave me, but something unreadable flickered in them. Amusement? Relief? Desire? Hell, I had no idea! This wasn't me. I didn't get flustered by men. That was the stuff of teenage dramas and rom coms—my life was not that.

'You have no idea how much I want this.' His body pressed into me, and I gasped as I felt him hard against my stomach. 'But you told me this couldn't happen, so I respected that. But sweetheart, I've never wanted something so much in my life.'

My breath hitched at his words, and I clenched my thighs together, the dampness between them building. I reached my hands up onto his chest and let them drift up to the curl of his hair at his neck. Charlie let out a low hum in his chest in response to my touch, which only served to push me on.

'Someone told me it's better to have something for a brief moment than not at all.'

He tucked a loose hair behind my ear before his lips placed a gentle kiss on my cheek. Teasing me. Goading me to ask for more.

'Tell me you want this.' He nipped my ear. 'Tell me that, and I'm yours.'

I thrust my hips into him, answering before I had the words out. 'I want this.'

Charlie didn't need any more permission than that. His lips crashed onto mine, all hunger and need. There was nothing gentle left. He grabbed my ass, and I replied by wrapping my legs around his waist.

'I need you.' His voice was low and full of intent against my neck.

'I'm all yours.'

The desperation for more was pouring out of us both. Like a woman possessed, I let my hands roam over his body. My fingers scraped down his chest, the need to remove the thin material between us too much. His hands wrapped themselves into my hair, pulling my head back to deepen our kiss.

'Bedroom?' His voice was rough.

'What? You don't want to take me right here?' I smiled on his skin as I trailed kisses down his neck. He let out a groan of pleasure before pulling himself back to look at me.

'As great a vision that is, I don't want our first time to be a quickie on the pool table.'

My mind started to race through his words. But before I could deep dive into my thoughts, Charlie had started to pull me towards the stairs.

'Don't overthink this, sweetheart.'

Chapter 21

Overthinking was my MO, but as I lay on my back watching this gorgeous man strip himself of his shirt, my mind was blank to anything other than what I wanted to do with him. I crawled forwards on the bed and slipped my fingers beneath the top of his jeans, relishing the feel of his muscles tensing under my touch. Unable to be patient any longer, I tugged at his belt buckle and pushed his jeans down, taking his boxers with them.

'Like what you see?'

I swallowed hard and tried to compose myself. 'It's more about the performance, if I'm honest.' I shrugged with as little care as I could muster, my tongue tracing along my lip a dead giveaway.

If this man did not hurry up, I was going to explode. Charlie leaned over me, gently pushing me up the bed.

'That mouth.' He smiled with wicked intent as his teeth nipped at my neck, sending electric shocks of pleasure through my body and down between my thighs. 'May I?' His fingers hovered at the edges of my T-shirt.

'I thought you'd never ask.'

He took the T-shirt and ran his hands up my stomach as he pulled the fabric up and over my head. His eyes never left me, and I flushed at his unwavering attention.

'Mmmmm,' he said, his eyes devouring me.

'What?'

I shifted on my knees, and he grazed one hand over my bra strap. His fingers moved with smooth, light motions as he slid a bra strap from my shoulder, then slipped the cup down letting my breast spill out.

His fingers moved within touching distance of my hardening nipple before focusing his attention on the other strap. I pressed into him, desperate to find the release I was craving. This was meant to be a quickie to get it out of our systems, but something about it felt more like worship. Something so much more.

'God, you're beautiful.'

I looked away, blushing under his gaze and words. I wasn't used to this level of attention. He was drinking me in. Like he was enjoying every part of stripping me of my clothes, my inhibitions. He made quick work of the rest of them, leaving me completely exposed.

'Don't.' His voice was firm. 'Don't ever hide yourself. You're perfect.'

His thumb rubbed gentle circles round one nipple, then the other, and I arched my back in response.

'That's it; relax.'

I closed my eyes and allowed myself to fall back on the bed, letting the sensation of his touch fill my overworking brain.

'Tell me what you like.' His finger and thumb pinched at my nipple, and I cried out in pleasure. 'Do you have any idea what you do to me?'

'I do now.' I smiled, my confidence growing with every word he uttered. Every reaction his body made in response to mine. His lips found my breast, and he sucked. Hard. His tongue made circles that caused ever increasing delight. His teeth found the perfect line between pain and pleasure. My hips bucked up towards him in reply, and he let out a growl.

'I asked you a question,' he said, his tone commanding an answer.

'I want you inside me.'

I reached down and felt him, long and hard.

'There's no hurry,' he said. His moves were considered, never rushed. It was all for me—every brush of his fingers, every lick of his tongue—it was all orchestrated to inflict pleasure on me. I was his to undo.

I groaned in protest, surprised how my body responded to his words. This wasn't what I was used to. I was being worshipped.

His kisses roamed my stomach, and his hands touched all of me.

'Can I kiss you?'

'I thought that's what we'd been doing?' I laughed.

'I want to kiss you here.'

His mouth dropped to my inner thigh, pushing my legs apart.

He pressed a finger into me, and my body rocked in response. But I couldn't help the urge to close my legs after years of failed attempts by men to make it enjoyable. I'd been made to feel like it was me, not them. Before I had a chance to enjoy the feel of his finger inside me, it was gone, his hand roaming across my inner thigh again. My body bucked against him, and his eyes caught mine. He must have seen the flicker of hesitation, because he moved back up beside me, his hand cradling my face.

'Next time,' he said, before pressing a kiss to my cheek. 'We have many other ways to have fun.'

'I hope they still include being naked.' For a split second I thought he was going to walk. I'd killed the mood with my stupid insecurities.

'Oh.' He kissed my neck. 'Every. Single. One.'

I tilted my head to the side to allow him more access, his free hand already trailing down my body. God, every touch of his hands had my body responding.

He pressed his palm to my centre, making me push up to meet him. His fingers circled slowly, sending me crazy with need.

'You're a tease.'

'You're impatient,' he countered, biting at my nipple, releasing a squeal of delight from me, before sliding a finger inside me again. My body was on high alert. He was in no rush; I was under no pressure. The combination was gasoline to a fire. I felt my body responding, his fingers learning where to touch.

'More.'

'Your wish is my command.' He pushed another finger inside me, stretching me further as he sucked hard on my nipple. The heat rose in my face, and an orgasm I hadn't expected to be so powerful was released with each thrust of his fingers.

'Charlie!'

'That's it, sweetheart.' He didn't stop until I collapsed back on the bed, my body still shuddering with aftershocks.

'*Now* I'm going to fuck you,' he said, his lips finding mine in the most delicious slow kiss. It felt intimate, and so much more than what this was meant to be. I pushed him back, determined to keep this the dirty one-night stand it was meant to be. No lingering kisses, no spooning.

'No,' I said.

'No?' He leaned back on his elbow, creating a space between us.

'I'm going to fuck *you*.' I sat up on my knees and let my hand run along his length. Charlie responded with a groan, his eyes darkening as I took control.

Charlie took me by the hips. In one smooth motion I was straddling him.

'Condom?' he asked.

While his hands never stopped their roaming, I leaned over and reached into the drawer.

'Let me,' I said, taking it and rolling it down him, enjoying the desire in his eyes. His hands wrapped around my ass, and I lifted myself up and started to move. Our rhythm was messy and brutal. But the wave was building inside me again as I watched him coming undone. The room blurred, and there was nothing but me and Charlie in that moment. Nothing else mattered.

***

Charlie's chest was warm and broad. I lay with one arm draped across him, the gentle rhythm of his chest rising and falling lulling my eyes to close. My mind had emptied of all the very real reasons this was a bad idea, and I was left with the overwhelming feeling of...happiness.

'What are you thinking?' Charlie asked, after some time. His words were separated by roaming kisses across my shoulder.

'How long it's going to take an old man like you to recharge.' I laughed before I'd even finished my sentence, as Charlie tickled my waist.

'I'm thirty-nine, not ninety-nine. And quite frankly, even then, the sight of you would be enough to get even the most infirm version of me ready.'

'Is that so?' I turned to look up at him, a glint of mischief in his eye. Not so old after all.

'We better make the most of our time then. This is a one-off thing, after all.' As the words left my mouth, they felt rough and dry. Like sawdust in my mouth. But whatever it was, it didn't matter. There was no room for anything else.

'Rissa, where you're concerned, I'm always a yes.' His thumb drew lazy circles over one nipple, then the other. I arched up to ensure I didn't lose the contact. His hand dropped over my thigh, and my legs opened wide, ready for what was to come.

I was done. Even as my hips started to move in sync with his touch, I knew that my only attempt at a one-night stand was going to be harder to get over than any relationship I'd ever had.

Chapter 22

'So it's over? We won?' Nav laughed as she chopped a cucumber into unimaginably tiny pieces.

'We need to raise the money first, remember? And we are still a way off,' I said, hugging my hot chocolate. It was strange though, since last night I hadn't thought about it as winning, or even what it meant. My night with Charlie felt like it had happened in a separate reality. One where our battle didn't exist.

'I was right then!'

'About what?'

'You guys just needed to shag.'

'Nav!'

'Don't *Nav* me. You know I'm right. Anyway, more important is why you're here with me and not going in for morning rerun?'

'Don't,' I groaned. I'd needed to get out. 'I left a note telling him where the coffee is.'

'I guess you're right. It's not like it can happen again. Chalk it up to a great one-night stand.'

Great it had been. Mind blowing, life changing... God, there weren't enough adjectives to describe it. If I was honest, the bar was low. Half an orgasm would have sufficed. But multiple over the course of the night was more than even I could imagine. He'd taken his time, responded to my body, and given me what I wanted.

'I'll give him credit though.'

'What for?'

'Shagging you even though your hair still looks like a traffic cone.'

I laughed at her comment and swatted a hand her way.

'But you can't go there again.'

'Hmmmmm.' I took a long sip of hot chocolate to avoid answering in full sentences. I wanted to believe that was all it was. A one-night stand. But I had a heavy weight in my stomach that told me that my feelings for Charlie were a lot more complicated than that.

'I'm serious, Riss.' Nav had put her knife down, which I was grateful for, because the look on her face reaffirmed her words. 'It has to be a one-time thing. No winners, remember.'

No winners. I knew that, and yet...

'Riss?' Nav's warning was clear. 'Think about it. This new deal is great for us. But he still leaves, goes back to his building empire, and you're left behind. No winners.'

'Fine. But enough about me. Are you ready to tell me what yesterday was all about?' I said, spraying more cream onto my hot chocolate. Turned out that much whisky on an empty stomach was not great for the head.

'Nope. But maybe he'll give you some answers.' Nav nodded towards the restaurant doors, and I turned to see a sheepish Clem walking towards us, his hands deep in his pockets, head low as he navigated between tables. I looked back to Nav, but found she had already disappeared.

'Riss?' His eyes weren't bloodshot anymore—the result of a proper night's sleep and some serious hydration. The shiner I'd given him was a beautiful shade of purple, but it didn't hold a candle to the embarrassment and shame scratched across his face.

'Hey,' I said, feeling uncertain before I wrapped my arms around his large frame. Despite being five foot ten, I still needed to reach up on my tip toes. 'How are you?' I instinctively breathed in his smell, checking for any telltale traces still lingering on his clothes from a night spent nursing a bottle. But there wasn't anything. Clean clothes replaced those from the night before, and soap had replaced the heavy stench of vodka.

'Can we talk?'

***

The sky was overcast, and the threat of rain hung in the air in a thick scent. Clem and I walked in silence for a while, before either of us said anything.

'I've got a problem, Riss.'

The joke was balancing on my tongue, but when my eyes looked up at him, it vanished.

'OK.' I nodded.

'I know we've been here before, but—' He stopped in his tracks and looked up at the moody sky. 'I almost hit you, Riss.'

'But you didn't.' I placed a hand on his shoulder.

'I can't do it anymore. I know that now.'

'Well I won't lie; I'm pleased to hear it.'

'I'm serious this time. I've joined one of those groups. I had my first call this morning.'

'Wow. You aren't mucking around.'

He nodded, his eyes not quite meeting mine. 'Figured it might help. I mean, I don't know if it will. I woke up this morning and felt nothing but shame. Turns out it sucks. I went online and found the first meeting I could and clicked on right then and there.'

'Do you not need to be in a circle in a room or something?'

'You can.' He nodded. 'Just not sure I'm ready for that yet.'

'That's amazing, Clem.' I linked my arm in his and pulled my coat a little closer as the wind picked up.

'Like I said, I'm new to all this stuff, and not quite sure how it all works, but I'm pretty sure I owe you an apology.'

'Don't worry—'

'No, wait. I've gotta say it first.' His eyes met mine, and he let out a long breath. 'I'm sorry. I'm sorry for my behaviour, and I'm sorry you had to get involved. It wasn't fair.'

I waited a beat before throwing my arms around him. 'Apology accepted.' My words were muffled against his shoulder. I stepped back and looked at my oldest friend. A feeling of love and pride swelled in my chest.

'I'm sorry I knocked you one.'

'Nah, I deserved it. Besides, good to see you've still got it. Got your old man's swing there.' He smiled.

We had reached the Shed, and I pulled the large sliding door open.

'So have you got one of those apologies for Nav and all?'

Clem winced and rubbed his shiner, although I'm pretty sure the pain was related to the mention of Nav and not my swing.

'Cheers, yeah.' He nodded. 'I'm working up to that, but I've got a feeling it's gonna take a bit more than an apology.'

'Coffee?' I asked, not wanting to push.

The looming rain of before was now pounding hard and fast on the corrugated roof of the Shed, making it sound far more dramatic than it was.

'You're going to be fine,' I said, as I handed him a hot mug before taking my seat next to him. We had pulled two plastic garden chairs to the entrance and faced out onto the water. 'You're not going to lose your boat. I promise you. I won't let that happen.' Thanks to Charlie's announcement, I was confident of that for the first time.

'I get what Charlie's said is great and all. But we still need to raise it.'

'We will.' We would raise the money, and we would save the Shed. No fishermen were going to lose their livelihoods on my watch.

'This is all I have, Riss. I chose the boat.' He paused over his words. *Was that regret I heard?* 'Everything else in my life might be a pile of shit, but this, this I have got right.' He picked at the fraying plastic arm. 'I can't keep a relationship going to save my life or maintain a social life outside of Aunt Val's.' He let out a sad laugh.

I went to object, but he raised a hand to stop me. 'I'm alright with it. For the first time in a long while, I think I will be. No more plasters, just facing my demons head on. One day at a time. And no more burning in the fires of the future.'

He caught my quizzical face and smiled. 'Someone said it in the meeting. Just means "don't sit in the misery of the future." Plenty of time to burn when you get there.'

His words sat with me as each of us settled into our own thoughts. Was I burning in the fires of the future? Was me ignoring my attraction to Charlie just that? Or was it self-preservation? Was I hiding from fishing so I wouldn't fail? Like I did with Dad?

'I'm sorry I wasn't there for you,' I said after a moment. 'I should have been.'

'Not your fault. This one is all on me,' he said, before taking a sip of his coffee. 'But this is— Christ! What the hell you trying to do to me?'

Our laughing was interrupted as Charlie came into view. Clem stiffened in his seat, and I placed a hand on his. 'Stay.' We watched as he walked towards us.

'What are you doing here?' I asked, confusion written all over my face. Thank god the fluttering starting up in my stomach was known to me and me alone.

'Good morning to you too,' he said, shaking off the umbrella he was carrying. His smile suggested he liked the idea he had caught me by surprise.

'I think I might be off,' Clem said, scraping his chair back. 'Mr Caulson, I'm sorry about yesterday. I was out of line.' Charlie had the good grace to nod in acceptance. 'Riss told me about the new deal. Thanks for giving us a fighting chance.' He turned and hurried away into the Shed and out of sight, leaving me staring back at Charlie.

'You ready?' Charlie said, looking at me as though last night hadn't happened. Which was good. Very good. I mean, it was best to pretend like nothing happened. After all, it was me that said it was a one-time thing. So that was great, super great. We were on the same page. Perfect. Super.

'For what?'

'To go to the hospital. I thought you'd want to get there for visiting at ten?'

I opened my mouth to reply and closed it again. How did he do that? Not only could he totally forget our night ever happened, but he also played the good guy.

'I don't need you to take me. I can get the—'

Charlie put his hand up to stop me. 'Let me make this little dance we do quicker. I know you don't need me to. You can walk the ten miles, get the bus, take a horse and cart, or whatever other unnecessary mode of transport you can think of to avoid taking the favour from me. But I'm here, and I want to. Nothing more, nothing less.'

There were a hundred things rushing through my mind, but not one managed to make it to the surface and out of my mouth into actual words. Instead, I stood up and started walking in the direction of his car.

***

'I'll be in the car if you need me. I have some work calls to catch up on, anyway.'

'Thanks.' I smiled, not knowing how to respond. Why couldn't I go back to only seeing him as a total dick? This Charlie, the one who drove me to hospital, apologised, and gave the town a fighting chance... He was too much to handle. He was someone I could... *No.* There was no point even considering that line of thought.

The rain had stopped, and the sweet smell of damp summer grass caught the air. Clouds moved fast across the sky, the sun cutting in and out on her mission to break through. My chest was a little looser as I walked up to the light brick, flat-roofed building. I had called the hospital first thing, and they had reassured me she was doing well. They wanted to keep her in another night, but she was up and moving and well enough for visits. The cold edge of the night before, when I had run through those doors, had dissipated.

I made my way down to the ward and pressed the green button on the wall. The automated doors swung open to reveal the morning hustle. I walked forwards to the reception desk and smiled at the nurse who looked up at me.

'I'm here to see Val Williams.'

The nurse's round face broke into a broad smile, and she chuckled as she pointed down the corridor. 'Third on the right. That's quite a lady you've got there.'

I smiled back in response, pleased to know Aunt Val was feeling well enough to let her enigmatic character shine through, as I took off down the corridor. There would be time enough to think through my night with Charlie. For now, I was here for Aunt Val. I was only grateful he wasn't making it awkward.

I reached the door and knocked before moving into the room. My breath caught, and all thoughts of Charlie momentarily vanished.

'Oh shit.' I rushed forwards. A machine beeped to her right, and tubes ran from her arm and nose.

'Now don't start your bloody fussing. I ain't dead, and I ain't gonna be anytime soon,' she said, slowly opening her eyes.

'Why didn't you tell me? Why did you keep it all from me?' The questions tumbled out as I took her thin hand in mine and perched on the side of the bed. I'd promised myself I wouldn't go head-on with the questioning, but seeing her there undid any restraint I'd thought I might have.

She let out a big sigh and sank a little deeper into her pillows. 'I was going to. Honest.' Her eyes told me she wasn't bluffing. 'But when you got home, I was so pleased to have you back, I didn't want no nonsense spoiling it. And with everything happening with Caulson, it seemed so unimportant.'

I made a dismissive noise and gripped her hand tighter. 'I can't believe I wasn't there to help. I should have been there.'

'I think you had bigger fish to fry.'

I held my breath. Did she know about Charlie? Did she know he was the one who had brought me here the night before? Did she know what had happened? Oh god, I bet she had the CCTV set up on her phone.

'I hear Clem made quite an exit. Nice shiner you left him with, though.' She winked.

Clem! Not Charlie.

I let out my breath and allowed my shoulders to drop. 'Right.' I laughed nervously. 'Yeah, he had a minute, but he's gonna be alright. News travels fast.'

'Hmmm, and my birdies also tell me that we might be in with a real chance at saving the Shed.'

'Jeez! Good to see the Telbury grapevine is alive and well.'

'Geoff called. Clem had contacted him. Told Geoff you'd seen him this morning.'

'Ah.' I waited for her to mention Charlie showing up at the Shed. But it never came. I sent a silent *thank you* to Clem for keeping that to himself.

After a few more minutes of gossip and checking on whether I had fed Johnny, I went back to what really mattered.

'What do I need to do?' I asked.

'About what?' Aunt Val looked at me confused and, after reaching over to her side cabinet, she popped a small tablet out of a tinfoil pack.

'For you, you idiot. What do I need to do?'

'You need to be happy. You need to do what makes *you* happy.'

'What about the pub? You need to cut your hours down. I've been reading about this. You need regular meals and decent sleep.'

'Don't we all?' She scoffed.

'I'm not joking. Missing meals and eating the wrong thing can have serious consequences. As we've seen.' I raised my eyebrows. 'And another thing is the smoking. It's got to stop.'

She picked up the packet of tablets from the table and waved it at me. 'Why'd you think I'm chewing this shit?'

'Good.' I nodded. Nicotine gum sorted, now just her hours. Prying them off her wasn't going to be easy, but it was for her own good...literally. 'I can do more, we can—'

'No.' She shook her head.

'No? You don't even know what I was going to say.'

'Yes, I do. And the answer is no.' She was shaking her head now, a growing determination in her eyes.

'Aunt Val.'

She put up her hand to stop me and shimmied herself higher on her bed.

'Let me,' I said, leaning forwards to adjust the pillows. Once she was settled, she looked up at me.

'I should have said this a long time ago, but I wanted to give you your space.'

'Said what?' I squeezed her hand, urging her on

'What happened to your dad is not your fault. You need to face up to his death and see what's left behind. It was tragic and brutal and life shattering. But the pieces are all still there, love.' It was her turn to squeeze my hand. A burning lump formed in my throat. 'You just need to pick them back up again.'

'What if I can't?' My voice was raspy and quiet.

'I won't let you make me your next excuse.'

'What about the pub?'

She shook her head again. 'Don't worry about the pub; I'll sort it. Got some plans anyway.' A small smile kicked up on her mouth, and she raised her eyebrow conspiratorially.

'It's not that easy.' I held on tighter to her hand.

'Of course it's not. But it is worth it. I'm not saying it's going to be better than before, but it could be just as good. Bit like them Japanese bowls.'

I looked up from where I had been focusing on the fray of the bed sheet.

'You know.'

I looked back at her blankly.

'Them ones they stick back together.' She clicked her fingers, trying to conjure the word she was looking for.

'What are you talking about?' I let out a sniffling laugh and wiped away a stray tear.

'Kinty something. Kinty... Kintsugi! That's it.' She threw her hands in the air. 'It's the art of taking broken pottery and putting it back together with gold or something as the glue to make it beautiful again. They ain't pretending that the break didn't happen. But they are re-building.'

'Hmmmm.' I nodded.

At the sound of knocking, we both looked up to the door to see the nurse from the front desk.

'I'm just here to do your obs. Don't worry; you don't need to go.' The nurse walked in, pushing her trolley.

Aunt Val waved a hand in the air. 'She's heading out anyway.'

'I am?'

She leaned in and wrapped her arms around my neck in the first unprompted show of affection I could remember since being a child. 'Go take some leaps of faith. Find your own neon leotard and jump. I know you can do it.' She pulled back from the hug and grabbed another chew from her packet. 'Christ, this stuff ain't doing anything.' She rolled her eyes, and her attention was already elsewhere.

***

I walked back outside, Aunt Val's words still swirling in my head as I approached the sleek black car. I could see Charlie tapping the steering wheel to a tune I couldn't hear. I took a breath and opened the door, before allowing my body to sink into the low, reclined shape of the seat.

'How is she?'

'She's going to be fine.' I nodded, knowing that whatever her plans were, she really was going to be fine.

Charlie started the engine, and we pulled out of the car park. My stomach twisted at a niggling thought that crept in as we turned onto the main road and back towards Telbury. There were no more reasons to spend time with Charlie, and despite all my best judgments and level-headed logic, I didn't want the time to end. It didn't need to be sexual. Charlie had shown that with his behaviour all morning. This could just be civil relations between two opposing sides. Peace talks, if you like.

I was pretty sure when Aunt Val told me to take a leap, she was referring to fishing, and maybe she had a point. But this would have to do for now.

'Are you busy this afternoon?' I asked.

'What did you have in mind?'

Chapter 23

There wasn't much in the way of food in the pub, but I scrounged up enough ingredients to throw together some sandwiches. Charlie had dropped me at the pub before heading back to his hotel for a shower and a change of clothes. We had agreed to meet in the main square in half an hour. I stuffed everything into my bag and grabbed a couple of cans of beer for good measure. Johnny ruffled his feathers on his perch, so I poured a handful of nuts into his bowl.

'Good boy. I'll be back in a bit,' I said, stroking his soft chest feathers.

'Bloody guests. Bloody guests.' Johnny stretched out his wings, and I stepped back.

'Really? I've been here weeks now.' But my hurt was short-lived as the door to the pub opened, and I turned to see Charlie's attack dog, David, standing looking back at me. A chill ran down my body and it wasn't due to the breeze that followed him in. He looked around, with the condescending gaze of someone who had no class.

'Can I help you?'

'Ms Williams. I was hoping to catch you.'

'Rissa,' I corrected, uneasy with how the word *catch* sounded on his tongue. He said nothing for a moment, instead scanning his eyes across the room.

'As you can see, I'm heading out, so if this can wait,' I said, indicating the bag on the bar.

'I know you think you're being smart.' He finally looked back towards me. 'And I'll accept you've been more of a pain in my ass than I'd have liked. But it won't last.'

My icky feeling was growing. I stuffed the remaining things into my bag, ready to make a quick exit. I didn't want to have to put this guy down, but if he pushed his luck, that was exactly where he was going to end up.

'Cryptic was never my thing, so if you've got something to say, I suggest you just get on with it. Otherwise you can leave.' I hitched the rucksack over my shoulder and stared back at him.

He let out a joyless laugh and smiled. 'Simple is probably best for someone like you. Here's the thing. Caulson Properties will buy that wooden shack you and your lot seem so attached to, and we will build on it.' He clapped his hands together in triumph. 'You might have Charlie convinced there's more to this place than a price per square metre, but I'm not.'

I nodded, moving forwards with conviction, needing him to leave my space. His small frame retreated. A hand leaned out for the door frame as he moved back too fast, needing to steady himself.

Pathetic.

'You have outstayed your welcome, and I no longer want to listen. Thank you for your assessment, but now let me be simple with you.' I leaned forwards with a confidence I didn't feel. But hell if he knew it.

'Fuck off.'

'Hmmm.' Another cold smile and chuckle. But I saw it. I saw the flash of fear in his eyes as he blinked one too many times. I saw the thought flicker across his mind that he was about to find himself forcibly removed, before he turned and walked out the door.

I allowed myself a moment to breathe. Despite knowing I could handle myself, my heart rate still betrayed the adrenaline running through my system. After a few minutes, my breathing had recovered. I pushed thoughts of David to one side and started looking forward to my afternoon.

Charlie had given me his word, and, despite previous misunderstandings, I trusted him.

***

'Is this legal?' Charlie said, as he sidled through the gap in the wired fence.

'Guess it depends on who you ask,' I replied, enjoying the look of uncertainty on his face.

'You.'

'Then yes. Yes, it is completely legal.' I walked off in the direction of the steps before he could quiz me any further. The fencing had been put up years ago, after a dogging society had found out about the demise of the hotel and decided it was a good place to stop and enjoy the view...whilst engaging in some other activities. The hotel on the hill had the best views around and also boasted the only access straight onto the water. Even if that access was now a questionable set of stairs.

'I'm getting the distinct feeling you've brought me here to get rid of me once and for all.' Charlie's voice caught up with me as I stood at the top of the steps. There was a light breeze skimming across the water, but the sun was bright. Myrtle's Cove lay in all her glory below.

'Now why would I do a thing like that?' I smiled a wicked smile, and gestured for Charlie to go first.

'If I wasn't suspicious before, I'm damn convinced now.' He moved in front of me and took hold of the slack rope that pretended to be a banister.

'You know I don't believe in chivalry,' I said, by way of explanation.

He nodded as he started down the steps. 'Hmmm, you might be right. As the man, I should go first, I suppose. Make sure it's safe.' He turned his head back towards me with the satisfied grin of someone who had just won our baiting game.

I refrained from replying, allowing him the win.

Damn him, playing me at my own game.

We carried on in silence, each of us watching our footing as we navigated the narrow path. But it was impossible not to sneak the odd glance at the specimen in front of me. Charlie's usual white shirt and suede shoes were gone, replaced with a white T-shirt that looked to have been made for him and him alone. The material winced at the broad expanse of his shoulders before falling away at his waist, where a pair of black board shorts took over. I knew our night together wasn't going to be repeated, but a girl could admire the view. Right?

A memory of trailing kisses down from his neck, across his strong broad...

No. Nope. Not helpful.

Maybe I didn't need to look. In fact, I didn't need to remember anything of the sort. Charlie had been nothing but respectful of that rule ever since. Not that I minded. It was good to have clear boundaries, no confusion. No room to misinterpret things. Super. Perfect. Just the way it should be. Eyes on the path, Rissa.

We reached the sand and stood side by side, taking in the view.

'This is unexpected.'

'It's one of my favourite spots. My dad used to bring me and Clem here when we were kids. We'd spend hours mucking around in the water, and then lie out and bake under the sun.'

'Your dad sounds like quite the man.'

'He was,' I said, smiling to myself as the memory came back.

Due to its small size and sandy bed, Myrtle Cove wasn't the favoured choice for those looking to pot crab or fish mackerel. But because it was protected on three sides, the water held its temperature well, making it perfect for swimming. I caught a glance of Charlie's face. He was looking out at the water and seeing it. Really seeing it. Seeing the beauty in the simplicity of it. The breeze caught in his hair, and the smell of his cologne reached me, making my stomach loop in misplaced anticipation.

'I didn't think you could do casual,' I said, to distract my overzealous pulse. I nodded at his T-shirt and board short combo.

'Despite what you might think, I am capable of switching off...sometimes,' he added. 'I admit, it's not something I do enough of. I'm trying to fix that though,' he said, with the sincerity of someone who was battling hard.

He helped me lay out the picnic blanket I had brought, before I started to unpack the random selection of food items I had put together back at the pub. A shiver ran down my neck at the memory of my run-in with David.

'Consider it a thank you,' I said, spreading my arms out at the display in front of us.

'What for?'

'Being there to help with Aunt Val. The chance to keep the Shed.'

I looked at him then, searching for any signs of the threat that David had landed on me hours earlier.

His eyes told me all I needed. There was no deceit there.

'There is no need for a thank you... Besides, you haven't won yet.' His tone was mocking and didn't feel like it held any real threat. No, Charlie wasn't lying...despite what his attack dog said.

I laughed at his words, amazed at how far we'd come. Joking about the Shed. *Talking* about the Shed! Christ, a few weeks ago, we'd have been lucky if this didn't end in a fist fight.

'Either way, I appreciate what you've done...more than you can know.' I kicked off my shoes and dug my feet into the warm sand. 'What will you do?'

'What do you mean?'

'When you lose.'

'Aha! I see.' He laughed. A noise that gave me far too much pleasure. 'If, and it is an if, I think I'm going to look at some other sorts of projects. Less of the ground up, and more fixer up. We'll see. As a kid, that's what I worked on. I would love seeing an old car being brought back to its former glory. My dad was never keen on me being in the garage with him, but I would make myself useful, listen. Fixing up those cars was peaceful.'

'Why?'

'Why was it peaceful?'

'No. Why did your dad not want you there?' I asked, before I had a chance to change my mind. This was the most open Charlie had ever been with me, and I wanted to know who he was. Who he really was.

He shrugged, a look on his face as though his thoughts had drifted into a somewhat painful past. 'Dad wanted the best. It came from a place of love, but it meant our lives, as they were, were not good enough. He wanted me to have nothing to do with it. Working with him at the garage would have been failure in his eyes.'

'I'm sorry.'

'He got to see the business succeed, and so he was proud of me when he died. I guess part of my years of blinkered work on the company was because I wanted his approval.' He let out a short laugh and shook his head. 'At least that's what my very expensive therapist tells me.'

I laughed too, thinking back to Aunt Val's assessment of me that morning.

'I hear you. My aunt had her own therapist words of wisdom for me when I saw her today.'

'And what was her advice?'

'Live my life.' I nodded, thinking back to our conversation.

'Sound advice.'

'How about yours?'

Charlie paused, the decision as to whether to divulge any more let out in a sigh. 'Focus on making myself proud by doing the things I love.'

'And are you?'

For a moment I thought Charlie wasn't going to answer, as he stared out at the water. 'I'm trying,' he said, turning to face me.

I held his gaze for a moment, before the intensity of it became too much and I turned away, hiding the blush on my cheeks.

'So other than bringing me to this beautiful cove, what's the plan?'

'Of course.' I smiled. 'You couldn't just sit and enjoy the sound of the waves on the sand.'

'Maybe for a minute.'

I laughed again, enjoying our easy conversation. 'I thought we could go for a swim.' I stopped and watched for the realisation to sink in.

'A swim?' His tone was cautious.

'I know you said you'd learned, but I wondered whether you had ever had a chance to go out in the sea?'

***

We stood on the water's edge, the water licking at our toes.

'Do we need to do some theory first?'

'Theory?' I repeated, unable to hide my amusement at how seriously he was taking it all. 'What sort of theory were you thinking?'

'Well'—he paused—'I'm not sure. Is there a certain technique that's best?'

'I think the best option is to just jump straight in,' I replied, as a small flicker of panic passed through his eyes. There was something endearing about seeing him this way. So out of control. So vulnerable. This was new; this was something different.

'We'll swim round the headland. There's a tiny cave there that they say pirates used to land their boats on.'

'Rissa, I don't want to sound too panicked here, but I'm not a strong swimmer.'

'That's alright. This is for you.' I chucked him a life jacket, which he immediately put on. 'And if all else fails, I will haul you back to shore.' I winked as Charlie took a few tentative steps into the sea, his body stiff with apprehension and the uncertainty only seen when people experience something for the first time. Like a small child arriving at the play park for the first time, not yet aware of the joy it will bring once they have figured it all out.

'Are you sure this thing will work?' he asked, tugging at the life jacket that was a bit too small for him, exposing two very defined muscles that seemed to be taunting me as they angled down below the line of his shorts.

'Rissa?' I looked back at his face, hoping he hadn't just caught me ogling him.

'I promise. Come on, start by wading out to me, and we can go from there. Just get used to the water first,' I said, swirling the water around me and reaching up onto my tiptoes as my body was lifted by an unbroken wave.

The sun had warmed the shallows enough to take the bite off it, but the Mediterranean it was not, and as Charlie waded further in, I watched as he did his best to suppress a yelp.

'Are you struggling?' I pressed, teasingly.

'No. In fact, I was just thinking how warm the water was.'

'Brilliant, then it's time to go all in.'

'All in?'

'Head under,' I said. 'Once you've done that, then the fear of it is done. Then we can focus on some swimming.'

Before I had a chance to say anything else, Charlie threw his head forwards and submerged his whole body, before reappearing, his mouth forming a perfect *O* and his eyes wide as the cold left him in shock.

'Nice.' I nodded, impressed by how well he held it together, and maybe a little by the water sparkling on his tanned skin. 'Let's get to it.'

The cove was a ten-minute swim. I turned and treaded water to look back at Charlie.

'Keep your strokes long and slow. The tide will tire you quickly otherwise. It's going to feel different to the pool.'

'That's an understatement.' A small frown line appeared between his eyes as he stared out at the water in front of him.

'How you doing?' I said, smiling at his look of pure concentration.

'I don't know. I should probably ask you.'

'You're doing great. Nearly there.' It was impossible not to admire him. The joy of unlocking something new, something unknown and realising the potential. Most people give up trying to master new things after a certain point, too afraid of ridicule, too afraid of embarrassment, failure. But Charlie had none of that, a man so composed and successful in his everyday life, yet prepared to throw it all out the window and embrace the fear of the unknown. The niggle in the back of my mind was hard to ignore. I was hiding from something I already knew how to do, and was good at.

We came round the headland, and the cave appeared before us.

The sea was calm, and the rocks leading out of the water were easy to scramble onto.

'Wow,' Charlie said, breathless as he stripped off his lifejacket. Water fell from his body, glistening in the sunlight. My now disobedient butterflies gave an unwanted flutter, and I averted my eyes. 'That was incredible. God, how have I never done this before? It's exhilarating.'

'I'm glad you enjoyed it.' I couldn't help but laugh; his joy was infectious.

I moved further into the cave, the cool dampness of its walls replacing the bright sunshine of outside.

'My dad used to bring me and Clem out here. Told us there was treasure still hidden in here. We were convinced we'd find it.'

'That's some swim for a kid,' Charlie said, as his eyes searched the cave.

'Dad said that to fish we had to swim. He always wanted to be certain we could hold our own if the worst happened.' I let out a hollow laugh. 'I guess it wasn't as useful as he thought.'

I felt the warmth of Charlie's hand on my shoulder, and found my body instinctively leaning into it.

'Let's see if any of that treasure is still here, shall we? You never know, might help you buy the Shed.' Charlie nudged into me, a wicked grin on his mouth. I feigned shock and swatted him with my hand.

'You're on, Mr Destroyer of Towns.'

Our searching produced nothing more than a half-eaten crab and some old fishing line, which I tied around my wrist to ensure it didn't get caught on any unsuspecting bird.

'So last one back to the shore buys the drinks?' Charlie said, as he stood beside me at the edge of the cave.

'You better get your wallet out then,' I said.

'I need to take this off though. It's holding me back,' he said, signalling to the lifejacket. 'I'm going to put it round my waist, and it will float next to me.'

Despite his obvious confidence, I had doubts about the loss of the life jacket. The breeze was getting stronger, and the sun was now spending more time hidden behind large, bulbous clouds than out shining on the water. Before I had a chance to dwell on my concerns any longer, Charlie stretched out his arms in front of him and pushed off, disappearing beneath the surface of the water.

'Whoa!' He resurfaced and threw his head back, shaking off his hair, the fear of before gone.

'I think I am going to need to take full credit for your speedy progress.'

'Is that so?' he said, treading water.

'Absolutely,' I said, keeping a straight face. 'It's all in the teaching, you see.'

'I see.' He nodded, playing along. 'I think you have forgotten one thing.'

'What's that?'

'The student. Without a good student, you'd have nothing.' A youthful smile creased his face.

'I don't know; even the most untalented of students can be brought to greatness through great teaching... Take yourself, for example.'

'I suggest you stop standing there looking beautiful and try keep up.'

With that, he turned and headed off round the cove, whilst I was left reeling from his words.

Chapter 24

I wasn't one for signs. I had no idea what my star sign meant, had never read a horoscope, held close certain lottery numbers, or seen coincidences as anything more than that—coincidence. However, as I stood at the counter of Mermaid's, and the long-haired teenager with better dress sense than I would ever be fortunate enough to have said, 'Just the two sausages left. Sure you don't fancy it? Share it with a friend?', I saw my sign.

Maybe it was an excuse; maybe it was the push I needed. Who knew, but the cellophane box in my hand was hot, and the smell of fried food was filling the corridor of the intimidating Townhouse Hotel. A thick, deep blue carpet runner ran the length of the corridor. Small wall lights gave out a golden glow, while black-and-white photos of the area hung on the walls.

After our afternoon swimming, Charlie had dropped me back at the pub, where despite my best efforts, my mind had been a jumble of second guesses and micro-analyses of every look and touch from Charlie. And yet he was unfazed.

My niggling curiosity had turned into full-blown annoyance towards Charlie's blatant rejection of me. He was so full of mixed messages. A tease, a player... I had been gaslit! Yes, that was it. He had me believe in something, then *poof*. Gone. But I wasn't standing for it. Nope.

But as I got closer to room 108, my confidence waned.

101

After all, it was me that had imposed the ban.

104

Of course he wasn't going to force himself on me. Hello, consent!

106

But he could have flirted. He could have hinted. Given me a sign. *Ha!* The irony. Things had changed between us. Not just because of his olive branch about the Shed. But in all the small ways he had shown me there was more there than suede shoes and an obnoxious bank account. It was becoming harder and harder to connect the Charlie Caulson who had held me as I cried tears and rubbed snot all over his chest with the evil property mastermind I was at war with.

108

The point was I needed to know. I needed to know if Charlie was being respectful of my wishes, or if he wasn't interested. If our night together had been nothing more than that. One night.

As soon as I knocked, the door opened, and a towel-wrapped Charlie greeted me. His chiselled stone chest on full display.

Breathe, Riss. Just breathe.

The towel was wrapped low on his hips, the distinct ab lines guiding my eyes down to what I knew lay beneath.

Behave!

235

'Rissa.' Charlie's voice brought me back. I shut my mouth, aware I looked like a drooling Labrador.

'Why don't you want me?' I blurted out, all hope of playing it cool gone.

'I beg your pardon?' His eyes widened, and an amused smile fell on his face.

'I mean, I get I'm not your type, but—'

'What's my type?' he interrupted.

I looked away, feeling the heat of his gaze too intensely.

'What?'

'You said you're not my type. What is my type?'

'Well, I guess...' I looked around the doorway, anywhere but the towel-clad Charlie, trying to think what his type was. 'Successful, runs her own company, bi-weekly facials, perfectly coloured hair, definitely never forgets to shave her legs. Or wax her bikini line. Scrap that, she'll have had laser removal, so shaving is a thing of her past. Has a body in a similar style to your...' I waved a hand up and down and swallowed hard before saying, 'Your physique.'

This was a disaster.

Charlie stood watching me, the *blink and you'd miss it* raise of an eyebrow the only suggestion he was even listening to my rambling.

'But you know what? It's fine. It really is. I get it. We slept together, and it meant nothing. You're able to move on fast, next building project, next woman. It's just who you are. Polite, professional, emotionless. In fact, I'm pretty sure there's a degree at one of your fancy universities called PPE.' My words were tumbling out of my mouth quicker than I had time to take a breath and realise I sounded like a complete weirdo.

Abort. Abort.

I looked down at the cooling box in my hand and then up at Charlie. 'I should go. I, um...I'm meeting someone. To eat with.'

Abort.

I gave a final nod to complete my car crash of a monologue and went to walk away, as Charlie, who had remained silent throughout, spoke. 'You're wrong.'

'Hmmm?' I said, as I turned to look at him again.

'Don't have any illusion that I don't want you, Rissa. I want all of you.'

I let out an unattractive snort of disagreement, which I immediately regretted. Charlie took a step towards me, and his presence smothered the air between us, leaving me breathless.

'You *are* the type, Rissa. You speak your mind at all times. You stand up for what you believe in with no fear, even when you are battling your own demons. You are spectacular.'

I was rooted to the spot. The space around me had become blurred, the man in front of me my sole focus, with the smell of the ocean still clinging to his skin.

'And in regards to waxing.' He smiled now. 'I want a woman, not a child.' His hand came up to my face, before it twisted a piece of my hair between his fingers. 'You said it wasn't going to happen,' he continued.

I opened my mouth to reply, but nothing came out.

'I won't push myself on you, Rissa. But if you say you want this, I'll give you everything.'

I inhaled, trying to push oxygen back into my brain, which was rapidly overheating.

'What do you want, Rissa?'

'I mean...' I tried to keep my tone casual, calm. But as Charlie's hand came up to my face, his finger tracing the line of my jaw, his eyes never leaving mine, my legs were ready to buckle.

'No more games,' he said, his eyes darting between mine.

'Kiss me.'

'With pleasure.' Charlie didn't miss a beat. In one swift movement, he wrapped an arm around my waist, pressing me against him, as the door behind me slammed shut.

'I need a shower, and you need a lot less on.'

***

The steam swirled around us, blurring the large bathroom from view. Charlie pressed my body up against the cool glass, pinning me there. I thrust my hips forwards, needing more connection. This man had lit a fuse, and there was no turning back. I didn't want to either. Charlie pulled away from me and held my face between his hands, and I groaned in frustration at the loss of contact.

'I meant it when I said I want all of you, Rissa. I didn't sleep with you the other night thinking it was a one-night stand.'

'You didn't disagree to it being that,' I said, as my teeth found the soft skin of his neck.

'I needed you to realise what we had was more than you were prepared to admit.' His hands pressed me back into the glass as he made his way down to my breasts, taking each one in turn, his tongue flicking over them, teeth scraping, causing me to yelp in pleasure.

'Can I kiss you?' he said, looking straight at me.

I knew what he meant. Before my doubts had a chance to squeeze their way in, I nodded.

'I need to hear you say it, sweetheart.' His fingers didn't stop making their languid circles, his lips finding the sensitive spot below my jaw.

'Yes, kiss me.'

Charlie dropped to his knees, water bouncing off his skin as he ran his hands down my thighs.

'Spread your legs.' His voice was firm, and I found myself obeying.

I looked down at Charlie, the water splashing off his shoulders, his hands roaming across my stomach. I clenched my muscles instinctively, feeling exposed.

'Don't.' He looked up at me, his chin on my stomach, hands resting on my hips. 'You are beautiful. Never feel ashamed of your body. It is damn perfect.'

I said nothing, trying my best to not focus on my unwaxed bikini line and Charlie's face moving to my inner thigh.

'You don't have to do this,' I managed, between his kisses that were slowly circling closer to my centre.

'I want this more than you could know, Rissa. But if you tell me it's not for you, I'll stop.'

'It's not that,' I said. His finger rubbed against my clit, and my legs betrayed me as they slid further apart. 'I know it's not much fun for you.'

Charlie let out a disbelieving laugh and stood to face me, but kept his body against mine, all of us fused together. 'I don't know what sort of men you have been with, and quite frankly I don't want to think about it too much. But I want to taste you.'

I took a sharp breath.

'Can I kiss you?'

'Kiss me. Please!'

Charlie knelt again.

His mouth landed on me, and I threw my head back against the glass, unable to silence my gasp.

How did it feel so good? It had never felt like this. This was... This was otherworldly.

'Sweet Jesus.'

'That's right,' he said against my skin. 'God, you taste perfect.' He tilted his head up, a wicked smile on his lips.

'Yes!' I was a different woman. I didn't cry out in pleasure; that wasn't me. But this man was a master. 'Don't stop.' I pushed my hips forwards, begging him not to keep going. His lips found me again, and his tongue swirled in almost painful circles as he inserted one finger and then another. My hands tried to grab at the glass to steady myself, but the smooth surface had me flailing. I reached out and gripped Charlie's hair as a low groan of pleasure vibrated against me. I held him there. Just. There.

'I'm going to make you come now.' His voice low and determined, his stubble rubbing on my already sensitive skin.

I tried to laugh at his arrogance, but the building pressure I felt told me he was right. So, so right. His tongue found my centre again, savouring my taste. My body responded as I gripped onto his hair. His mouth sucked and released, before he pushed another finger into me, finding the perfect combination. His rhythm picked up, my groans of approval only encouraging him more. Everything about it felt like worship, desire, lust, and yet so much more. Just like our night at the pub, this was considered, emotional, deliberate. My thoughts about what this all meant were quickly swept away as my pleasure rose through me, as he curled his fingers up, sending me over the edge.

As my arms fell down by my side, releasing him from my hold, he kissed a trail of lazy kisses up my stomach. He took my chin in his hands and pressed his lips to mine, the taste of my pleasure on his tongue.

***

By the time I had recovered, we were wrapped in the duvet of his super king bed. My head rested on his chest, listening to the steady beat of his heart. I never wanted to leave that room. I wanted that moment, that place, to stay frozen in time. Nothing about me and Charlie made sense, but in that moment, it all felt so simple, so right.

'What are you thinking about?' he asked, pressing a gentle kiss to my shoulder.

Could I tell him what I was really thinking? Could I tell him I was terrified by the feelings I had for him? Terrified that it left me with nothing other than heartache to come?

'Your new plan to get more balance with work.' I guess not.

'Ah.'

Was that a hint of disappointment in his voice?

I rolled over to face him. His hair was ruffled, and god, if it didn't undo me again.

'You said earlier that you needed more balance.'

'I did.' He nodded, raking his long fingers through his hair. 'I do.'

'Do you think you can?'

I had no idea why I asked. It wasn't my business. I didn't need to know. But that was the problem—I wanted to know. I wanted to know everything about him. The good, the bad, the downright ugly.

He pressed his head back into the soft pillow and sighed.

'For the longest time, building the business was all that mattered. I needed it to be a success. My parents had sacrificed everything for me to do it. I needed to make them proud. It was my obsession. But in the success of the business, the rest of my life stalled. I never let anyone in. Not fully.'

'I understand that,' I said, because it was true. Despite our reasons being worlds apart, I understood Charlie's approach. I'd done the same. Block out everything else and don't give anything a chance. If I'd let joy in, passion, love, it would have been a betrayal to Dad. Of what he was no longer able to have. So like Charlie, I'd put blinkers on.

Charlie's words stirred me back to where we were. 'But I think the truth is, I wasn't ready. I hadn't met someone who rocked the ground beneath me. Who made me want to sacrifice.'

The air between us became heavy, and Charlie held my gaze. I took in a breath and said the only thing I could to keep any level of self-preservation alive.

'I should go.'

I rolled over and swung my legs over the bed, feeling a chill on my skin now I wasn't wrapped up next to him. I sat with my back to him as I scanned the floor for my clothes that had been discarded at different points on our way to the shower.

'Stay.' The word landed on me. It felt like a hand taking mine.

I said nothing for a moment, allowing it to rest in the air between us.

Finally, I said, 'Why?'

Charlie pulled on my wrist, coaxing me to look at him. He sat up now, the sheets pooling low on his waist.

Christ, keep your eyes at head height, Rissa, or you've no chance of making it out.

'Because you want to.' His fingers moved to my face, pushing my sex-ruffled hair behind my ear. 'Because you know there's more here than sex.' His fingers moved down my cheek, stroking the outline of my jaw. 'Because the feelings I have for you are too strong not to be real, and I want to know if you feel them too.'

My head tilted into his hand as he cupped my cheek. I knew it was mad, but I couldn't help it. I couldn't see anything but the man in front of me. The man who had held me as I'd cried over my guilt about Dad, who had helped fix my truck, had driven me to and from the hospital, had taken the time to learn about Telbury and our way of life. That was the man in front of me. That was the man asking me to stay, and hell, wild horses weren't going to keep me away.

I leaned forwards and pressed my lips to his, my hands reaching into his hair. I wasn't brave enough to tell him that I was falling for him. That I was free falling, and I couldn't see the ground anymore. Instead, I pulled the sheets back over me and draped a leg over his as I felt him go hard against me.

'You're insatiable.'

'Only for you.'

I was so screwed!

Chapter 25

The summer sunrise burst through the window and scattered light across the room. I rubbed my eyes open and was greeted by the most delicious view of Charlie. Low hung jogging pants. No shirt. He was standing at the window with his back to me. All firm lines and bite-me-smooth skin. He had a phone to his ear and was talking quietly.

'Thank you. I'll confirm in the next fifteen.' He disconnected the call and, as if he could feel my gaze, turned around.

'Good morning, beautiful.'

'Morning.' I blushed and averted my eyes, unused to such attention.

'I have a surprise for you,' he said, walking back over to the bed and placing a kiss on my forehead as though this was normal. As though this was how we spent each and every morning. How was that possible? How could this man feel so natural to me?

'What is it?'

'Ah, now that would be telling.' His kisses trailed down my neck as I wrapped my arms around him, pulling him back into the bed. 'No. No time for that.'

I held him by his shoulders and looked up at him as he hovered above me. 'Are you telling me you don't want to have sex with me?' I joked.

'Oh sweetheart, there are so many things I want to do to you, I barely know where to begin.'

A shot of anticipation travelled down between my thighs, and uncensored thoughts fogged my mind. 'I realise you might not be ready for everyone to see us together yet. So early morning is our opportunity.' My racing thoughts must have been written across my face as Charlie cupped my cheeks and said, 'Don't overthink this. There's just one rule this morning.'

'Oh yeah?' I leaned into his hand, feeling my pulse slow under his reassuring touch.

'No work chat. This is just me and you.'

I swallowed hard and nodded, the realisation that I had in fact not thought about our ongoing war since arriving at his room the night before now weighing on me.

Now you're in trouble.

***

'How did you—'

'I made some calls.' He shrugged, but his eyes sparkled with satisfaction at my open-mouthed surprise.

'Of course you did. How did you know I could ride?'

We stood in a car park just outside of Telbury, on a small country road. There was a 4x4 pickup truck with a two-horse box hooked on the back. A man stood with two tacked-up horses facing us.

'Call it a hunch. You ready?' Charlie asked, as we stepped forwards and took the reins of our respective steeds.

I let out a disbelieving laugh. 'I guess so. I didn't even know you rode. Was it on a polo pitch you learned?' I mocked as I stood on the positioned box and swung my leg over.

'The estate where we lived had a city farm close by. One free lesson a month if you cleaned out the stables... I cleaned a lot of stables!'

I cringed at my own assumptions. I should have known by now that he was full of surprises. Charlie had worked damn hard for what he had, and who was I to judge that?

'I'll meet you back here in a couple of hours,' said the young groom who had delivered us the horses, saving me from my internal chastisement. 'Enjoy.'

***

We rode in companionable quiet as we got a feel for our horses. Maisy—my horse—had a long mane that fell in waves down her dapple grey neck. Charlie was on an all chestnut firecracker whose tail swished from side to side with each stride forwards. I tilted my head up to the rising sun and allowed my legs to wrap around Maisy's middle, feeling her respond. Her ears twitched back and forth, waiting on the next command.

We had fallen into a gentle rhythm as we made our way along the narrow lane that led to the vast sand dunes and long sandy beach. Telbury was snuggled between the rocky cliffs to the west, where the best crab in Cornwall could be caught, and the tourist beach to the east. The tall hedges that lined the road made each corner a surprise reveal, but beginnings of sand and sea crept through the hedgerow in fragments. Maisy picked up the pace, and the steady *clip-clop, clip-clop* of before was replaced with a skip and a scuff on the tarmac. Charlie trotted to catch up with me; his chestnut tossed her head back and forth impatiently.

'Are you ready?' he said, the carefree smile on his face swelling my heart. Relaxed Charlie was by far my favourite.

'The question is, are *you*?'

We squeezed through a gap in the hedge, thorny branches scratching my legs, before the beach spread herself out in pure, tide-smoothed glory. The water was on the retreat, and given it was still early, it was yet to be filled with tourists trying to bake under the Cornish sun. I felt my body tense in anticipation, a spark of something igniting in me. Maisy's ears pushed forwards, and my reins went slack as she stretched her head high.

'Try to keep up,' I said, with a backwards glance. I pressed a gentle heel into Maisy's side. It was all the encouragement she needed. I leaned forwards and she threw her front legs out, the wind picking up around me as I took off down the beach.

'Woohoo!'

My voice caught on the wind and vanished. Tears streamed down my cheeks; my mouth hung open in a childlike grin. I could hear Charlie gaining on me and urged Maisy forwards. Sand threw up around us, catching me on the cheek. I hadn't felt this light in years, and as I turned my head to watch Charlie coming up behind me in full gallop, my heart beat faster, and I let out a real laugh. It was hard to remember the last time I had felt such joy. The thunder of hooves on sand got louder, and before I realised it, Charlie was beside me.

'Is there anything you're not exceptionally good at?' he shouted into the space between us.

'I'd say you're holding your own.' We pulled up and slowed to a steady trot.

'Fancy a dip?' I asked, the smile that had found its way onto my face when I'd woken up next to him growing wider with every minute in his company.

We steered towards the water, our horses obliging as we waded out into the shallows. I looked over at Charlie and opened my mouth to speak but closed it again as I looked at him and him at me. Our communication was a silent one. One that took me by surprise. One that scared and thrilled me all at once. Words unspoken but felt. My body fizzed with energy, and my chest burst open, allowing this man in front of me to take my heart in his hands. The problem was, I had no idea if I was ever going to get it back.

***

I pressed my head into the sand and stretched out. I closed my eyes and allowed the bright light to filter orange through my eyelids.

'This is perfect,' I said, sighing out the clean sea air.

'I'm glad you approve.'

After a few minutes of content silence, I turned on my side, resting my head on my elbow. 'I think you're getting better at it, you know.'

'What's that?' He turned to look at me, mirroring my position. His beautiful face caught in the sun, turning his eyes a shade of green I didn't know existed.

'Relaxing. You've been still for at least five minutes.'

He let out a soft chuckle and rubbed a hand over his day-old stubble as though mulling over my remark. 'There's a lot of things I've discovered recently.'

'Care to share?'

He looked back at me, his smile replaced with something so much more intense. A look that had me straining to hear his thoughts. His hand came over my waist, and he pulled me close against him, his nose running along my neck.

'When I kiss you here, I can feel your pulse quicken beneath my lips.'

'Mmm,' I said, leaning into his touch, a smile on my lips.

He kissed my neck, and I chuckled.

'Mermaid's Fish Bar does in fact produce the best fish supper in the country.' His hand ran along my waist, turning leisurely circles with his fingers, igniting goosebumps across my skin.

'Fishing is so much more than giant nets out in the sea.'

I stilled at his words.

'Telbury is so much more than what I thought.'

'Mr Caulson, have we caught you in our net?' I hitched one leg over his and pressed a kiss to his lips, unable to wipe the mischievous grin from my face.

'You have no idea.' He returned my kiss with force, pulling me on top of him.

'Well'—I sat up and looked at him—'whilst we're in this little truth sharing moment, I should probably admit something too.'

'Oh yeah?'

'Don't look so smug.' I nudged his shoulder as he sat up to face me. 'The day I took you out fishing?'

He nodded, as the memory of how it ended came back to me.

'You might have had a point. I've been hiding from this life ever since Dad died. In fact, I've been hiding from life. Working at the home was an escape from thinking about it all. I was so busy looking after the residents, it stopped my brain from thinking about what happened.

'And now...' I thought about it for a second. *And now?* 'Now I know that I belong here. I belong in this community. And as much as I loved my job as chief trashy magazine reader to your mum, I think I'm better suited to being at sea.'

'She definitely misses your company. But if she could see you here, the way I have, she would be blown away. I'm proud of you, Rissa. You know where you belong; you know what you're meant to be doing. It's a precious gift.'

'Why, thank you.' I tilted my head to the side and smiled.

'That is not to say you are not the single most frustrating person I have ever met.'

'Way to ruin—'

'I haven't finished.' He pulled me down to the sand and pushed the hair from my face. 'But you are also the most mesmerising woman I have ever been in the company of.'

My skin came alive at his touch and his words. They were cheesy, and in any other reality, I would have shivered with embarrassment. But right now, as I lay back onto the sand with Charlie moving over me, our mouths pressed to one another in a slow, lazy kiss, I felt content. Happy. Give me all the cheese, I say. What shouldn't have felt good, felt great.

The man I should never have liked had me in the palm of his hands, and I never wanted it to end.

Chapter 26

I pulled my high ponytail tighter and stood up to assess my crop top and tracksuit combo. My phone pinged, and my heart did its daily short circuit.

It was official. I was a teenage girl. If my phone beeped, my heart skipped a beat. Vital oxygen bypassed my brain. I knew I was falling, and I didn't care. We were raising the money. We were going to hit the target before the deadline. There was no reason I couldn't get the man and the dream. Life was good.

Aunt Val had come home from the hospital, and I had been focused on settling her back in and making sure the fridge was stocked with all the right foods. It had also taken a minute for her to get used to her daily injections of insulin. In the week I'd been focused on Aunt Val, I hadn't seen Charlie once, but our contact was constant. Late night phone calls about everything and nothing, random daytime texts telling me he was thinking of me. We hadn't spoken anymore about the Shed and the fundraiser, but we had it in the bag.

Charlie: Have fun tonight. X

I smiled at the phone. Smiled! Pathetic. I knew it, and yet the smile stuck even as I started typing.

Rissa: Thanks. Shame you can't come. I'd love to know what your song is.

Charlie: Where are you?

Rissa: Getting ready.

Charlie: There's a little something for you downstairs... Keep your energy up.

I jumped from my seat and skidded down the stairs. Aunt Val stood at the bottom, an immediately distinguishable Styrofoam box in her hands.

'I don't know when Mermaid's started making deliveries, but I'm telling you, this has bad news written all over it.'

I rolled my eyes at her and took the box, inhaling deeply as the scent of batter wafted up to me. 'Hush your moaning. It's food. Not a marriage proposal.'

Aunt Val gave me a suspicious look and muttered something under her breath before walking back behind the bar. Her usual grumpy demeanour was back, but with an extra edge, given the cigarette withdrawal she was facing. The doctor had made it very clear that the smoking had to stop, as it was playing havoc with her sugars. Begrudgingly, Aunt Val had agreed, and was now not to be found without a packet of nicotine gum swirling around in her mouth.

'And we need to discuss this outfit.' She nodded at my low-slung sweatpants and sports bra.

'It's tradition! The Spice Girls are living legends. Anyway, our routine is flawless.'

'What time is Nav getting here, anyway?'

'Any minute now. Don't worry,' I said. 'We've got this. I know we're not as good as Clem, but trust me, we'll MC the shit out of it.'

'Maybe,' she grumbled, whilst half-heartedly wiping a cloth over the bar top. It was Clem who'd taken on MC duties at the pub's impromptu karaoke nights over the years, but given his recent revelations, he'd decided to stay away. The door swung open, and Nav appeared, dressed in her Union Jack dress and bright red wig.

'You could have got changed here, you know,' I said, laughing as I helped her with the trunk of food she was dragging behind her.

'Nah. I love the looks! Part of the fun,' she said, trying to catch her breath.

'Ever the exhibitionist.'

'Don't you know it. Now, let's get ready to raise some money!'

***

'You ready?' Nav said from the door. 'Got quite a crowd building down there.'

I gave my ponytail one final tighten and turned towards the growing chatter and laughter coming from the bar below. I stopped on the final step and took in the scene in front of me.

'Wow,' I said, more to myself than anyone else.

'I know, right?' Nav replied.

I felt the same swell of pride I had felt the night we gathered to discuss saving the Shed all those weeks before. And now here we were, on the home stretch. The space was packed with locals, tourists, and everyone in between. Aunt Val had thrown her doors open for all and everyone.

The response had been overwhelming, and we had had to cut off the sales of the tickets due to capacity. It was amazing how many people wanted to help. They wanted to see Telbury thrive, as it was. Not as something new and shiny, but in its current form. There was a balance to be had between tourists and locals. We needed each other. But no one could grow so big that the other was smothered. It was a delicate balance that needed constant checking.

'Oi, popstars. Get your arses down here,' Aunt Val hollered from the bar. Nav and I laughed and jumped to it. A roar went up as we stepped onto the stage and took the mics.

'Good evening, everyone,' I said, beaming back at the crowd of smiling faces.

Another roar.

The drinks were flowing, and everyone was in the right mood for fun and spending money.

'As you all know, we're here to save our Shed. Telbury has been a fishing town since before the disciples were doing it. We have multiple generations of fishermen with us here tonight, and you are here to help save their jobs.' The crowd started stomping their feet in approval, and I gave them a minute before I held my hand up to quieten them again.

'But more than that, you're here to help save our way of life. This whole town is connected to the fishing. From the restaurants who buy the fish, to the dock workers who fix our boats, fishing is the beating heart of Telbury. We know change comes for us all, and we need to learn to move forwards, but we must hold onto the things we know are good for us.' I looked out at the silent pub and swallowed down the lump in my throat. 'So with that said, we need your money. And lots of it!

Tonight is about letting loose, singing your hearts out, and putting that cash behind the bar. Ain't that right, Aunt Val?'

'I'm ready for ya!' she shouted out, causing the room to cheer once more.

The crowd sang and clapped with each act. The singing was appalling, but the enthusiasm was spectacular. We were there to save Telbury, and I felt like I could almost touch the finish line.

Chapter 27

'You look beautiful,' Charlie said, his voice low and just for me, despite the fact the restaurant was full, and the chatter around us more than drowned his words out to anyone else.

'I'm in grease-stained jeans and a T-shirt.'

'Exactly.'

My cheeks flushed, and I rolled my eyes. I was still getting used to his compliments, but I couldn't deny the effect they had on me.

'Although...' He paused.

'What?'

'I'm kind of missing the two tone hair.'

'Shut up.' I laughed and leaned my head in towards his.

'Do you think this is a bit brazen?' he asked, giving a quick look around the restaurant.

'Yes.' I laughed. 'But to be honest, people round here have kind of got used to you. It's a bit like having wolves reintroduced. You're wary, but keep your distance, and it's generally fine.'

'I don't think that makes me feel particularly reassured,' Charlie said, before taking a sip of the water in front of him.

'Besides, there is nothing untoward about this,' I said, waving a hand around. 'It's a business lunch.'

'True.' He nodded before leaning across the table, voice low. 'Although your foot running up my leg might suggest a different sort of lunch. Thank god for long tablecloths.'

'Agreed.' I laughed.

Nav's was busy, and no one was paying us any attention. Apart from Nav. I hadn't told her anything concrete about Charlie and me, but she was suspicious by nature, and my newfound joy was knocking her off balance. I caught her eye and waved. She raised an eyebrow and went back to giving instructions to the chefs.

Charlie was back from London. He'd stayed longer than I'd hoped, but after his mother had a fall at the home, he'd wanted to be near her.

'How is she doing?' I asked.

'Alright. I think it was more of the shock than anything. She'll be fine though.'

'I'm hoping to see her, you know. I need to head back up and clear the rest of my things from my rental. Now I know I'm staying here, I've given notice on the room. I've still got some things at the home too. Would you mind if I popped in to see her?'

'She'd love that.' Charlie smiled. 'She asked after you the other day. She'd be delighted to see you, I know.'

As our conversation flowed, I found it hard to understand how we had got here. Or where it was going. After all, the last of our fundraising was the summer ball in a few days, and after that, it would all be over. The Shed would be ours, and there would be no need for Charlie to stay. I stomped the thought from my mind and looked out at the harbour beyond. It was time to enjoy the moment for the moment itself.

The waiter came over to the table and placed our food down, before a noise outside caught us all by surprise.

'Sounds like someone's not happy,' he said, the ever-professional smile of a well-trained waiter on his face.

We turned to where the noise was coming from. The movement caught my eye first. The two men I could see had their backs to us, but the indomitable size of Geoff was unmistakable.

'Is that Geoff?' Charlie asked, looking in the same direction.

'I think so.'

'Is he alright?'

I looked back to the plates of food and focused on the divine smell wafting from the pasta in front of me. 'I'd be more worried about whoever has pissed him off. Let's eat.'

Before I had a chance to put my fork to my mouth, the sound of crashing stopped me in my tracks.

'I think I'll just go check everything is alright.' I stood to leave as Charlie mirrored my move.

'I'll come with you.'

But we didn't get any further, as the door to the restaurant was thrown open and Geoff stormed in with Clem right behind him.

'What the—'

'Rissa!'

'Geoff,' I said, registering the clenched fists and deep-dug frown between his eyes. The look he gave Charlie would have been enough to send many running to take cover.

'Everything alright?'

'Did you know?' His voice was barely contained, and if all eyes hadn't been looking at us before, they were now.

'Geoff, you're going to need to be a lot more specific.' My gut was telling me something was very off. The last time I'd had this feeling, my dad had gone overboard on Saoirse. And now that same cold drip of fear was trickling into my stomach.

I looked behind Geoff to Clem. He had said nothing, but his eyes never left Charlie.

'Tell her,' Geoff boomed.

The restaurant was silent now. The waiters had stopped serving, and my feeling of impending doom was flashing red in my brain.

'Geoff, you're going to need to use more than three words to—'

'*Tell* her!'

I took a step back, shocked by the anger in his voice.

Clem placed a hand on Geoff's shoulder and whispered in his ear. Geoff nodded, and Clem moved forwards.

'Riss, it's over,' Clem said.

'What's over? Christ! Will someone please explain?'

As if on cue, the door to the restaurant opened, and the narrow, tight-suited frame of David walked in.

'Charlie?' I turned to look at him. His hand had found mine at some point, and I squeezed hard, desperate for some reassurance. 'Charlie, why is everyone in the restaurant?' I was staring at him, willing him to give me some sort of communication that everything was going to be OK. Because it was, right? That's what we'd agreed. We could face it. Together.

Charlie's face turned a shade lighter in the space of a few seconds as he watched David walk up towards our table.

'Tell me what's going on, Charlie.' I said, my fingers squeezing his, hoping to find the space that was just me and him. Hoping he could end this nightmare.

'They fucking bought it,' Geoff said, no longer waiting. 'It's over. They bought it, and it's done.'

Charlie went to open his mouth, but shut it again. His gaze had left mine and was on David, who stood with a folder under his arm.

'They fooled us, Rissa. The whole fucking time. Just a big joke. There was no deal. There was no fair fight. They had us,' Geoff said.

'Ah, you've told her then.' David stepped forwards. Geoff lurched, but Clem was ready and had him held.

'Now now, there's no need for that.' David tutted.

'David, what are you doing?' Charlie asked, his tone threatening.

'I've the signed contract here, Mr Caulson. The Shed is officially ours.'

'He was right.' I shook my head in disbelief.

'Who was right?'

'Your attack dog. He visited me at the pub the other day. Said we wouldn't win. Said you'd buy the Shed.'

Charlie reared back at my words. 'Tell me when he was there. I need to know.'

'What you need to do is get lost.' Geoff's tone was deadly and left no room for argument.

Charlie tried again, but the noise was becoming muffled. I stumbled back, and my connection to Charlie was gone. He reached for me, but I was quicker.

'Don't touch me.' My voice was no more than a whisper, but with a direct hit at Charlie. The air was trapped in my throat, and I had the feeling I was about to be sick.

'If you give me a minute. This is not—'

'You know what; we don't need your big words to describe something we already know. You won. Spin it however you like, but it don't change jack,' Geoff said.

It was all crashing in around me.

Breathe, Riss, just breathe.

My hand clamped onto Geoff, and I opened my mouth to speak, but there were no words. It was the water again, crushing me, pushing me under.

'You lied. It was all lies. I've just had a call from the Marshalls' lawyer. Caulson Properties went in with some joke offer, and they've accepted. Paid ten times what it's worth. It's done. Over.'

'I mean, it *was* a very generous offer,' David said, his enjoyment in the situation dripping from his words.

I watched in slow motion as Geoff made another launch at David, but he slipped out of the way, and Clem dragged Geoff out the side door of the kitchen, into Nav's office.

'You need to leave.'

'Rissa, please trust me.'

'Trust you?' I looked up at him. 'Trust you? I did. *We* did. Geoff's right. You won; it's done.'

He moved towards me, but Nav was there.

'I want you both out of this restaurant. Now,' she said, before wrapping an arm around my waist and guiding me away.

'Rissa?' Charlie's voice was distant and muffled.

I felt nothing. No sadness, no anger, no pain. Nothing. It would come. I knew it would come, but right then and there? In that moment? I felt nothing. He had betrayed me. Us. All of us. And I had let him.

I had trusted him, and in turn, so had everyone else. We had lost the Shed, and it was on me.

Chapter 28

'Here.' Nav pressed a steaming cup into my hands.

I gave the best smile I could muster and allowed the sweet chocolate aroma to fill my nose. Despite our all too public showdown at Nav's the day before, word had not yet spread about us losing the Shed. We knew it was going to come out, but with only a few days to go until the ball, we wanted to wait. Everyone had put so much effort in, and it seemed only fair they got to enjoy it.

'I don't have a plan yet, but it's going to be alright.'

I reached out a hand and placed it on hers. 'I love your optimism, but it's over.' I looked up and surveyed the decorated hall as we both sat silent.

'How are you doing?' she asked, taking a sip from her own cup of chocolate delight.

'I don't know,' I said honestly. 'I just can't believe he lied. It doesn't feel real that the Shed is gone.'

'That wasn't what I meant.' She widened her eyes.

I picked at the paper rim of my cup and avoided eye contact.

'Riss.'

'How did you know?' My eyes flitted back across the hall. We had almost finished decorating. It felt strange to be holding the ball. But the tickets were sold, and too many people had done too much to not have it go ahead. We may have lost, but at least we would go down in a cloud of gold confetti, loud music, and too much alcohol.

'Oh, Narissa Williams,' she cooed. 'You're my best friend in the entire world. How could I miss that sparkle in your eye? It's been missing so long, it shone brighter than anything else when it came back.' She nodded her head from side to side with a smile. 'It took me a minute to figure out the source. But when I saw Charlie's had that same shine, it was pretty obvious.'

'I'm sorry.' I dipped my finger into the cream and scooped out a small chunk of brownie.

'Sorry? Why?'

'For... Well, you know. The whole sleeping with the enemy thing...literally.' I let out a short laugh, but there was no humour in it.

'Oh please!' She batted away my words with her hand.

'No, I'm serious. It's my fault. If I hadn't taken my eye off the ball, if I'd listened to my head and not my—'

'Heart?'

'I was going to say something else.' I raised an eyebrow.

'No.' She shook her head. 'It might have started out as sex. But that's not what it is now. You have fallen for that man. And I'm pretty certain he's so far in he doesn't know which way is up.'

'Nav.'

'I'm serious. I don't have an explanation for it all. Call it a gut feeling.'

I said nothing. She might be holding on to unsupported hope about there being more to Charlie's actions, but she was right about one thing. I had fallen head over heels for that man, and now not only had I lost my dream of fishing, I'd lost him too. It wasn't like I hadn't known it could happen. That had always been the end result. One of us would lose.

Lowering my head, I groaned. I had no idea how we were going to share this news. Fishing in Telbury would come to an end after four hundred years. The livelihoods of Clem, Geoff, and too many others to name would come to an end.

'You're going to stay though, right?' Nav asked.

'What makes you say that?' I shifted my body to face her, a worry in her eyes I wouldn't have believed unless I'd seen it.

'You're not going to run again?'

I put my cup down and took her hands. 'No. I'm not going anywhere. I'm back for good this time.'

Nav's shoulders dropped, and she gave a quick nod of her head.

'Although'—I groaned at the thought of it—'I'll have to head back to London soon. I need to collect my things. I gave notice on the room I was renting and need to clear my stuff out. Also, I left the home so quick after Aunt Val called, I said I'd go pick my things up, save them sending a box down here.'

'Want me to come with you?'

I smiled and wrapped my arms around my best friend. 'Thank you. But I'll be OK. I'm going to wait until after the ball.'

'Here you are, Chef.' Luke walked in through the main door, carrying three large boxes stacked on top of the other.

'Ah! Just in time.' Nav pulled back and looked at me. 'Come on. Wallowing allocation is over. You have a quota, you know.'

***

The hall looked perfect. The tables were set, each with a glass bowl in the centre with a submerged ship lying on a bed of stones. I had raised the question as to whether a sunken boat was the best look for a party celebrating our fishing fleet, but Nav said aesthetically they looked far better than having one bobbing around. I stood in the centre of the hall and admired all our work.

I was functioning, moving through the motions of the day, but there was nothing more than that.

'Are you sure the tables shouldn't be a little more spaced out? I'm worried that when the waiters are trying to get past they might have a hard time,' Nav said, shuffling chairs a few centimetres from one side to the next.

'Does it matter? I mean, everyone is going to be so pissed they're not going to care,' Luke shouted over from the kitchen.

Neither of us replied, instead we rolled our eyes. This mundane distraction had served its purpose for my bruised and battered heart.

'Maybe he's right. Let's leave it for now,' Nav said, low enough that Luke wouldn't hear. 'Come and have a look at this sound system with me. I have no idea how it works. Unless it's a cooking appliance, my knowledge on technology is zero. Give me a Thermomix any day, and I'll troubleshoot the heck out of it!'

I looped my arm in Nav's and smiled. 'Thank you.'

'For what?'

'Distracting my brain with this, so I don't go back to a heap on the floor.'

***

'We need Val,' Nav said, after we had spent an inordinate amount of time staring at the sound deck.

'No, no, no. We've got this,' I said, looking over it suspiciously. 'Have you got instructions?' I pressed a random combination of buttons and watched as the large black box in front of us came to life.

'It looks like a control panel for NASA, not a sound system.' Nav peered around the back, as if someone might have left the instructions on a sticky note somewhere. 'I know we said we weren't going to discuss it anymore, but there is one good thing you can take away from the whole Charlie thing,' Nav said, obscured entirely now by the large black box.

'I'm pretty certain there's nothing. But go ahead.' I picked up a loose wire and held it up before plugging it in to a random socket on the panel. I handed Nav a microphone while I flicked a few more switches, hoping it wasn't about to blast all our ears out with some terrible high-pitched squeal. Nav tapped the top of the microphone and made some professional sounding *one two, one two* noises—to herself, as no noise left the microphone.

'Well.' She paused, thinking for a moment as I flicked switches and pressed buttons in some vain hope I was having an effect on the microphone. 'The whole fight with Caulson Properties got you back out on the water.'

As much as I didn't want to admit it, there was some truth in her words. Although I hadn't taken Saoirse out fishing, I had taken some steps in the right direction. God, the irony!

Nav put the mic to her lips and addressed me, as though to a crowd waiting on her every word. 'And we can't forget this man has given you *the best sex of your life*.' The microphone burst into life, broadcasting Nav's voice across the room.

'*Shit. Sorry*.' Her voice boomed across the room again.

I snatched the mic from her hand before any more of my private life was broadcast.

'Really?'

'Sorry, I didn't think that was going to happen,' she said, with not nearly enough sincerity, as she did her best to keep in a laugh.

'You think?'

'Don't stop now,' Luke shouted, before turning his back to us and wrapping his arms around himself, in a childlike display of two people making out.

Nav threw her middle finger up at him and walked back round the NASA control panel, looping her arm in mine.

'You know you will have to speak to him.'

'Why the hell would I do that?' Being in his presence seemed to make me lose my head. I was not falling for his fancy words and charm anymore.

'I'm not saying today. Just...when you're ready. Closure, Riss. It's important.'

***

He stepped out of the pub as I walked around the corner. The pub. Aunt Val's pub! My stomach lurched, and I considered turning round and hiding out of sight. But I wasn't that person. Not anymore. I was going to face this, one way or another. I twisted my watch around my wrist and took in a breath.

You've got this, Riss.

He must have felt my eyes boring into him as he turned and stopped.

'Rissa.' His voice was low, and for the first time since I'd known him, unsure.

'Why are you here?'

'I've been calling you.'

'I blocked your number.'

'Can we talk?'

'Why are you here?'

'Rissa.' He said it again, his tongue rolling over my name in a way that still gave me shivers. But I wasn't buying it anymore. I shook the feeling and stood my ground.

'Either answer my question or leave. I'm done with your bullshit.' I could feel my face growing flushed, but my voice was still steady. His eyes didn't leave mine, and I cracked first, needing to break the connection. I let my gaze shift to the calm water beyond the sea wall and the gulls, swooping and calling.

'If you just stop for a second and think rationally—'

'Rationally?' My voice betrayed me, and I took a step back.

'You know what I mean.' He ran his hand over day-old stubble, instant regret marking his face at his choice of words. 'You tend to jump before seeing it all.'

'This is the most rational I've been since you arrived in this damn town. Irrational was believing you. Irrational was allowing myself to be taken in by some rich, entitled, self-involved nobody.' I knew I was ranting, but I didn't care. With each word, I waved my hand in his direction, as though indicating to each of the parts of him that held these insults. 'I don't need you. I don't need you to feel sorry for me. I don't need you to pretend this is all some big mistake. I'm all good, thanks, and I'm not your damsel in distress. Find your ego trip somewhere else, because I'm not it.'

I stopped to take a breath. His gaze was unwavering and his face unreadable. I didn't know what else I expected from him. There was nothing he could say that would make what he'd done any better. But I guessed my breaking heart was scrambling to find the light, find anything that might mean it was a mistake, that I had heard Geoff wrong. That everything Charlie and I had shared wasn't one big fat lie.

'I trusted you.' I laughed, unable to ignore how stupid that sounded when I said it out loud. I wanted to say more, so much more, but I felt the exhaustion of the last twenty-four hours creeping through my body, weighing me down again.

'I'm not guilty of what you're excusing me of.'

I nodded and let out a snort of disgust. 'That's all you've got?'

'I need you to trust me. I need you to remember what we have is real.' He took a step towards me, and it took all I had to stop my heart from crashing through my chest.

'Don't.' I shook my head and held my hand up to stop him. 'Nav told me I would need to speak with you. I didn't think it would be this soon, but—' I shrugged my shoulders. 'Here we are.'

Charlie's fingers found mine. For the briefest of seconds, I allowed myself to remember that feeling. The trip on the beat of my heart when he smiled at me, the swoop of my stomach when I'd see him unexpectedly.

'Had,' I said, my voice struggling to stay steady.

'Pardon?'

'You said what we have. It's what we had.' I pulled my fingers away, clenching my fist to dampen the fizz of his touch.

'Rissa.' He tried to take my hand again, but I moved out of his reach. If I didn't know better, I'd think it was pain in his eyes. But I did know better.

'I fired David.'

'Why? Because he got in there first?'

'No.' Charlie scraped his hand through his hair. 'His behaviour was unacceptable. What he said was wrong. Do you hear me? If I'd known—'

'What? You'd have what? Done exactly the same but with prettier words?'

'Rissa.'

'You can't have it all, Charlie. You showed me that. You get one true love. Some choose the person; others, the job. You have only ever chosen the job.' Looking at it, I didn't know why I'd ever thought it would be different this time. 'I shouldn't have expected you to be anyone other than that.' My voice was calm, or maybe it was resignation. I forced the lump in my throat back down and looked straight at him. 'Maybe

273

there was a moment where I thought I could have both. That there was a way to have it all.' I smiled a weak smile at the naive memory and shook my head. 'There is no situation where I don't choose Telbury, the fishermen, this way of life. And there is no reality where you don't pick Caulson Properties.' I sighed, some twisted relief at bringing it to a close. 'So I guess that takes us full circle.'

I didn't wait for a response. Whatever he had to say was not something I wanted to listen to. I pushed open the pub door and let the latch click behind me. I crouched down and hugged my knees to my chest, as undignified sobs left my body.

Chapter 29

How's a girl meant to wallow with a broken heart and a shattered dream if she's not left alone? They didn't wait to be invited in, like normal people. No, they barrelled in with no concern for common courtesy.

'Right, time's up.'

'I'm tired. It's not even nine.'

'Yeah, three hours late, if you ask me.' Clem nudged my leg out the way as the sound of the curtains opening told me they weren't going anywhere. I peeled the duvet down to below my eyes and looked out at the two of them staring back at me.

'I'll meet you downstairs in ten. Got a coffee on, and I might even rustle you up some toast.' Aunt Val smoothed down her skirt and walked out the room.

'Well?' Clem asked, prodding me again after I had put the covers back over my head.

'What?' I whined. 'Why are you here?'

'Nav's busy at the restaurant, and we've got shit to do.'

'Are you and Nav talking again?' I peeked out from behind the duvet, my eyes wide.

'No.' His disappointment was obvious. 'But I'm working on it.'

I covered my head again. Was there no joy left in the world?

'Plus, you can't wallow. It doesn't suit you. Be miserable and heartbroken, but at least get up and do something. Besides, you need to get out on the water. Time for avoiding it is over.'

'New and improved Clem sucks.' But he was right.

Since when was Clem giving out the advice?

'Fine.' I surrendered. 'I'll come. But only because I'm worried I'll have Geoff in here next if I don't get up.'

Clem laughed. 'Don't tempt him.' He nodded in the direction of the door Val had just left through.

***

I turned the key and listened to the low rumble of Saoirse waking up. Smoke puffed out the back, and the gentle hum of her rhythm settled into place. I moved around the deck with confidence, working through my checks before heading in to the wheelhouse. Clem was right. Wallowing didn't suit me. My heartbreak needed to be smothered in jobs and business, not with blankets and hot water bottles.

'Did she ever tell you why he was there yesterday?' Clem asked.

'No,' I said, cranking up the speed as Saoirse moved out of the harbour and onto the open sea. Despite finding me in a heap by the door, Aunt Val had given me nothing… In the way of information, that is. She had given me a hug and called in a favour at Mermaid's for them to drop off two fish suppers for us. But despite my constant pestering about why Charlie had been at the pub, she was giving nothing away.

'Hmm.'

'What does that mean?' I flicked on the autopilot and joined Clem out on the deck.

'I think there's more to it.'

'To what?'

'It.' He swung his arms around as though referring to the world, life in general. 'I mean, the guy said you could trust him, right?' He leaned back on the railing and re-lit the rollie in between his lips.

'You're right.' I nodded. 'Just like if some random person down a dark alley offered you a brown paper bag and told you to trust him.' I rolled my eyes. 'Clem, the guy is about as trustworthy as Mogget in The Old Kingdom.'

Clem looked back at me blankly.

'Garth Nix? *Sabriel*? *Lirael*? Urgh, I gave you the collection to read. You know what, it doesn't matter. The point is, he cannot be trusted.'

'You and your weird kids' stories.' He laughed, interrupting me.

'They're not weird. Those *books* are master classes in morality and hidden meaning,' I said, resisting the urge for a longer lecture.

'Look, all I'm saying is I have a feeling there is more to this.'

I knew arguing was pointless. Clem's new, enthused approach to life—that now included daily meetings at AA—also meant he had developed an inability to see someone or something as all bad. Even if that person happened to be responsible for the certain demise of our entire fishing fleet.

We stood silent for a moment, both rocking with Saoirse as she pushed through the water.

'Where is Charlie, anyway?'

'Who knows? Who *cares*?' I lied. 'Probably counting his money and laughing at us all for being such idiots.'

Clem's question stayed with me longer than I'd have liked. *Where was Charlie? Would his team now just appear and get to work? How long did we have left?* I had a million questions that led to even more questions, none of which I had an answer for. No more Shed, no more fishing... And before I could stop my heart from having a say, the thought of no more Charlie entered my head.

***

'Looking at this, I'd say we're close. I suspect they're all in a bit of a mess to be honest, but nothing unfixable, eh,' Clem said, staring down at the plotter after we had gone back into the wheelhouse. The plotter was a key tool in making sure we shot our lines right and in our spot. Clem had done his best to work my dad's lines, but recently it had all become too much. The chances they were where they were meant to be was slim. Especially given some of the early summer winds.

We were approaching the pots, and my heart rate had kicked up. The last time I had been out here, doing this, I'd lost Dad. My confidence had grown in the last few months, with Saoirse, with the sea, but this...this felt too big.

Clem stepped out onto deck. Following him out, I took a huge gulp of sea air. I waited for the inevitable pressure to build in my chest, the closing in of my throat, the ever-rising panic that always left me rigid. But it didn't come. Instead, the air went down and filled my lungs. The gentle spray tingled my lips, and the breeze kicked up my hair. My mind was focused. There was no room for my heart ache, no room for fear as the boat rocked from side to side.

'What you doing?' I asked, as Clem picked up the hook and started looking out on the water.

'Hooking on.'

'Don't you think you'd better bring us alongside?'

'Nah.' He waved a hand in dismissal. 'Think you've got this one, Riss.'

I didn't say anything and walked back inside, dropping our speed as we approached the lines.

I looked out beyond the bow of the boat and squinted. The sun was bright and reflected off the water, making it almost impossible to spot any distinguishing objects on the surface. Once he had hooked on, we could start reeling them up. If the lines had been worked, you would hopefully be greeted by plenty of lobster, crab, whelks, or whatever it was you were fishing, but today was a tidy-up job.

'There!' Clem shouted.

I looked out and squinted at what I hoped was the beginning of the line.

'Yeah, that's it,' he said, leaning over the railing. I felt the panic rising in me. He was leaning too far out.

'No,' I said, pulling us away.

'No?' He straightened and looked back at me.

'It's not right. Too much movement.' I was shaking my head, a cold sweat beginning on my skin.

'OK,' Clem said. If he was annoyed, he kept it hidden. 'Let's go again.'

I nodded and went back into the wheelhouse to turn her back round. It wasn't the same. The sea was calm, and the wind hadn't kicked up, obscuring my view. But the feeling was there, the knot of fear that twisted in my chest, rising to my throat, causing me to gasp for air.

'That's it, Riss, a bit more.' Clem leaned forwards as I slowed alongside.

'No. No, it's not good.' I pulled Saoirse out and heard Clem swear in frustration.

'Riss, you've got this.'

'Do I?' I shouted. 'Do I? Because I'm not sure.'

Clem dropped the hook and walked over to me, placing his hands on my shoulders.

'You've got to push through this. It's your only way forwards. We ain't leavin' till you succeed.'

'Shit!' I stepped back, shaking my head and walking out onto the deck, trying to calm my breathing.

'This is a waste of time. Just, you do it, and we'll head back.'

Clem looked at me and said nothing.

'What? It's true. What is the point? There's not going to be a fishing fleet in too long anyway.' I threw my arms up in the air. Clem said nothing and kept staring.

'Say something, dammit!'

'What do you want me to say?' His voice was calm, his expression unchanged.

'Something, anything. Agree with me...or don't, but don't just look at me.' I waited for what felt like minutes before Clem responded.

'You're upset.'

Oh, sweet Jesus!

'You're upset, and you think it's because the Shed is going. And it is, in part. But a big chunk is because you fell in love and got your heart broken.'

'I don't...'

'Uh.' Clem waggled a finger in my face. 'I'm speaking now.'

I shut my mouth.

'But what you haven't figured out yet—and don't get me wrong, it took me a while too—this'—he swung his arms around—'this has nothing to do with any of that. So what? You missed the can? We'll go again. So what if the lines have been fished over? These things happen. You know that. It's not about you and the universe being out to get you. It's just that you weren't here, so you lost your edge. But for god's sake, stop finding the excuses. This is where you belong. Stop hiding.' Clem nodded with finality and walked back into the wheelhouse. I followed him and stood at the door.

'I'm not hiding.'

'What's that?' Clem mumbled, before carrying on with his completely tuneless and lyrically incorrect rendition of Christina Aguilera's classic, "Genie in a Bottle."

'Clem.' I shoved him. 'I'm not hiding.'

'I heard you. I just wanted to see how hard you were going to try and convince yourself.'

I raised an eyebrow expectantly, and Clem sighed before turning down the music and facing me.

'You want to be a fishermen, but whatever happens you find an out.

I get that it's been tough, and what happened that day was fucking shit. But it wasn't your fault. The Shed being sold is not your fault.'

'They're pretty good reasons, Clem.' My tone was defensive, but his words were hitting somewhere soft and bruising.

'Those are all excuses. None of 'em stop you from fishing. Find the solutions.' He shrugged, as if it were that simple. 'Your dad would be gutted if he knew your reason for not fishing was him. If we have to fish elsewhere, we'll fish elsewhere. Look, I'm no happier about this Shed situation than you, but there are answers.'

I leaned back against the small window and said nothing. Clem had shot an arrow and hit my soft bubble of security right in the centre. I hadn't seen it as excuses—they were reasons to me—but both were stopping me from doing what I loved.

'Anyway.' Clem placed a hand on my shoulder, his goofy smile breaking the tension. 'Can we please get these damn pots in before we lose the tide back in?'

I looked back at him, not sure how to respond.

'You good to get it?'

I turned my back to him and turned Saoirse full circle, pushing out clouds of smoke as we came back on ourselves. Maybe I was destined to fail, but I might as well find out.

I watched again as Clem leaned over, stretching out to hook on. Hook at the ready. Steady line. I relaxed my shoulders and kept watching. Maybe the answer was to keep going? Maybe failure only occurred when you stopped trying? You couldn't fail if you kept moving forwards.

Clem was right. It couldn't all have been for nothing. The sun broke from behind a cloud, and the warmth of it hit my back. I knew it wasn't Dad, but it felt like a reminder that he was always with me, always standing behind me, urging me forwards. Never in front, blocking my path. I watched Clem tip forwards, then pull back.

'Got it!'

Chapter 30

There was a low buzz of content chatter pouring from the open double doors. The evening was warm, and the sky was smudged pink and orange. I braced myself at the sight of so many people. So many people with no idea what we'd lost. So many people, people who would know the truth by tomorrow. That this had all been for nothing.

Heartbreak was a bitch, but while getting ready for the event, I'd also found that it was nothing a strong highlighter and lipstick couldn't mask for a few hours. I knew that my face had a subtle glow from two days at sea, and I'd even managed to find a dress that didn't have my usual grease stains or rips in it.

'Hey, Riss.' A hand landed on my shoulder, and Clem sidled up next to me.

'Hey. Goodness, you look...clean!' I laughed, stunned at the smartly dressed man next to me.

'I could say the same about you.' He looked me up and down, his disbelief that I knew what makeup was clear.

'I didn't know if you were going to make it.'

'Nor did I,' Clem said, his eyes giving away far more than his words.

'I'm really glad you're here.' I reached up and wrapped my arms around his neck. The soft smell of soap washed over me, and I stayed there, not wanting to lose the connection.

'It's not your fault, you know,' he said, as though reading my thoughts. 'We can still fight. And we will survive whatever happens.' He looked at me briefly before I broke eye contact, looking out at the happy people.

I felt tears prick the sides of my eyes and released my hold.

Not now, Riss. Too many tears had been cried already.

I nodded and brushed away imaginary fluff from his shoulder. 'You look very nice, Clem.'

'So do you.' He smiled, recognizing my need for the conversation to be over. 'Shall we?' He held out his arm and linked mine through his.

My heart had been broken. I had failed in my promise to the town, but I was still there. I couldn't have been prouder of our town. I took a breath and readied myself for the toughest evening of my life. The noise rose around me, and a young boy I recognised as one of the skippers' sons handed me a glass of something pale and fizzy. I wouldn't want to say champagne, as I was pretty sure the budget hadn't stretched that far. My first sip, though, confirmed it was alcoholic and good enough to suit my needs.

Clem and I walked in together, smiling at friendly faces all wanting to congratulate us. I took a long sip, hoping the bubbles might soften the stab in my chest.

'Rissa... Oi, Riss.' Nav's voice travelled over the content hum of voices in the hall. I turned and waved. Her face changed when she saw whose arm I was on.

'Guess that apology is still a work in progress?'

'Could say that,' Clem mumbled. 'Think I'll head over to the others.' He nodded in the direction of Aunt Val, who was holding court. The story of her collapse at the beach had taken on new proportions since she had got out of hospital, and it was in no small part down to her retellings.

Before Clem had taken a step, the circle around Aunt Val shifted to reveal...him. I stiffened on Clem's arm, and he looked down at me confused, before following my gaze to what I had seen.

'What the—'

He stood beside Aunt Val, a smile on his face as she said something that had the people with them laughing. The ground beneath me started to tremble, and I blinked, trying to refocus my eyes. This wasn't possible.

'Keep your cool.' Clem's words were low, and a clear warning for me not to make a scene. But I was so far from listening to reason. I pushed off his arm and marched over to where they stood.

'There you are!' Aunt Val called out, throwing her arms in the air. 'I've been looking for you.'

'Is this some sort of joke?' I hissed as I approached, looking between her and Charlie.

The smile on his face had now vanished, and he stood silent next to her.

'Rissa.'

'No.' I shook my head. 'Aunt Val, I'm sorry, but no. This man is the reason we have lost everything. He tricked us. What possible reason could you have for allowing him to be here? He is not to be trusted.'

The crowd around us was growing as my voice grew louder.

'Rissa, if you let me explain—' Charlie said, stepping forwards.

'Don't. Even.' I threw a hand in the air to silence him, cursing my heart for still picking up pace at the sound of his voice. I turned my attention back to Aunt Val who took a long slug of her beer, looking far too relaxed for my liking. Had she hit her head when she fell? Had the doctors missed something?

'When you're done, I'll explain, shall I?' she said.

I went to say something, but she took my hand and pulled me away from the group.

'Sometimes...' She shook her head as she guided me to far end of the hall. The crowds were up by the dancefloor, so we stood alone.

'I wanted you to be the first to know.' She took my hands and found my eyes with hers. 'It only got confirmed as I arrived at the hall. And I was so excited...'

'What is going on?' I said, trying not to raise my voice.

'We won, Riss. We only bloody went and won!'

'No.' I shook my head in despair. 'No, we didn't. They gazumped us. They went and paid some stupid amount...'

'Darling, I love you, but boy, you're shit at not storming in with your flame throwers burning.'

I stared back at her, floored by her words.

'Charlie came to see me.' She waited for a reaction, but I gave none. 'That day he was at the pub. He said he'd tried talking with you, but you wouldn't have it. Which I understand.' She put a hand up in acceptance. 'See, I'd had a thought for a while now. Then I got the call from Charlie, and it all came together. Like it was meant to be, you know?'

'No, actually. No, I don't know. What came together? What thoughts?' My patience was all but gone.

'Charlie had no idea about the sale. It was that awful guy that worked for him going rogue. He only found out when you did at Nav's.'

I rolled my eyes, but she squeezed my hands to focus me. 'The minute he knew, he started putting a plan together. He spoke with the Marshalls' boys and said that offer was dead in the water. But they had got a sniff of what good money looked like by then and wanted more than the original asking.' She waved a hand in the air as if bored of explaining. 'Charlie told them they would have one last offer, and it was a take it or leave it. I knew we were going to need to raise more money, but we didn't have the time. So I came up with a new solution. One that suits everyone.'

'What?'

My patience was gone.

'I sold the pub,' she said, with uncontrolled delight. Her eyes sparkled, and she laughed as the words spilled out. 'I've been wanting to get rid for a while now, and when Charlie came to me, I thought here's my chance. This way, we save the Shed and the fleet, and I get a retirement. Everyone's a winner!'

I had no words. My head was swimming, but none of my questions were forming into full sentences. Aunt Val looked back at me, as though expecting me to join her in her happy dance.

'This is a good thing, Riss. A great thing! We saved the Shed.'

'The pub.' It was all I could manage.

'Oh, and that's the other great bit. Charlie has said you can stay in the pub. He's not going to do anything with it. Says he's got some other project. Part of a rejuvenation thing.'

'I need some air.' My words were clipped and my breathing short. I didn't want to hurt her. Despite what she was telling me, she seemed genuinely pleased. I wanted to be happy. To feel the elation I saw on her face. The Shed was safe, and the fleet was safe.

'Rissa?' She squeezed my hands and pulled me back. 'Don't you see? *You* did this. You saved the town. You helped that man fall in love with this town, with the people. You opened his eyes to what we already knew. We don't need changing, not like that. He fell in love with you.'

Her words hit, and I looked back at her.

'Don't be too hard on him, eh? He didn't betray you, or us. He might have dropped the ball a bit with that man who works for him, but only because he was so focused on you.' She laughed again. God, who was this new woman? Since when was she one for love and happiness?

'I'm gonna get back. More people to tell the happy news to.'

I smiled.

'And before you say it, it's one of them non-alcohol ones.' She held up the bottle in her hand as proof. I nodded, not trusting myself to speak, and leaned in to give her a quick hug before she hurried off back to the group we'd left behind.

I watched her rejoin them all, a cheer going up as their beer bottles met in the air. I needed to get out.

The evening air rushed over my face like a cool, damp cloth, soothing my raging cheeks. I pressed my back into the hard stone, tilting my head up to the sky. I knew he was there before I saw him.

'Can we talk?'

I said nothing, but I didn't move. The music had kicked up a gear in the hall, and the steady thump of the bass vibrated through the wall. Charlie took a step towards me, and his scent caught on the breeze, my heart jumping frantically in my ribcage. I hated how my body still responded to him.

'I take it Val explained everything?'

'In her own way.'

'I'm not touching the pub.'

'Until someone offers you enough money. That's how you work, isn't it? The business always comes first. Did you tell Aunt Val that bit?' I said, nodding to the open doors of the hall. 'We didn't need you saving us. We needed a fair fight. When are you going to realise that not everyone needs saving? I thought I made it pretty clear to you that I can stand on my own two feet.'

There was a flash of amusement in his eyes.

'What?' I snapped.

'I bought a pub I don't want, to help save a fishing Shed that I had planned on developing. For you.' He let his words sit there. 'I chose you, Rissa, with all your brashness, all your shoot first and ask questions later attitude, all your determination, your love of this place. I chose you because I fell in love with you. Because you're my number one. Because I want you to have your chance at your dream. Because this place deserves to be more than a number on the bottom of a balance sheet. Because I want to be more, for you.'

I opened my mouth and closed it.

'Rissa, when I said David was wrong to say what he did, it's because that was never an instruction I gave. My time here in Telbury...' He paused, thinking about his words. 'With you. It's shown me so much. But not least that the Shed was not mine to take. I asked you to trust me, because I wasn't able to tell you my plan. I needed to get things in order, so the offer Val put in would be the only one available to the seller. I told you a long time ago you could trust me. I wasn't lying.'

I wanted to wrap my arms around his neck, pull his mouth onto mine. I wanted to feel the heat of his body against me. But my feet wouldn't move.

'I know you by now, Narissa Williams, and I have no doubt you're running through all the possible ways you think I'm going to screw you over. And that's fine.' He smiled. 'I can wait.' He reached his hand to my face and rubbed the pad of his thumb against my flushing cheek, and it took all my strength to resist the pull of his warm touch.

I dared to move my eyes up his body and meet his. He was looking back, waiting for me.

'Rissa, I love you. From that first day on the harbour.' He smiled at the memory. 'You intrigued me. You challenged me. You reminded me of the things I had long forgotten.'

I wanted to fall into his arms, breathe him in. Be happy. But I didn't. I couldn't. This love came with conditions, bought conditions. Buying the pub was just another Shed. It was an asset to trade. Bricks to knock down and rebuild.

'I can't do this.' I shook my head to free myself of his touch. Despite every part of me wanting to hold on.

'Rissa.' He went to take my hand, but I stepped back.

'No. I know you think this is love, and maybe it is. God, what would I know?' I half laughed at the absurdity of it all. 'But I can't do this.'

'Why?' It was a challenge.

One word I didn't have an answer for. *Why?* Why couldn't I be with this man? The one man who challenged me and intrigued me and seemed to love all of me. *Because.* Because loving him would be to turn my back on my dad. Because loving Charlie came at a price. Maybe not today, but it was always going to be there. His part in saving the Shed. The debt owed. I wanted to push it away, pretend it didn't exist, but wasn't that what we had done up until now?

'To love you feels like betraying everything I love. I can't see how that will ever be acceptable.' Hot tears stung my eyes. 'I have to go,' I said, as the first rogue tear broke free, but Charlie's voice caught me as I made to walk away.

'I will prove that you can trust me, Rissa. I know you can't see it at this moment, but this is the real deal. I choose you.'

I didn't turn and look at him, instead walking away before my heart burst from my chest.

***

I knocked once and pushed the already ajar door open as the familiar voice called me in.

'Oh, Rissa, my dear girl!'

Mrs Lesley sat in her chair by the window. Sunlight was filling the room, but she had a thick wool blanket over her knees. I winced at the sight of the bandage wrapped around her head, and the deep purple bruising to her hand.

'How are you?' I asked, as I walked over.

'Much better for seeing you, that is for sure.' She smiled, her pale blue eyes catching in the light. 'Come, sit. Don't worry, I'm team Telbury. I told that son of mine as much as well.'

I let out a laugh and allowed myself a deep breath out.

'I think Telbury is team Charlie now.'

After his deal with Aunt Val was made public, the whole of Telbury was singing his praises.

'I brought you something,' I said, keen not to dwell on the topic of Charlie longer than necessary. I hadn't seen him since the ball, and although my heart was still aching, distraction was my answer. 'I wasn't sure if you'd have the latest or not.' I pushed her gossip magazine across the table.

'You star.' She beamed at me before her eyes looked on the glossy front page and her fingers thumbed the pages. 'Have you seen him?' she asked after a moment, not looking up from her magazine.

'No,' I replied, all too aware of who we were discussing. 'Not since the ball.' It had only been a week, but the pain of not having him in my life was cavernous.

'You know, his dad meant well. He worked hard, harder than he should have, really. He wanted better for Charlie, and when he saw it was something he could have, he told him to take it and never look back.' She stopped and turned the page, her eyes still fixed on the magazine. 'I think Charlie was so afraid of letting his dad down, he was prepared to let himself down. For years, he pushed on, making more and more money, but moving further and further away from who he is. But then he met you.' She looked up at me. 'You reminded him of who he is. Who he wanted to be. Thank you.'

'I'm not sure that's—'

'Oh, it is.' She nodded. 'You know, he's a good man, really. I'm not telling you this so you'll give him another chance; I just don't want you to end it thinking he's something he isn't.'

I didn't say anything. The truth was, I knew Charlie wasn't bad. He had shown that in so many ways to me. But I couldn't move forwards.

'You can call foul whenever you want dear, and maybe I've spent too long perusing the therapist section of these damn magazines that I'm reading too much into this.' She closed the magazine and smiled before looking out the window. 'Is there maybe a little bit of you that came to see me today to confirm for you that he's one of the good ones?'

I opened my mouth to reply, with what, I had no clue. But Mrs Caulson closed her eyes and shook her head. 'Don't worry dear. You don't need to answer that. It's just a thought.'

I sat back in my chair and joined her in looking out at the garden below. Maybe she was right—maybe I had come looking for an answer, or maybe I'd just needed to collect my belongings and wanted to check in. If I knew the answer myself, I wasn't able to see it. All I did know was the hole of not having Charlie in my life anymore was vast and cold. Protecting my heart was no longer feeling as comforting as it had in the past.

Chapter 31

One week later....

'Who's a good boy? Yes. Yes, you are.'

'Is that necessary?' I said, as I walked through the pub door and dumped my bags on the floor.

'Is that?' Aunt Val nodded at my clothes.

'I had a fight with the oil,' I said, by way of explanation. I kicked my boots off at the door and stripped my overalls down to my (almost) clean jeans and T-shirt before taking a seat on a bar stool.

'Ah, be a good boy now,' she said, as she handed the peanut to Johnny.

'Is that peanut butter?' I asked, looking from the plate on the bar and back to her.

'If I've got to make so many bloody changes, then maybe it's about time Johnny did too,' she said, not taking her eyes off him. 'He doesn't seem to mind it too much.' She picked up another nut and dunked it into the spread. 'Besides, this o__ one of them no palm oil ones.'

'Got it.' I smiled at her reasoning.

'How are you doing?' She wiped her hands on a cloth and looked up at me. We both knew she wasn't talking about my current struggles to get Saoirse out fishing again. I had spent the best part of the last week burying myself in paperwork and boat jobs, making sure I was ready for the inspection that would allow me to fish commercially again. But that wasn't what she wanted to know about.

'I'm good,' I lied. What was the point in being honest? My heart was broken, and I couldn't fix it. Nothing more to say.

'Hey, it's just me.' Nav pushed open the door. 'I'm early, but Luke's finishing up at the restaurant, so thought I'd just come on over.'

It was quiz night, and given Aunt Val's instructions to *do less* from the doctor, we had all stepped up to help. Tonight, Nav and I were on duty.

'What we discussing?' she asked, hopping up onto the bar stool next to me.

'What a plonker this one is for still refusing to give old posh chops a chance.'

'Really? This is such a dead conversation. Anyway, why do you care?' I glared back at her as she busied herself pouring two pints.

'Because I'm sick of your moping.'

'I'm not moping.'

'Please!' she said, dropping the pints down onto the bar.

'Am I moping?' I turned to Nav.

'I mean...'

I took a long sip of my beer and slumped forwards.

'I realise you haven't asked for it, but I'm going to give you my take on it all.' Nav swivelled on her stool to face me. 'You love Charlie and are being your usual stubborn self by refusing to admit that maybe you were wrong. He told you he was trustworthy, and he wasn't playing. He really wasn't. He came good.'

'At a cost,' I interrupted.

'Bullshit. He's not doing anything with this place. You know it, and I know it. Your pride is like a big fat wedge in your way.'

'You pick guys that have no chance of ever being in the game.' We both turned, wide-eyed, to look at Aunt Val. 'You pick the ones who don't have their shit together. Who couldn't handle you even if they could hold down a job. Who threaten to destroy your town,' she continued, raising an accusatory eyebrow. 'You never gave the man a fair fight.'

I snorted at the irony.

'Snort all you want, but it's the truth. In that head of yours, you knew it was always coming to an end. Always waiting for the disaster. You never had to go all in. Never had to commit. Never gave it a chance. Poor sod was always going to lose against you. No matter what he did.'

'That was unexpected.'

'I do pay attention, you know.' She turned her back on us and pulled a steaming tray of glasses out of the dishwasher.

'Even if that's true. You can't have both,' I said, with finality. My carefully constructed walls were starting to fray and show the shoddy workmanship that had been used to construct them. I needed to draw a line under the conversation.

'Can't have both of what?' Nav asked.

'You have to pick; it's just the rules. Dream love or dream job. You can't have both.' I shrugged and took a long sip of beer.

'Pah! What crap are you talking now?' Aunt Val didn't even turn around to look at me as she dried one glass and hung it back up. Then another. And another.

'It's not crap. It's true.'

Hold firm, Rissa. Hold. Firm.

'You see, there you are again,' she said, as she hung another glass from the hook above the bar, reaching up, her white blouse momentarily untucking from her trousers.

'There I am again, what?'

'Hiding.' She dropped her arm and retucked her shirt before pointing an accusatory finger at me. 'Finding an excuse. You can have whatever you want. Find the solution! Jesus, what sort of modern-day woman are you? He loves you.'

I turned my attention to Nav for moral support, but she sat with another handful of Johnny's nuts in the palm of her hand. Her eyes flicked from me to Aunt Val as though watching two heavyweight fighters size each other up. Waiting to see who would blink first. Aunt Val let out a long, exaggerated sigh and reached for something below the bar.

'I didn't think it would have to come to this. But you're even more stubborn than your old man was.'

I gave her a quizzical look as she pushed a brown envelope across the table.

'What's this?'

'Don't think that honouring your dad's memory means never being happy. You can still hold onto him and be happy all at the same time.'

I felt the familiar lump in my throat rise at the mention of him. Aunt Val placed her hand over mine and smiled. 'You're allowed to do so,

Riss. With whoever you choose.'

'But what if he's not the right one?' The words came out of my mouth before I had a chance to realise I was thinking them. 'What if I've got it wrong and he's no good? What if it all ends in disaster anyway?'

She let out a small laugh, her eyes full of warmth. 'Oh love, you ain't got no choice in that. Surely this whole situation with the Shed has shown us that. There are always what ifs, and we don't get to decide any of that. Just how we react to them. So what if he's not the forever guy? Anyone with one eye can tell you two are hook, line, and sinker right now.'

I winced at her fishing pun.

'Sorry, couldn't help myself.' She smiled that mischievous smile of hers and squeezed my hand, and with it released some of the heaviness surrounding us. 'Besides, I've got a feeling about this one.' She winked, nudging the paper closer to me. 'Before you open.' Her hand froze on top of the envelope before she said, 'See this for what it is, and not what you think it is.'

'Huh?' I said taking the envelope and ripping the seal.

'Just... You'll see.'

I pulled the paper out and allowed my eyes to scan over it.

Rissa,

My nephew and I finished Artemis Fowl and the Last Guardian *the other night. Consider this my* Artemis Fowl *sacrifice moment...just crank it up from YA. ;)*

FACT: The pub is yours. Always was, but now it's official. It was no more mine to have than the Shed.

FACT: I love you. I've said it already, but it's the truth, and it's not going to change.

THEORY: You love me too, but need to give yourself permission to fall all in...or maybe that's wishful thinking? Either way, the above stands.

Yours, always,

Charlie

P.S. I'm going to be around for a while. Turns out there's a derelict hotel on a cliff top that needs some love. Rebuild what we have. That's what they say, isn't it?

I could feel the tears building again and swallowed hard to push the sharp pain in my throat away.

All the things I'd seen as obstacles, as signs he was trying to control the situation, had been the complete opposite. Charlie had chosen me. Telbury. *Us.*

'Oh shit,' I said, already standing up.

***

What was I thinking? I wondered, as I stepped out of the truck. The wind kicked up, spreading hair across my face. My stomach took a lurch, and I sucked in air, forcing my shoulders to relax. I had left the pub in a state of urgency, but now as I stood here, I had no idea how to move forwards. Or if he was even here.

After scanning the line of parked cars, I turned back to look at the hotel. Ivy clawed its way up the front, and some large holes in the roof allowed pigeons free access in and out of the building. It was one hell of a project. A man in a yellow hi-vis walked up to me, one of those querying smiles on his face.

'Can I help you?'

'I'm looking for Mr Caulson. He's not here, is he?'

'Follow me. He's up at the site. Watch where you're walking; it's not pretty.'

Since the last time I had been up at the hotel, scaffolding had been erected around the entire building. The noise of diggers and drills battled with the sound of the waves hitting against the rocks below. The cove where Charlie and I had been was submerged under the waves, now at high tide.

'He's just over there.' The man pointed in the direction of a group of people. 'Put this on,' he said, handing me a hi-vis jacket like his and a hard hat.

I stood and watched for a moment, my confidence of before gone. But I didn't get long to compose myself, as my presence was noted by the others in the group facing me. Charlie turned, and a look of confusion filled his eyes. I made an awkward wave and walked towards them.

'Hi. Sorry to interrupt.'

'Hi.' Charlie looked back at the group, and they all seemed to get the message this wasn't a conversation for all. I waited for them to leave.

'I—' I looked up as a steel beam was winched into the air, men on either side grabbing it by the ends. 'I wanted to see what you were doing with the hotel.' I swallowed hard. I should have planned for this moment. Should have written down some notes first. I had got caught up in my emotions while reading his letter. But now? Now I had no clue what to say.

'Would a tour help?'

A tour. A distraction. 'Yes. Yeah.' I nodded, warming up to the new plan. 'A tour would be great.'

'Sure.' Charlie smiled.

We walked the site for fifteen minutes or so, Charlie pointing out things, me nodding and making polite noises of approval.

'It's definitely a do-er upper,' I said, as we came round the front of the hotel. The breeze had picked up, and the gulls lay on the wind just beyond the cliffs. 'I guess you'll need to leave soon. Leave a team here.'

'I'm going to run this one. Call it a passion project, if you like.'

'Are you allowed to do that?'

'I can do what I like. It's my company.'

I felt a warmth come over me, a settling of sorts I didn't know I had been craving at his words. At him being here.

'I'm taking the company in a new direction,' he said, looking back at the building. 'Caulson Properties will now only take on projects of rejuvenation. We're moving out of the second home market.'

'But that's where the money is.'

'Maybe'—he nodded in agreement—'but not the important things.' His eyes locked with mine, the butterflies that had never died, even after all the drama, launched into flight in my stomach. For a moment we stood silent, before Charlie spoke.

'Rissa, why are you here?'

I looked away, trying to buy more time, but Charlie moved closer. His fingers found my chin, and he brought my gaze back to his.

'Why are you here?'

'I don't have a speech or anything.'

'OK.' He suppressed a laugh.

'I got your letter,' I conceded.

He nodded.

'And the Deeds... Thank you.'

'Like I said, it was never mine to have.'

I nodded but stayed silent. I looked down at the dirt beneath my feet and wondered how long it was going to take to regrass it all. If that was the plan of course. Maybe it was all going to be gravel, or—

'Rissa.' Charlie was closer now, and my breath caught in my throat. 'Why are you here?'

'I don't know how to do this,' I admitted. My arms flapped down by my side. Honesty. That was the only option.

'OK.'

'I'm not one for the big declarations...not these sorts anyway.'

Charlie smiled but left space for me to continue.

'And...'

I took a deep breath and let it out, dropping my shoulders. 'I'm sorry for not trusting you. I was wrong.'

Charlie said nothing. Just kept his eyes on mine.

'I pushed you away because I didn't think it was ever possible for it to work. And if I'm honest, I still don't know what it looks like. I mean...' I let out a laugh at the absurdity of it all. 'I'm going to be fishing full time soon, and I'll be working stupid hours, and you—' I thrust an arm out in his direction. 'Well, you...'

'I what?' He took another step towards me. Close enough the wind blowing around us was blocked from moving between us. Close enough that the glint of amber in his eyes was visible. Close enough that the words on my tongue disappeared.

'You work.' I swallowed hard as Charlie cupped my cheek, setting an unexploded box of fireworks off inside me.

'I'm not going anywhere. Rissa, I'll make this build last the next thirty years if that's what it takes to convince you. Your life is here, your career is here, which means it's exactly where I will be.'

'What if I can't give you all the things you want?'

'You already do.'

My excuses were running thin, and my defences had all but crumbled.

'Can I kiss you now?'

'Yes.' My response was no more than a sigh as Charlie's mouth landed on mine. His arms wrapped around my waist, bringing me into his chest. The last of my uncertainty disappeared as I melted into him. Charlie deepened the kiss, and I let out a whimper of satisfaction.

'Wait,' I said, pulling back.

'What is it?' he asked, his hands stroking the hair around my face.

'It seems too simple.'

Charlie let out a laugh and shook his head. 'It is simple, sweetheart. You showed up.' He nuzzled into my neck, sending shivers up my spine. 'I can't ask for anything more. You'll tell me how you feel when you're ready. But this, right now. This is more than enough.'

I pulled his face to mine and kissed him hard. Maybe there was no need for big speeches. Maybe showing up was enough. Being there, always. That was a love I could give and a love I knew Charlie was already there for. I had no idea how it looked, or what was to come, but in that moment, it didn't matter. We were exactly where we were meant to be.

I was living for the now. No hiding in the past or burning in the future. I was here, and that was enough.

Epilogue

Three months later...

'I'm late, I know,' I said, as I jumped onto the jetty.

'Late? Sweetheart, we'll be lucky if we're there before Val.'

'Quit your whining. Have you got my clothes?'

Charlie held up a bag, and I blew him a kiss.

'Five minutes, tops.' I did a final knot on the rope securing Saoirse and grabbed the bag from Charlie.

'Time check?' I asked, as we pulled open the door of the Shed.

'Three minutes. Let's see your genius at work, shall we.'

I leaned up and kissed him, 'I love that you think me getting ready in record time is something to be proud of.'

Charlie kissed me back, holding my arms. 'Mmmm, it is true, but your timekeeping is not.' He turned me round and tapped my bum. 'Go.'

'Good day?' I asked, as we half-jogged towards the pub.

'Not bad. The roof is almost watertight so we should be able to start work soon. We'll need to decide which of the original features we can restore. How about you?'

'Oh, you know, just fishing and enjoying the water. Nothing to complain about.' And I wasn't lying. Life was damn near perfect. My licence had come through, and I was getting used to being out on the water. Charlie was busy with the hotel renovation, but we made it work. Time was not our friend, but I was doing what I loved, with my person by my side.

I shook my arms out in an attempt to get warm.

'Cold?'

'I mean, a jumper would have been good,' I said, shivering against the coming autumn wind.

'My options were limited.'

'I know, I know.' I rolled my eyes. I only had a few things at Charlie's place, something he found very frustrating. He had been asking me to move in from the day we'd made things official. He said he was too old to play around. He knew what he wanted, and that made it simple for him.

We reached the pub, and the sounds of chatter and laughter spilled onto the cobbled street out front.

'Shall we?' Charlie pulled the door open for me and gestured for me to go in.

'Still got the chivalry going on, huh?'

'Always.' He winked and moved in behind me.

Johnny Cash was playing through the speakers, and the room was filled with fishermen and locals. Everyone had made the effort for today. It was a changing of the guard moment in Telbury history. Turned out not all change was bad.

'What time do you call this?' Aunt Val called, from her spot behind the bar.

'I know; I got caught up on the boat.'

'If I could count the number of times your father said that exact sentence, I'd be richer than your man there.' She nodded in Charlie's direction.

'Here, let me help.' I walked behind the bar. 'Besides, this is your leaving do. You're not meant to be working at it.'

'Nonsense, what else am I gonna do?'

'Relax?'

'Pah.' She waved my suggestion away with her hand. 'Got months of that coming up, haven't I? More importantly, are you sure you're going to be able to look after Johnny? He's a sensitive old thing, you know.'

'We have been through this too many times to count.' I rolled my eyes and took the glass she had taken from the hook and flicked the tap.

'He's going to be just fine,' Charlie said, from his side of the bar. 'Isn't that right, Johnny?'

Johnny stretched his wings out and flapped as Charlie dropped a few peanut butter dipped nuts into his dish. They'd come a long way from their rocky beginnings.

'Hmmm. If you're sure.'

Aunt Val wasn't ready to admit it, but even she could see that Charlie and Johnny had a bond.

'Just think, by tomorrow evening, you'll be landing in Egypt, at the beginning of a great big adventure.'

Her face lit up at the prospect, and if I had ever needed reassurance that her selling the pub was the right decision, that was it.

'You've got my itinerary, haven't you?'

'Yep. All printed and ready to tick off as you go.'

I wasn't sure I would call a five-month road trip across Egypt and North Africa relaxing, as such, but it was as close to relaxing as Aunt Val was ever going to get. Her plan had taken shape fast, and before long, she had signed up with an agency that specialised in tours for women. Aunt Val walked off to chat with another customer, and I turned my attention back to the gorgeous man in front of me.

I slid another pint glass under the tap and filled a second glass, before sliding one across the bar to Charlie.

'Never gonna be a glass of wine, is it?' He smiled a wicked smile.

I leaned forwards over the bar and looked down at his shoes. 'Never going to be practical, are they?'

'It doesn't matter.' He took a sip of the beer and smacked his lips. 'I'm actually starting to like it.'

I gave another glance down at his shoes before locking eyes with his. 'Me too.'

The sound of the last order bell ringing broke the moment and the room fell quiet.

'Right you lot, this is supposed to be a party. I'm gonna be out of here tomorrow; you can all sulk then.' Aunt Val's voice rose up as she stood on her stool, giving her five foot three frame a good view over the pub.

'Speech!' Geoff's booming voice carried across the room, and a chorus of agreement went up.

'Alright, alright.' She calmed the room. 'Let me just say this.' She paused and looked out on all the loving eyes looking back at her. 'Telbury has been my home for the last forty years, and thanks to all of you lot and what we achieved together, it will continue to be until I'm taken out in a wooden box. But I need a new adventure for a minute. I need to explore some of this vast world and see what else is out there, safe in the knowledge that Telbury will be here waiting for me when I get back.

'Now I know what you're all more worried about is whether you're gonna get a nightly pint, so don't worry. I've got it covered. Your pints are safe.'

A cheer went up at Aunt Val's words.

'But for now, I want to thank you for coming, and thank you for saving Telbury. Without you lot, there is no Telbury.' She stopped again and took a breath. Aunt Val never cried, but she did pause. She did look up at the ceiling and then down at the floor, before tilting her head from side to side. 'Right, that's enough of all that. I'm only gone five months. I'll be back before you get a chance to miss me.'

With that, she stepped off her stool and turned the dial on the music up, the room cheering as she made her way around the bar to chat with her adoring fans. My attention was taken away as I watched the pub door swing open.

'That's a sight I wasn't sure I'd see again,' I said to Charlie.

'It doesn't look completely healed; I'll be honest,' he replied.

We watched Nav come through the door, with Clem following behind. It was awkward and stunted, but Nav managed a weak smile to Clem for holding the door open as she carried a hamper in.

'That looked almost friendly,' I said, as she slid the hamper across the bar.

'Huh, I wouldn't say that. But it's an acceptance,' she said.

'Well, it's a start.'

Nav mumbled something under her breath, but I didn't push it. I still didn't know what the full story was with those two, but whatever it was, they needed time to figure it out.

'Hello, Caulson.' Nav nodded at Charlie.

'Nav.' He nodded.

'How is the slow life treating you? Still not tempted back to the big city?'

'No chance,' he said, not missing a beat. 'Turns out life down here isn't that slow after all. This one certainly keeps me on my toes.' He raised an eyebrow at me, and I felt the now familiar flutter of excitement in my stomach at his words.

'What about when you finish this hotel? Then what?' Nav was testing him—her protective best friend streak had not been completely placated by Charlie's decision to stay.

'I'm not sure yet. But whatever it is, it's wherever this one is.'

'Urgh.' Nav made a gagging noise and carried on emptying the contents of her hamper onto the bar. 'Your loved-upness is too much for me.'

'Let me make it even worse for you, shall I?' Charlie held out a hand and gestured for me to come around from behind the bar.

'Can I have this dance?'

I let out a disbelieving laugh and watched Nav drop her head into her hands.

'I give up,' she groaned.

Charlie pulled me closer to him, and I looked round the room.

'No one is dancing.'

'I don't care.' He smiled. 'You've been out before sunrise the last three days, and I've missed you.'

'Ahhh.' I tilted my head to the side. 'Miss me?'

'More than you know.' Charlie pulled me up against him and dropped his mouth to my neck.

'You sure you can handle it?' I asked, already sure of the answer.

'What do you mean?'

'This life. It's not for the fainthearted. Early mornings, long days. It's a guarantee.'

'I meant what I said.' His lips moved across my hair as he started to sway our bodies to the sounds of Johnny Cash. 'This is your time. You just need to know I'm here. I'll always be here.'

I dropped my head onto his chest and smiled, a feeling of peace washing over me. I had found my person. I had found the man who would pick me each time. The man who would put me first. The man who was here to let me shine.

'Hey,' I said, looking up at him. 'I've been thinking about your offer.'

'Oh, yeah?' His eyes sparked like a child on Christmas morning.

'Yeah. I think we should give this living together thing a go.'

'Is that right?'

'I mean, I can't deny your water pressure is a lot better than mine.'

'That is true.' He smiled and kissed my neck.

'I do really love your shower.'

'Mmmm,' he said, before picking me up off the floor. 'I love you too, Rissa Williams.'

Acknowledgements

Well this is all a little strange! Writing the acknowledgements to my debut novel feels utterly surreal, and yet a really long time coming. Rissa and Charlie's story has been with me for a long time, and if it wasn't for the support and encouragement of the people around me it would never have come to be in your hands.

Writing books seems a little like raising children to me. It takes a village. It is certainly true of my two young boys and it is definitely true of Gone fishing. There are so many people who have helped bring this book into the world and they all deserve my thanks. The barista who gave me my tea and croissant for free when I was wrangling my newborn and really not feeling like getting my edits done was ever going to be possible. Thank you. Your gesture of kindness made my day and I went home, got baby to sleep and smashed out an hour of edits.

To Ashley, for being an all round rockstar. Any and all accuracies as to fishing and boats, is down to you and you alone. You gave your time so freely and answered every question I had, however ridiculous it must have seemed. For anyone looking to read about a real life fisherman, go and read her wonderful book My Fishing Life.

To my writing group, Sally, Susana, Penny, Steph, Chris and Meera.

You saw Gone fishing in her rawest form and your encouragement and notes were invaluable in pushing me on.

To Emma, you have been a source of constant advice and encouragement throughout the mad journey that is self publishing. Your notes on my later drafts undoubtedly helped shape the book that I now have. You are the truest example of how wonderful the online writing community can be. Thank you! And anyone needing a little cowboy romance in your life, check this lady out, she really knows how to weave a story. @emmalucyauthor

To my parents, I don't think I'd get much done without you to be honest! You are my biggest supporters and knowing you'll be proud whether 100 people read this, or 5 is good enough for me.

To Jade, you already got the dedication so don't expect a lot from me. Just kidding! Thank you for never seeing my writing as anything other than a priority. You have given me the greatest gift in allowing me the space to put my writing first. Thank you.

Finally, thank you lovely reader. Whether you're the only one, or one of many, you are here, and for that I am eternally grateful. Thank you for taking a chance on an unknown debut. I really hope we meet again to find out what on earth went wrong with Clem and Nav?!

In the meantime, please reach out on Instagram, I'd love to hear from you.

A xx

About the author

Alice Calliva is a romance author based in Scotland who loves nothing more than creating worlds that explore humankind and all their beautiful imperfections.

When she's not running through dialogue in her head on the school run, or trying to hit her word count when the kids are in bed, she can be found out in the garden trying to keep her vegetable patch alive or on a hill somewhere with her dogs.

To stay in touch, sign up to Alice's newsletter at Callivabooks.com, or say hi on Instagram @callivabooks

Leave a review!

I can't thank you enough for taking the time to read Gone fishing. If I can ask one more thing of you, it would be to ask you to leave a review. Reviews are unbelievably helpful in spreading the word about a book. Goodreads or Amazon whatever your preferred platform may be!

Printed in Dunstable, United Kingdom